What was Ryan doing here? Now?

From appearances it seemed the years had been wonderful to him. He was still tall, lean and broad-shouldered. His hair was still thick and slightly unruly. The slash in his cheek—he'd hated it when she'd called it a dimple—was deeper, even more arresting now than it had been in a twenty-two-year-old face. Light laugh lines around his eyes only added to his appeal, as did the mature shape of his jaw and sensual mouth.

But most compelling of all, the self-confident bearing that had distinguished him as a young man had bloomed to complete assurance in the older Ryan. The visual impression was of a pure, unadulterated male in the prime of life.

After all the intervening years, he looked familiar and strange and dear. Bree's every instinct urged her to wrap her arms around his waist, to laugh up into his face, as she would have done twelve years ago. The urge was so strong that, had it not been for the patent differences in him, she might have succumbed. And she would have regretted it deeply....

Dear Reader,

The editorial staff of Silhouette Intimate Moments is always striving to bring new and exciting things your way: new authors, new concepts in romantic fiction and new ideas from favorite authors. This month we have once again come up with something special.

Emilie Richards is one of your favorite authors, as your letters have made clear, and this month she embarks on a project that will delight her current fans and undoubtedly win her new ones. Tales of the Pacific is a four-book miniseries set in Hawaii, Australia and New Zealand, and the cast of characters who fill the pages of these books will make you laugh, make you cry and make you fall in love—over and over again. Of course, each book stands alone as it presents one very special story, and in *From Glowing Embers*, the first book of the series, Julianna Mason and Gray Sheridan will capture your heart as they strive to mend the hurts of the past and rebuild their marriage. Theirs is a love story that will truly leave you breathless.

Also this month, look for delightful treats from Paula Detmer Riggs, whose first book was part of our March Madness promotion, Marion Smith Collins, and an author who's new to Silhouette Books but not to fans of romance, Andrea Parnell.

As always, Silhouette Intimate Moments is the place to find love stories *for* today's women *by* today's women. We hope you'll enjoy them as much as we do.

Leslie J. Wainger
Senior Editor

Marion Smith Collins

Better Than Ever

Silhouette Intimate Moments

Published by Silhouette Books · New York

America's Publisher of Contemporary Romance

SILHOUETTE BOOKS
300 East 42nd St., New York, N.Y. 10017

ISBN: 0-373-07252-X

First Silhouette Books printing August 1988

Printed in the U.S.A.

MARION SMITH COLLINS

has written nonfiction for years, but only recently has she tried her hand at novels. She is already the author of several contemporary romances and has no plans ever to stop.

She's a devoted traveler and has been to places as far-flung as Rome and Tahiti. Her favorite country for exploring, however, is the United States because, she says, it has everything.

In addition, she is a wife and the mother of two children. She has been a public relations director, and her love of art inspired her to run a combination gallery and restaurant for several years.

She lives with her husband of thirty years in Georgia.

This book is dedicated to Shannon Harper.
They all should have been!

Chapter 1

Set midway along a block of other houses of the post-World War II era, this one seemed to have a personality all its own. Or perhaps the personality of its owner had stamped this house with uniqueness. At any rate, it didn't wear the practical brown or gray trim of the other houses on the block.

Ryan O'Hara checked the address, parked in the shade of an oak tree and contemplated the redbrick dwelling. A sun-dappled porch spread across the width of the facade of the house like a smile. Above the porch roof the second-story windows, framed by lemon-yellow shutters, sparkled in the early-morning sunlight. The scrap of lawn was neatly trimmed and fenced with the same white wooden picket fence that rimmed the porch. A lilac bush guarded the walk. He could smell the heady scent of the blossoms through the open windows of his car.

A kid on a skateboard, wearing a sophisticated head-phone set, rolled through the scene, dipping and dashing along the sidewalk to the beat of unheard music.

With a sigh Ryan got out of his car and headed up the walk. He might as well get this over with. It was not a meeting he looked forward to.

At the sound of the doorbell, Briana Regan Fleming tossed her pencil aside and rose to pad on bare feet from the dining room into the entrance hall. She almost opened the door without checking the peephole. The New England morning sunlight was streaming in through the window of the dining room where she'd been working—what threat could possibly be abroad on such a beautiful day? Or so early in the morning? It was not quite eight o'clock.

Maybe she assumed her mother, who had stopped by earlier for coffee on her way to work, was returning. Maybe she was simply distracted by her thoughts and plans. Or maybe she was a fool. But at the last minute something warned her and, closing one eye, she peered with the other through the tiny circle.

She could hardly believe what she saw. Ryan O'Hara stood there on her front porch, looking touchingly familiar but at the same time looking nothing like the Ryan she'd last seen twelve years ago. Not conscious of the movement, she took one step back. What was Ryan doing *here*? *Now*?

She placed one hand, palm flat, against the white wood panels and reached out for the knob with the other. But instead of opening the door immediately, she put her eye to the hole again.

From appearances, it seemed the years had been wonderful to Ryan. He was still tall, lean and broad shouldered. His hair was still thick and slightly unruly; its color was that of toast smeared lightly with cold butter. The slash in his cheek—he'd hated it when she'd called it a dimple—was deeper, even more arresting than it had been in a twenty-two-year-old face. Light laugh lines around his eyes only added to his appeal, as did the mature shape of his jaw and his sensual mouth. The mustache was a new addition, coffee-colored, very full, very masculine. She supposed it was the style they affected in Texas.

But most compelling of all, the self-confident bearing that had distinguished him as a young man had bloomed to complete assurance in the older Ryan. The visual impression was one of pure, unadulterated male in the prime of life. Bree chewed on her bottom lip.

His stance touched a memory, too. His feet were spread slightly apart, his navy-blue jacket was unbuttoned, and one hand was thrust impatiently into a pocket of his gray tailored slacks. She had seen him stand like that a hundred times. With his free hand he reached out to jab the doorbell again.

The action provoked an unwilling smile. Ryan had never shown much patience when he'd had to wait, even if it was only for someone to open the door. He had been one of the restless ones, productive and untiring, who needed their hours filled as others needed oxygen to breathe.

After all the intervening years, he looked familiar and strange and dear. Her every instinct urged her to throw open the door, to wrap her arms around his waist, to laugh up into his face, as she would have done twelve years ago. The urge was so strong that, had it not been for the patent differences in him, she might have succumbed. And she would have regretted it deeply.

Instead she straightened, preparing herself for this meeting. She turned the brass knob and let the door swing silently inward.

Their eyes met. For a long moment neither of them moved. Then, crossing her arms over her breasts, Bree leaned her shoulder against the doorjamb, casually waiting for him to speak first.

He smiled that same slow, sexy half smile that she wished she *had* forgotten and treated her to an appraisal that was just as thorough and curious as hers had been. She owed him, she supposed, having certainly taken her time before opening the door.

Over the years Ryan had learned to guard his facial expression against his thoughts, but never had the ability cost him so much. Bree had always been beautiful in his eyes; the years had added a maturity that made her breathtaking. She was thinner but the weight loss was the natural evolution from the shapeliness of a young girl to the full-grown slenderness of womanhood.

Barefoot, she looked like a sexy advertisement for the tight, faded jeans she wore. The oversize sweatshirt hung on her, but in the most delightful way imaginable, its folds smoothing out only over the high curve of her breasts. Her neck, above the stretched collar, was long and slender. Her oval face was devoid of makeup and as lovely as ever. The most startling change was her hair. She'd always worn it short. Now that brown-to-black tumble framed her face and curled loosely down her back to just below her shoulders, adding to her sexuality.

His gaze returned to search her eyes again. His powers of observation came into play as he tried to identify something new in those midnight-blue depths. When he put a name to it he was sorry he'd made the effort. He pushed the disturbing information to the back of his mind. Whether Bree had grown hard or not was no concern of his.

Bree forced herself to stand still for Ryan's long study. She kept an expression of polite inquiry on her face.

"How are you, Bree?" he said in the baritone that could always send echoing vibrations through her. But there was something different about his voice now. Not only the deeper resonance that was the normal mark of maturity, but something else.

She had it—the drawl. The typical Boston accent had been softened by a definite Southern drawl. Its effects threw her.

When she didn't answer immediately, he bent from the waist, tilting his head slightly, that playful Irish smile lighting his gray eyes. "Hi. It's me, Ryan."

Bree allowed a smile of her own to soften her lips. "The O'Hara boy who used to play up the street? I'll have to see some identification," she said finally, wondering if he could hear the slight unsteadiness in her tone as clearly as she could.

The quality of his laughter, falling lightly on the summer air, stirred something deep within her. "Why?" he asked. "Have I changed so much?"

She shrugged, but she kept her eyes on his. "The mustache, the Southern drawl, I guess."

The brief drawing together of his brows, the flash of an emotion other than amusement in his expression, was gone before she could identify it, to be replaced again by the effortless Irish charm. "Why, darlin', how could you possibly forget your very first husband?" he teased softly, deliberately accenting the Texas cadence in his voice, waiting for her to respond to the memory.

And her brain reacted on cue. The Tom Thumb wedding when they'd been four. He'd been the groom. She'd been his "awful wedded wife." A wider smile fought its way to her mouth. Then her brain went too far. The first time they'd made love, when he'd repeated the vows word for word.... "Till death us do part ... till death."

Death had rendered them asunder; but of course not his, nor hers.

His words flashed other memories to the surface of her brain, too, like strobe lights illuminating, for a split second only, an image here, an idea there.

The same expression she'd wondered about seconds before now halted the images. He'd followed her train of thought. Even after all this time she knew him so well that she had only to search her mind for an instant to identify it, and the identification was painful. In his stone-colored eyes she saw a new, harder edge, obscured by his deliberate teasing, but there.

"That was a long time ago," she reminded him.

The amusement faded from his face. He ran a hand around the back of his neck. The gesture was familiar, too. Frustration, embarrassment, feeling at a loss—any of those things could have prompted it. God knew, they both had excuses for feeling at a loss.

"Yeah, well, I guess you can't live in Texas for eight years and not bring some of it back with you," he said.

"I guess not." After she'd heard the smooth tone in his voice, her own clipped accent sounded a bit harsh to her ears.

"I realize it's early. May I come in?"

The brisk question brought her back to herself, out of the past, into today. "Of course, Ryan. Come in." She stepped aside, all at once realizing what she must look like, with her hair streaming down her back, barefoot, without makeup, in faded jeans and a sloppy sweatshirt.

Facing every woman's nightmare of being confronted by an old love, she was more irritated at her conventional response than with her actual appearance. "I didn't mean to be rude. I'm...it's just that...that..." As he passed her she got a whiff of something musky and masculine.

Not since she'd learned that Ryan O'Hara was moving home for good to the city where they had both grown up had she felt really flustered—not until now. She sighed quietly. At least he wouldn't think she was trying to impress him.

"It's been a long time?" he finished helpfully.

"Yes," she murmured.

"And you weren't expecting to see me." He seemed puzzled.

She closed the door behind them and leaned against its panels. "Yes."

"You were expecting me?"

"No!" she said quickly. "Oh, drat. Stop finishing my sentences for me." She pushed herself away from the support of the door. That was something else Ryan used to do—his mind was always one beat ahead of anyone's. "I mean, yes, I wasn't expecting to see you." She shoved her hands in her jeans pockets. "Not until the wedding this afternoon, anyway." By then she would have been among old friends and fully prepared for this meeting.

Though the wedding and reception were to be small, a majority of the members of their high school graduating class would be there today to see Kathleen O'Conner, who had postponed her own happiness to nurse her aging mother, finally marry Craig Cowan, whom Kathleen's friends had dubbed the most patient fiancé in the world. Bree was standing up with Kathleen as her matron of honor.

"It'll be good to see the old crowd again," he said.

"Everyone's looking forward to seeing you, too." She paused. "You haven't really changed," she lied.

"You have," he said. "You're more beautiful than ever—" the pause lasted for only a millisecond, or maybe it wasn't a pause at all "—and I hear great things about your public relations work. Or is that what they call it now?"

She ignored his first comment. "Media consultant is the latest term. Who knows, next week it might be something else. But it is you who deserves the congratulations, Ryan." At thirty-four Ryan had come a long way in his field. He was the youngest man ever to be appointed commissioner of police for the city of Boston.

"Thanks."

Bree thought he winced, but she couldn't be sure. She was not really surprised that even after twelve years the subject of his career touched a tender spot somewhere in each of them.

Ryan sent his gaze around her small entrance hall, papered with muted blue and ivory stripes. A half-circle pedestal table against the wall held a tall basket of ivy. Another basket was reflected in the mirror above the table. Stairs led to the second floor. A living room off to the left, the dining room and kitchen to the right—the floor plan wasn't anything unusual in this neighborhood of modest homes. But what Bree had done to the inside of the house was. He could see a corner of the living room through the archway. He felt an urge to explore. "Nice place," he said instead, finally returning his gaze to her.

"Thank you," Bree murmured automatically, leading the way into the dining room where she'd been working. She realized her mistake—she could have handled this meeting better in the formality of her living room. But the error was one she couldn't rectify without being obvious. "My office," she explained.

"I thought you had an office downtown."

"I do. The nice part of being your own boss is the flexible hours; the hard part is that the work has to be done regardless." Two years ago, after the death of her husband, she had returned to Boston from New York and gone into business for herself. "I picked up a group of Italian seafood processors at the airport last night and delivered them to their hotel. Their plane didn't arrive until ten-thirty, and then there was a wreck in the tunnel, so it was after one before I got home. I decided to work here this morning." It was going to be all right, thought Bree with a certain relief. The conversation was flowing more smoothly than she'd expected.

Ryan raised a brow. "I didn't know a media consultant was expected to be a chauffeur, too."

"Normally I'm not. But there was no one else available last night. You do what you have to." Within limits, she added silently. Those Italian men . . . She indicated a chair at right angles to the one in which she'd been sitting. "Have a seat. Would you like some coffee?"

He had paused on the threshold, then followed her into the dining room; now he hesitated, his large hands curled over the back rail of the chair, as he eyed the portable personal computer, the open briefcase, the papers strewn over the table. "Yes, thanks. Unless—it looks like I've interrupted something important," he said, indicating her work.

"I was just going over some notes on the Karastonian foreign minister's visit next month. You'd be familiar with that," she said wryly, grinning.

The tiny impression at the corner of her mouth was still there when she smiled.

Ryan quickly dragged his gaze away from her mouth. Yes, he was familiar with the impending visit of Nicholas Theodor Saber, the foreign minister from the tiny country on the Mediterranean near where Greece and Bulgaria meet Turkey. "Am I!" he said with a nod and a grimace. "The trip promises to be a first-class security headache for the Boston police department."

"Oh, it won't be so bad. Have a look. I'll get our coffee," she offered, and left him there.

While Ryan waited, he scanned one or two of the papers on the table. As a free-lancer, Bree must be called on often to oversee the visits of dignitaries—their transportation, lodging, entertainment, scheduling. The minister was evidently a history buff and wanted to see everything of significance in this historic city. The photocopy of the list of requests was two pages long. Bree had made notes in the margins; some of the places had check marks next to them, others had been crossed out. He had seen the original, typed on heavy cream-colored stationery bearing the palace crest.

Ryan found it difficult to keep his thoughts focused on Bree's notes. He finally gave up and dropped the pages.

This encounter with her had been harder than he'd expected. He pulled out the chair but remained standing to examine his surroundings more closely.

Her house was as neat inside as it had appeared from the outside.

Where other houses of the same type—her mother's, his father's—were cluttered with the accumulation of years of living, the furniture and accessories here were almost stark in their contemporary simplicity, giving the rooms an aspect of open space that the others lacked. An illusion, true, but skillfully done.

Yet the house maintained a cozy atmosphere that was appealing. The colors were simple; white—lots of white— marine blue, peach and, of course, the green of her plants. Bree had always had an exceptional rapport with plants, both inside and outside the house. He smiled slightly as he remembered filching tomatoes from the patch in her mother's backyard and eating them right off the vine; even unsalted, the fruit had been pungent on his tongue. He hadn't had a tomato since that hadn't seemed watery and flavorless.

She returned with a tray that she placed on the corner of the table between them. A cat had followed her in, a tiger cat that purred around her legs until they were both seated.

Ryan didn't like cats, and this one was particularly ugly. He ignored the creature, which now sat at the edge of the rug, eyeing him haughtily and suspiciously. "Do you still raise tomatoes?" he asked.

Bree's eyes flashed with amusement at the memory, and Ryan forgot the cat. "Do you think I'd admit that to you? The king of the tomato bandits?"

He grinned unrepentantly. "They were delicious. I couldn't resist." Suddenly, for some reason, it was important for him to know that at least this small part of the past hadn't changed. "Do you?"

She relented. "Yes, I put them out a couple of weeks ago. But they won't be ready to pick until July."

His mouth curved as he recalled how protective she was of her plants, how she coddled them until the fruit was exactly right for picking. "Will you save me one?"

"Sure," she said lightly. "Maybe two."

Well, thought Bree, that was the end of that topic. One can only get so much mileage from tomatoes. But she was pleased that he'd remembered her penchant for gardening. She concentrated on her coffee for a minute.

Ryan leaned back, pretending to relax in his chair but really wondering how quickly he could end the meeting and get the hell out of there. He certainly had enough to occupy his time today. Seeking another topic, he gestured at the yellow legal pad on the table in front of her. "It looks like you're a stickler for detail."

Bree picked up the pad for a minute, glanced over her handwritten notes, then let it drop. It represented many hours of preparation, and it was her greatest opportunity since she had begun her own business to prove her worth as a public relations—or media—consultant. This job would take her out of the category of a small firm into the more important strata that drew in the large accounts. "This is the first job of such scope that I've handled completely on my own," she explained. "I was lucky to get the contract. I want everything to go smoothly." She looked at him. "As I'm sure you do."

"I was surprised to hear that you're free-lancing. Why didn't you just go to work for the public information office? I thought they would be handling this job, anyway."

"They've had some budget cutbacks and are understaffed right now. They've found that it's cheaper to contract certain jobs." She shrugged her shoulders under the sweatshirt. "Besides, I worked as a city government employee when I was in New York. I didn't like having to answer to anyone else. Especially not a bureaucrat."

He forced his expression to remain noncommittal. Maybe he was being overly sensitive, but her words were like a slap in the face. He worked for city government. He had to answer to bureaucrats, and politicians, too. He didn't like some aspects of his job, either, but considered them necessary evils. A police department unchecked by freely elected officials would be a fast route to a dictatorship. "I can see why you wouldn't respond well to authority," he said mildly.

Bree looked up as she realized what she had said. "I didn't mean it that way, Ryan," she said.

"Of course you didn't." He took a swallow of his coffee.

Finally Bree could stand it no longer. "Ryan, why are you here?" she asked him.

He studied the liquid in his cup for a minute, his expression unreadable. Then he raised serious eyes to hers. "Because we haven't seen each other in twelve years. And we were once engaged. This afternoon at the wedding reception all the people who know us best will be watching like hawks to see how we react to each other. I thought it would be easier on both of us if we met privately for the first time. I don't relish being grist for the gossip mill. Do you?''

Bree hesitated, her cup halfway to her lips, almost wishing he hadn't been so honest. But she couldn't argue with his reasoning. She sipped and put the cup down. ''Not particularly,'' she agreed. ''Though I'm not sure there's any way around it. We may be living in a city, but in many ways South Boston is like a small town.'' She relaxed against the back of the chair. ''But why didn't you call first? Were you expecting to take me by surprise, too?''

He appeared genuinely rueful. ''I take it you didn't know I was coming. She was going to call.''

''Who?'' Bree asked, afraid she knew.

''Your mother... I had stopped by to see Father Brotsky this morning and was there when she got to work. She must have been too busy—''

''Oh, no!'' Bree raked her hand through her long hair.

''She thinks she left her keys here. I offered to pick them up.'' His voice trailed off and his brows rose in surprise when Bree uttered an explicit word he'd never heard her use before. He chuckled. For the first time, the humor in the whole situation hit him. ''Why, Briana Regan! Shame on you! What's the matter?''

''Come with me,'' she barked, and jumped up from her chair. ''I should have known when she showed up on my doorstep at 7:00 a.m. She *never* stops by to see me on her way to work.'' In the kitchen, where her mother had sat drinking coffee only a short while ago, she sank to her knees and crawled under the round oak table. There were the keys in plain sight, right where Frances had left them when she'd ''accidentally'' spilled the contents of her purse.

Accidentally my foot, thought Bree. Deliberately—or the Pope wasn't Catholic. "Damn her. She couldn't have missed them." She scrambled to her feet again. He was so big and so close that she had to catch her breath. "Either you've been had, commissioner, or I have. I'm not sure which." She slammed the offending keys down on the table.

Ryan parted his jacket and planted his hands on his hips. "What are you talking about, Bree?"

For once she was glad of an excuse to vent her Irish temper. "I'm talking about Frances Q. Romantic. Ever since she heard the announcement that you were coming back to town she's become a master at innuendo and subliminal suggestion. She thought if you came by unexpectedly I'd be so overwhelmed I'd fall into your willing arms—always assuming they'd be willing—and we'd live happily after, incidentally providing her with grandchildren." She paced a few steps and back again, her bare feet not making as much noise as she would have liked. "She's never forgiven me or Dirk for not producing any of those," she added in a bitter undertone.

Ryan watched her hair whip around her shoulders like a cape. The morning light coming in through the windows above the sink glinted among the dark strands. "Did you and . . . your husband not want children?" he asked quietly. Then he wondered why. "Damn, I'm sorry. That's certainly not any of my business."

"Whether we did or not doesn't have anything to do with this," Bree answered with a snap, coming to a halt in front of him. "He's dead, and it doesn't matter anymore, and my mother has no right—"

He held up a hand. "Hey, calm down. You're getting upset over nothing."

"It isn't just her, either."

"What do you mean?"

"Everyone has taken an interest. Father Brotsky asks if I'm looking forward to your return to Boston. My friends look at me sideways every time your name is mentioned in conversation. Do you remember the Stallings?"

"The couple we used to go sailing with? He's in advertising, isn't he?"

"That's them," she responded flatly. "He uses my firm occasionally. The other day in my mail I got a copy of the article about your appointment—as if I hadn't seen it—with a note saying we'd have to come to dinner."

"So? Bree, we were very close—for a long time. It's only natural for people to be interested. Once they realize that we've no intention of becoming involved again, they'll back off."

He was amused, damn him. She shot him an angry glare. "I take back what I said earlier. You've changed a lot. Don't you *mind* being manipulated?" she demanded.

The half smile faded from his mouth. His expression seemed to freeze into one of disapproval. "No one can manipulate me unless I allow it," he said calmly. "And yes, I mind when they try. But let's get back to the subject of your mother. I doubt that Frances would attempt any matchmaking between us, especially in light of our past history. She knows me a lot better than that."

"Ha!" Bree snapped, too quickly. "*You* don't know *her*." Then she became aware of the coldness in his gaze, and his words finally registered. "What do you mean, she knows you?" she asked softly, wishing she'd left the question unasked as soon as the words were out.

"We've corresponded off and on for years." He slid his hands into his pockets and rocked on his heels, seeming to search for the right thing to say. "You are the last woman on earth I'd ever get involved with romantically. We were friends for a long time, Bree, and I'd like for us to be friends again. But you're too damned dangerous for anything more. Self-protection runs too deeply in you. There's no way in hell I'd ever let you have another chance at my heart.'' He shrugged. ''And your mother knows that as well as anyone.''

He had spoken slowly, as though making his way through a minefield of dangerous phrases, but with complete determination to get it all out. He meant every word of that soul-spoken promise, she realized. Every stinging word. Self-protective? Was she?

Though she recognized the truth behind his accusation, though perhaps at one time she had deserved even harsher criticism, that had been twelve years ago. She was upset to find that his words still hurt her. But she'd be damned if she'd show it. Her chin rose a notch as she allowed more anger to seep in—this time directed at him—bolstering her wounded pride. ''If you feel that strongly, how do you think we can possibly become friends?''

He shrugged offhandedly again. ''It's no problem for me.''

The statement told her more than anything could have that there was no emotion left between them. Memories, perhaps, but no feelings. Why, suddenly, did that knowledge leave her with a hollow place in her stomach? Still, his rather cruel judgment had been unnecessary. ''Friends it is,'' she agreed lightly, but inside she was seething. ''Now that you have all that out of your system, you can leave and let this cold bitch get to work.''

''Don't put words in my mouth, Bree,'' Ryan warned her, his own anger a sudden thing. ''That wasn't what I—''

She spun on him. ''That's *exactly* what you called me. You may have couched it in more diplomatic terms, but it's what you meant. How do you know I don't have feelings other than self-protection? You're very quick to judge someone you haven't seen in twelve years."

Ryan didn't bother to deny that. He was furious with himself for losing his temper, and he was furious with her for having the power to provoke him. "And whose fault is that?" he demanded angrily. "Just who dumped who twelve years ago?"

She inhaled sharply. "You don't know me, Ryan," she said, her manner firm and unbending. "The woman you knew is gone forever."

She was furious, but the hurt was there, too—in her voice, in her eyes—and he took no pleasure in knowing he was responsible for it. What the hell had happened to him between one second and the next? "Ah, damn it, Bree—"

"I think you'd better leave," she said calmly. "Now."

He stared at her for a long minute. "I think that's a good idea," he said finally. He grabbed the keys and spun on his heel.

She heard the front door close behind him and slowly released the restriction she'd imposed on her spine, all the fight gone out of her. After several minutes she straightened, reentered the dining room and unhurriedly reached for the yellow pad filled with scrawled notes.

Gripping the keys in a tight fist, Ryan closed Bree's front door behind him. He was proud of his restraint; he didn't slam the damn thing hard enough to loosen the hinges. He ran lightly down the steps and strode toward his car.

He'd obviously overestimated his own control when faced with Briana Regan in the flesh. He'd resisted the feelings that had threatened from the moment she'd opened the door, but he hadn't resisted sufficiently. The meeting had turned into an emotional ambush when all he'd wanted was a private but civilized reunion.

In mental preparation he had taken himself back to the beginning, to the early days of childhood, to the innocent time before they'd fallen in love. He should have been reminding himself of the end. That had been his first mistake. No, his second—his first had been going there at all.

Sure, he'd wanted to see her. They'd grown up within a block of each other, played together, gone to the same schools, the same church. He'd always loved her parents, and particularly her father.

He'd been closer to Brian Regan than to his own father, who had never approved of his choice of career. And when his mother had made it clear that she was solidly on the side of his father, Frances had been the only woman in his life who seemed to understand his ambitions.

You didn't just write off friends of thirty-odd years. Or maybe you did. Maybe it would be best to stay as far away from Briana Regan—Fleming—as the city would allow, he thought, clamping his teeth together hard. He fished for his own keys and jammed one in the sports car's ignition, for once taking no pleasure in the motor's soft growl.

Minutes later he parked in front of the school and got out of the car. He was relieved to see that Frances wasn't at her desk. He wasn't sure he could be courteous to anyone at the moment. He dropped the keys beside her telephone and turned to leave.

Outside the office door he almost crashed into a diminutive nun in a black-and-white habit. "Ryan O'Hara. How nice it is to see you. I see you haven't slowed down at all."

"Sister Theresa," Ryan said, steadying her with a hand at her elbow. She'd been one of his favorite teachers, and he hated to brush her off, but he needed to get out of here. "I'm in a hurry right now," he explained. "You will be at the wedding this afternoon, won't you?"

She smiled, her sweet, round face framed by the starched white wimple. "Of course, Ryan. You hurry along. I know how busy you must be."

The rebuke was gentle but clear. Ah, hell. He relaxed, all the anger draining out of him at once. "I'm not that busy, Sister. Let me walk you back to your classroom."

"Thank you, Ryan." She was pleased by his offer. "Just let me check my mailbox."

As they walked he was lovingly grilled on the state of his health, his mind and his soul. Finally they came to the door of her classroom, the same room where he'd sat all those years ago, listening to her quote the poets. Keats and Shelley rolled easily off her tongue. She had a little more trouble with the bawdy words of Chaucer. The smell of chalk and books and that red stuff the janitors used to keep down dust when they swept took him back to his childhood. How cavernous this hall had seemed then. Nostalgia swept through him.

"And isn't it a coincidence that Bree has returned to Boston, too, after all these years? Where do you plan to live, Ryan?"

From her tone she might as well have been asking where *they* planned to live. Ryan narrowed his gaze, suspicion glinting in his eyes, but she looked as innocent and angelic as ever. He suddenly had a clear view of what Bree had meant. Father Brotsky, the elderly priest who had been principal of the school since Ryan could remember, had asked the same question when he'd come by early this morning to visit. Not quite as blatantly, but now that he thought back, it had been right after a comment about Bree.

Hell, he was imagining things, and Bree was overreacting. "I haven't made a decision yet, Sister. I just got in a few days ago."

"And your parents must be enjoying having you with them for a while."

"They left yesterday for California, to visit my sisters."

Sister Theresa was only taken aback for a minute. Then she smiled and patted his hand. Everyone knew that Ryan and his parents had always been distant with each other. "Well, I hope you'll decide to stay in the neighborhood, Ryan. We need young, vigorous blood in South Boston."

"I'll think about it," he promised.

He returned to his car and headed for the city, doing just that—thinking. Should he return to the old neighborhood or find something downtown, closer to his job? He certainly couldn't stay with his parents after they returned. He and the dour old man who was his father had grown farther apart, if that was possible, over the eight years he'd spent in Texas. He'd hoped things might have changed, but by the time he'd taken them to the plane bound for California he'd been relieved to see them go.

Shaking his head, Ryan turned onto the Summer Street Bridge, which led into the middle of the city. Downtown would be more convenient, he decided suddenly. Maybe Back Bay. He'd start looking for a place on Monday. Then he'd be spared even the occasional meeting at the market. The only time he'd have to see her was at weddings and funerals.

"Damn it!" he said out loud when he realized where his thoughts had led. He hit the steering wheel with the flat of his hand. Briana Regan—Fleming—had been there at the back of his mind the whole time, ready to subconsciously dictate even his choice of a place to live.

Bree glanced down at her watch. Over an hour had passed since Ryan had left. She hadn't accomplished a thing. Disgusted, she threw down her pencil and stood, stretching, pressing her fingers into the small of her back. She might as well dig in the garden. The way she felt right now, the weeds didn't stand a chance. On the way out the back door she gathered up an old pair of gloves and a trowel. Then she dropped the gloves. Today she needed to feel the fresh earth.

She'd been on her knees working for fifteen minutes when the emotional storm that she'd been trying to escape hit her hard. She sank to sit cross-legged, feeling the dampness of the ground through the seat of her jeans.

Maybe she shouldn't try to supress it any longer, she thought. Maybe she could use the memory as a catharsis. The trowel hung loosely from her limp fingers. Ryan... Twelve years. Less than half that time had been happy and content for Bree. "Oh, God." Her ragged whisper was a prayer for relief from a hurt that had never completely gone away. The scene from which the ache sprang was forever burned on her memory.

The blowup had occurred after her father's funeral. At twenty-two she had still been the light in her father's eye, his "precious child." And she had been almost mad with grief. A frenzied psychotic had put a bullet in her father's chest, the same broad chest where she had laid her head when she'd been a tired toddler seeking peace and security, where she had wept when her beloved dog, Goldwin, had died.

They had called Brian Regan Supercop. So what did that make the psychotic? Superkiller?

That day, after the coffin had been lowered into the ground, after the mourners had departed, she had given Ryan an ultimatum—give up your ambition to go into police work or give up me. She would not substitute one broad uniformed chest for another. Ryan had turned as white as the lilies beside her father's grave.

"Bree," he said in a choked voice. "I loved him as much as you did. Your father was my hero. In two weeks I graduate."

"With a degree in criminal justice," she said bitterly.

"Darling, I know you're miserable, but you can't mean this. We love each other."

She felt hard inside, like a piece of petrified wood, and she knew her expression mirrored that rigidity. "Miserable is a mild term for what I am feeling," she said bitingly. "I mean every word, Ryan. I will not marry you if you continue with your plans to become a policeman."

He stared at her, stunned. "Why now? Why here, over his grave?" he finally whispered, shaking his head in disbelief.

"I can't think of a more appropriate place, can you?" she answered.

Birds sang, unheard. The heat of the sun settled on her shoulders, unfelt. But the dense stillness between them, which seemed to stretch into forever, was tangible.

Slowly Ryan straightened. His shoulders moved beneath the jacket of his unrelievedly black suit. It was not like a shrug, it was more an effort to adjust a burden he hadn't been aware of carrying until that moment. "I've been accepted to law school, Bree. My career plans have never been a secret. How can you ask this of me?" he pleaded in a low voice.

She was deaf to the entreaty in his voice. "How? Look over there at my mother!" She pointed at Frances, who stood in the shade of a nearby tree, talking to the priest. "All her married life she has waited day by day, hour by hour, for the phone to ring, for a uniformed officer to come to the door." She fought the hysteria in her voice. "Day before yesterday, he came. And do you know what her first reaction was? Before the grief set in, before the realization that her husband was gone forever, before she began to think about how empty her life was going to be, she admitted to me that she felt relief not to have to expect him anymore.''

He schooled the expression that clearly reflected his shock and tried to take her hand, but she buried her fingers in her pocket. "I won't live like that, Ryan, afraid all the time. My fear would kill my love; eventually it would kill all my feelings."

"And what do you think you're doing to me?" The words fell like stones between them, heavy and sharp. "You've always known what I planned to do with my life. Do you think my love for you would survive giving up my ambitions?"

Selfishly, she hadn't thought of that. Now it only added to her determination to end their engagement immediately. They stared into each other's eyes with only the smallest premonition of the pain that was to come. Bree was the first to look away. The limousine provided by the funeral home stood at the curb, its door open.

Bree turned toward the vehicle; Ryan started to follow, but Frances stopped him. She had rounded the grave site without either of them noticing. "Let her be for now, Ryan. She'll come around," she counseled gently.

Her steps halted by her mother's words, Bree turned to stare slack jawed at them both. Then she spun away, resentment lengthening her stride.

"She needs some time to adjust. But she loves you," Frances went on.

Her mother, who needed comfort herself, was offering comfort to him. The words echoed in Bree's disbelieving mind as she climbed into the limo and closed the door. She could never, *never*, be so magnanimous.

Ryan called. He came by. At last he begged.

Bree saw what that did to him, and the sight was almost too much to bear. For she loved him; she would always love him. She didn't want that love to turn to hate or pity. Her mind was made up. Finally she asked him not to come anymore.

When Frances learned of her dictum, she was angrier than Bree had ever seen her. "If you want to be a fool, that is your prerogative, Briana. But this is my house. I shall decide who comes into it."

So, immediately after graduation, Bree moved out. She went all the way to New York to take a job she'd been offered in the public information office of the city.

During the many nights that followed, when she lay aching and lonely in her bed, she wished her ultimatum unspoken. But common sense always reasserted itself with the light of dawn. She'd done the right thing—for her and for Ryan.

Five years later, after Ryan finished law school, after he moved to Texas to work for the Houston police department, she married Dirk Fleming. Five years after that, her husband was the victim of a traffic accident.

At Dirk's funeral, her mother didn't say anything, but her thoughts were plain to read. Even while she held her daughter, supported her in another kind of grief, her expression spoke plainly. She had had more years as a policeman's wife than Bree had had as a stockbroker's.

The sun beat mercilessly down on Bree's head. She felt a cool nose push against her hand, smelled the rich earth caught tightly in her fingers. She opened her hand, brushed off the dirt. Then she picked up her ugly old cat and buried her face in his fur. "Gig, I'm going to have to be very careful."

Chapter 2

Ryan was practically knocked off his feet when one of the homicide detectives came bursting out of the office as he was coming in. "What's going on, sergeant?" he asked the woman at the front desk while glancing after the harried officer.

"We just got a floater, commissioner," said the woman, referring to a body found in the river. Starting to get to her feet, she looked somewhat uncomfortable when Ryan waved her back to her seat. "Excuse me, sir," she said when the telephone rang.

His job didn't officially begin until Monday, but like most officers of the law he was hard-pressed to stay away from the center of the action. He had made up his mind that he wasn't going to be the kind of commissioner who sat in a properly decorated office and waited for the department heads to come to him. So when he'd arrived this morning he had set off on a random tour of the building.

Money, money. The bane of all administrators was money. His predecessor had done a remarkable job, but how much more could have been done with enough money? He smiled to himself. Of course, he would put in a request for a budget increase; the mayor had as much as told him he was expecting one when he'd made the appointment.

Though the entire building was understaffed, from what he'd seen in the last three hours the homicide detectives seemed to be the most overworked. It was a sad commentary.

"Where was the body found, sergeant?" he asked when the young woman hung up.

"The Charles, sir." The Charles was one of the two rivers that curved through the heart of the city. "Near the Harvard Bridge," the sergeant explained.

"Is the captain in?" He nodded toward the office of the chief of homicide detectives.

"Yes, sir. Go right in."

"Sergeant, check with your boss first to see if he's tied up," Ryan said very patiently.

The sergeant looked surprised. She punched a button on the telephone and received instant permission for the commissioner to enter.

Austin Maxwell came out from behind his desk. "Ryan. It's good to see you." They shook hands with a warmth that testified to their friendship.

Maxwell was a relocated Texan. He had been well up the chain of command of the Houston homicide task force a few years before when his wife, an executive with a major insurance company, had been offered a vice presidency. The only catch had been that they'd have to live in Boston.

Maxwell had not hesitated. He'd resigned immediately and flown to Boston to apply for a job. The Boston police had been delighted to get him—he was a crack investigator—but the more macho members of his hometown force had given him a hard time about hanging on to his wife's coattails. He'd had his revenge when after only four years in Boston, he'd been named chief of homicide detectives.

Aside from the fact that he was impressed by the department's arrest and conviction record under Maxwell's direction, Ryan liked Maxwell and his wife and daughter immensely. The two men had laughed about exchanging hometowns and since had made it a point to see each other on visits home, whether in Boston or Houston. When Ryan had flown up to interview for the commissioner's appointment, Austin had been the first person he'd contacted. Now he sank into the chair opposite Austin's desk.

"I hear you've got a floater," he said.

"Yeah, among other things," drawled Maxwell as he settled into his own chair. They talked for a few minutes about active cases. Finally Maxwell, noting Ryan's restlessness, said, "You want to go down to the river?"

The question should have been a rhetorical one. Senior officers seldom took an active part in the investigation of an as-yet-unidentified corpse found floating in the river. But Maxwell knew Ryan. "I think so. You going?"

Maxwell stared at him for a minute. Then he shrugged his massive shoulders. "Hadn't planned to. But what the hell, it's a nice day. May as well."

Ryan's half smile was approving. "We'll take my car."

"Hot damn." Maxwell slapped his knee and stood up. "Let's go."

Ryan's smile grew wider at Maxwell's enthusiasm. The older man loved the sleek, superbly engineered Black Widow as much as Ryan did. The car, which had plenty of horses but no chrome, was Ryan's baby.

The ride was short. In less than fifteen minutes they stood silently on the banks of the river looking down at the water after having viewed a gruesomely mutilated nude body. The features had been obliterated by the force of a high-caliber bullet. At close range. The fingers had been hacked off at the first joint. The only thing they could be certain of was that he was a middle-aged male of slight build, approximately five-ten, with olive skin and a fairly old appendicitis scar. Someone had wanted to be absolutely sure that the man wasn't identified.

Ryan had seen many bodies—too many of them—and the very fact of murder ignited a sense of personal outrage. But mutilation never failed to make him physically ill. How could a man do something so inhumane to another man?

If you ask too many questions like that, he cautioned himself, you may find you're in the wrong business. But he wasn't. He believed with an unswerving conviction in the importance of his job, no matter what the cost. He stepped out of the way of a police photographer.

And it had definitely cost him. He clenched his jaw, this time firmly denying Bree admission to his thoughts. He had a demanding job to do, and too many adjustments to make to let himself get involved in a situation that could only go nowhere. He should be thinking about this murder and the questions it raised: when had it been committed, who was the unidentified victim, who had killed him, and why.

He thought about offering Bree an apology at the wedding this afternoon. He supposed he owed her that for his cynicism this morning, though he hadn't meant to imply that she was a cold bitch. If she interpreted that way... He shrugged. After today he would make sure their contact was minimal.

A police ambulance was backed up to the curb. One team of forensics experts was giving the ground a thorough, almost delicate, going-over; another was supervising the loading of the body into a standard black zippered bag. A man in diving gear approached Ryan and Maxwell. "Looks like he was pitched several days ago, Lieutenant. No ID, of course. We found that on the bottom near the piling."

The man pointed to an ordinary concrete block, fairly clean, that could have been filched from any number of construction projects in the city. "The body would have been under longer, but they used this." He held up several pieces of something twisted to resemble rope, made up of strips of a woven fabric, like an old sheet. The fibers were different from cotton, however. They appeared thicker, more like linen, and loosely woven. The homemade rope had practically disintegrated in the water, unraveling enough to release the body to within sight of the surface.

Maxwell took one of the soggy pieces and fingered it as though expecting a message. He shook his head. "Well, this is all we've got right now. Get it over to the lab and ask the coroner to get a move on on this one," he said, turning away with a move that told Ryan that the chief of detectives was as affected as he was by the mutilated body. "Let's get out of here," he snapped. "Unless you want to hang around. I can get a ride back to headquarters with one of my men."

"No, I'm ready," Ryan answered.

Maxwell climbed in the front seat. Ryan joined him there, buckled his seat belt and started the car.

"Why the hell do you subject yourself to something like that, O'Hara, when you could be sitting up in your office reading neat, cleanly typed reports?" Maxwell demanded. His anger was palpable, filling the car with accompanying tension.

Understandably. Murder brought out the rage in good policemen. He glanced across at his friend. "Would you?"

Maxwell didn't answer.

Ryan thought for a moment. His explanation had to be as clear as possible. He wanted his words to make the rounds, first to the other department heads, then filtering down until every cop on the beat was familiar with the new commissioner's philosophy. And he knew Austin would get the message out if he asked him to do so.

"You can pass this on, Austin. When I took this job, I promised myself never to let my work become a matter of statistics. You and I both have known cops to become dehumanized from sitting at a desk too long. They begin to think in terms of cases and paperwork rather than people. I'll follow procedure. I won't interfere in the running of your department as long as you do it effectively. But don't ask me to step back, because I won't do that."

Maxwell glared at him with grudging respect. "Natalie wants you to come to dinner," he growled.

Ryan nodded, agreeing with the deliberate change of subject. He knew it would take time for his ideas to sink in, time for some of the more experienced officers to understand the way he operated. Even Maxwell, who was his friend, had never been subordinate to him, and it would take some getting used to on the part of the older man. "Thanks, I'd like to see her again." He smiled. "She is some woman."

"That she is," Maxwell agreed.

They arrived back at headquarters. As they were getting out of the car, Maxwell said, "I'd better warn you that Natalie will pull all her unmarried friends out of the woodwork."

Ryan's hesitation lasted only for a heartbeat. Then he grinned. "That's okay, too. Let me know when you hear something about those fibers."

The venerable old church and school shared a kitchen. Bree parked her car in the lot nearest the school because it was closer. She tucked her purse under her arm and took the huge oblong tray of cakes from the front seat of her car. She was deliberately a little early. Her mother would be sure to read something into tardiness, something totally inappropriate, like anxiety or agitation over seeing Ryan again.

She slammed the door of her car with a twitch of her hip and crossed the parking lot. At the entrance she encountered a problem—how to get the door open with both hands full. She tried hooking her elbow into the handle, but that didn't work.

Suddenly, from within, a shadow loomed on the other side of the frosted glass. She stepped out of the way, a smile of thanks already in place. But the smile faded when she realized it was Ryan.

"I was watching for you. You looked like you could use some help." His tone was not warm, not indifferent, but somewhere in between. He propped the door open with his body and held out his hands.

"Thank you." She surrendered the tray, brushing past him to enter the building. After the scene between them this morning, why in the world would he have been watching for her?

He stopped just inside the door, and she had her answer. "Bree, I want to apologize for this morning," he said quietly.

She lifted her guarded gaze to meet his. "I'm sorry, too, Ryan. I suppose I'm quick to jump on the defensive where you're concerned."

"I didn't mean for us to argue. I came to your house because, as I told you, I thought it would be easier for us to meet privately." He started to add something but stopped when he saw the fixed expression on her face and waited for her to reply. He'd said enough to ease his conscience, anyway.

Her mouth softened slightly, her lips relaxing into a semblance of a smile. "You were generous to think of it. We're going to make everyone around us uncomfortable if we can't be at least amiable toward each other. The last thing we want to do is mar this day for Kathleen and Craig."

"The very last," he agreed. One side of his mustache tilted, and he nodded to the tray he held. "Sorry I can't shake on it."

"You just keep a good grip on that tray. Those are the wedding cakes," she said lightly.

This was a different Bree from the woman of this morning, thought Ryan, taking sidelong glances at her as they headed down the hall toward the kitchen. This one was glossier and far more elegant than the urchin in jeans. The mass of dark hair had been styled into a sophisticated chignon. In the rose-colored silk sheath and matching scrap of a hat, her New York polish glittered as brightly as the luster on her lips. To distract himself from the way she looked, he thumbed up a corner of the foil covering the tray. "Did you say wedding cakes? Plural?"

"Yes. Kathleen thought she and Craig were too old for all the traditional wedding frivolity. She didn't even want a reception. I convinced her that cakes and punch and coffee weren't frivolous."

At a break in the line of paint-chipped lockers, they passed the open door of a classroom. A nun was at the blackboard, explaining the intricacies of algebra. They walked under a countdown banner, strung across the ceiling, that read: 3 More Days of School, the three having been wedged in among a bevy of crossed-out figures beginning with fourteen.

A feminine squeal from inside the next room slowed Ryan's step. He glanced in and came to a halt. A grin spread across his face as he indicated the door with a jerk of his head. "Will you look at this?"

Bree backed up to look inside. It was the biology lab. She shuddered but laughed softly, remembering. "That poor frog."

"Yeah." He resumed his pace. "You saved my face that day, you know."

"I know. I'll never forget your expression. Who in the world would have believed that big, strong Ryan O'Hara, with ambitions to be a cop, would almost faint at the sight of a disassembled frog?"

When she looked up she had to smother a groan. Not again. At the mention of the job his expression had suddenly returned to the closed, hard look. It seemed that whenever they were about to relax a little bit some casual remark reminded them abruptly of the reasons for the animosity between them. Hard feelings and too many memories marked their relationship and were impossible to ignore. They would forever have to tiptoe around each other.

"I realized a long time ago that you did the right thing when you called off our engagement."

"Ryan, please—"

"A lot of marriages break up because of the job."

What he meant was that it would have taken a woman with strengths she didn't have, thought Bree, but she kept quiet about that. Instead she said evenly, "You've been through a lot worse. I heard about your getting shot."

It had happened not long after Dirk had been killed, only days after she'd moved back to Boston. She'd been at the end of her strength emotionally, and when the news had reached her she'd had to fight a strange but compulsive urge to fly to Houston immediately, to be with him until he mended.

Ryan's thoughts homed in on the first part of her statement. Nothing could ever be worse than having to choose between the woman you loved and your lifelong ambition, he thought, then shrugged, noting how pale her skin had become. "The shooting was two years ago," he said dismissively, wanting to forget. Bree would never know the story of the day he'd been shot, or of the weeks when he'd been recuperating.

"I was so relieved when I knew you were going to be all right," she admitted, unable to curb the hint of softness in her voice.

"Thanks," he answered shortly.

This man had been such an intimate part of her life... Suddenly a bell rang sharply, reverberating through the empty hallway, startling them both.

Bree recovered quickly. "Hurry if you don't want to be trampled." She gave a little laugh, quickened her steps to reach the door to the kitchen and held it open for him just as the classrooms emptied and the hall exploded with youthful energy. The door swung shut behind them, muting the sound.

Ryan chuckled. "Were we ever that wild?"

"We were worse." Tossing her purse onto a chair, she reached for the tray. "I'll take that now." Her fingers made contact with his on the silver handles.

It was the first time they'd touched, the first feeling of skin on skin. The reaction went through her like wildfire, spreading heat up her arms, across her shoulders, down her spine. Her eyes flew to his—and held.

Outside the door a shrill whistle, the kind that was made with two fingers between the lips, pierced the heavy awareness and brought Bree back to herself. "Thanks for the help, Ryan," she said briskly, placing the tray on the counter. "I have to find Kathleen. Why don't you go in?"

Without a word, Ryan relinquished the tray. When her fingers had brushed his he'd felt the effect jolt through him like an electric shock. And she'd felt it, too. "See you later," he muttered, and left, grateful to escape.

The service was simple, but the power and tradition of the wedding vows, spoken by friends of long standing, touched everyone who witnessed the ceremony in the small chapel off the sanctuary. Pretty Kathleen, capable of such incredible strength, stood beside Craig, who had a face like a thug and the kindest eyes imaginable.

Ryan caught himself repeating the words as Kathleen and Craig pledged their love to each other. He clenched his jaw in disgust when he realized what he was doing. They were words he would never say. "To love and to honor" was a belief to which he no longer subscribed. Oh, it was all right for this couple; these two had been tested and come up steel. But they were an exception.

Overcome by a rush of sentiment, Bree fumbled slightly when she was asked to produce the groom's ring. But it wasn't her own wedding she was thinking of. And it wasn't her late husband's face she saw reflected in the candlelight. Kathleen smiled and took the gold band from her trembling fingers.

Later, at the reception, Ryan paid his respects to the bride and groom. Kathleen and Craig were absorbed in each other, looking as though the sun were shining for them alone today.

He got away from them as quickly as good manners would allow and wandered restlessly around the reception hall, greeting old friends, seeing faces he'd forgotten. Time had acted with more subtlety on some of them than others. Some had reached the station-wagon age with grace; others seemed to be fighting it all the way.

He listened to snatches of conversation covering topics such as children and mortgages and family vacation plans with a strange, uneasy impatience that he put down to the discovery of the body in the Charles rather than the emotion of the service he'd just observed.

Murder, particularly a murder as grisly as the one they'd discovered today, was mind-stunning. Thank goodness the press hadn't yet gotten hold of the details of the discovery. But it wouldn't be long, he knew from experience, and then the siege would begin. This was the kind of story the press jumped on. Murder, mutilation, lack of identification. First they would plague Maxwell, then the harassment would progress to his office, and finally the mayor would be hounded.

Resolutely Ryan put the conjecture about the murder out of his mind. Everything that could be done for the moment was being done. This was neither the place nor the occasion for such thoughts.

Marilee O'Neal—Caitlin, he thought, silently correcting himself—was ladling out punch. He went over to speak to her. "How are you, Marilee?"

She had always been a little bashful, he remembered, but there was no trace of shyness in her smile now. "I'm fine, Ryan. Welcome home. Punch or coffee?"

"Punch," he said.

"It's good to see you again," she said as she handed him the glass cup.

"How's Colin? And let's see . . . two kids, was it?"

"Three," she answered. "We had our third little boy in December. Colin couldn't make it for the wedding, but he'll be here shortly and you can see him for yourself. Congratulations on your position."

"Thanks." He leaned a shoulder against the wall behind them and gave her a grin. "You're looking good for an old married woman, Marilee."

Her brown eyes sparkled with fun. "You're looking good, too, O'Hara. Have you seen Bree?"

Treat it lightly, he cautioned himself. "Yes, I have," he said with an easy smile, and drained the punch cup. "She's as beautiful as ever, isn't she? Where are Kathleen and Craig going on their honeymoon?" The casual compliment and the change of subject earned him a doubtful glance. Maybe they'd get the message when they realized he wasn't going to react.

"To Bermuda, I think."

"They'll enjoy Bermuda. I was there a couple of years ago." He pushed himself away from the wall. "See you later, Marilee. I'll be on the lookout for Colin." Pleased that he'd handled the situation, he handed her the cup and joined Father Brotsky by the water fountain.

The Polish priest, who had been assigned to be principal in a predominantly Irish school forty years ago—"until something more appropriate opened up"—was tall and spare, an Ichabod Crane in a Roman collar. His lips pursed thoughtfully, adding lines to a face already marked by seventy years of living. "Ryan." He nodded somberly.

"Father." Ryan greeted him with equal sobriety, fully aware of what his next lines were supposed to be. "It was a beautiful wedding, wasn't it?"

"Yes, but I'm sorry they didn't opt for the high mass."

"I'm sorry, too, Father."

"Ah, well, they're married. That's what's important in this life—marriage, the family, loyalty to one's church and community."

Father Brotsky had made it clear this morning that he presumed Ryan's appointment would mean extra patrols in the area and a sympathetic ear when a good kid needed rehabilitation more than incarceration. Ryan had grown up right here in the neighborhood. It was his home. He'd buy a house. He'd be around for mass. All those things were expected of him; Ryan hadn't the heart to correct the priest's assumptions.

"Have you thought about my suggestion that you join the church softball team?"

Ryan's brow cleared. "Yes, sir, I have. As long as it's clear to the rest of the team that my job has to come first, I'd like to."

"Good," said the priest, his mouth spreading into what was for him a broad smile. "The first practice is next Friday, a week from today, at seven o'clock. I will send you a copy of the schedule. As I told you this morning, we've had trouble getting good players. The team's performance has been less than distinguished over the last few years." He touched his chin, musing, and amended the statement. "Our Lord appreciates honesty—the team's record is rotten."

"Father, I haven't played in years," Ryan reminded him.

"But you were very good back then. If I remember correctly, you lettered in three sports. And you appear to have taken care of yourself. I'm sure it won't take you long to get back in the swing of it. We can certainly use some new blood."

Father Brotsky shuddered at his own word, and Ryan subdued a grin. The priest had told him about Tim Callahan's clumsy somersault on the outfield grass going after an easy pop fly last year, and about the resulting nosebleed.

"Ah, I see Colin has arrived. He needs to be out on the softball field, too. The exercise will help to eliminate that potbelly he's beginning to develop. Excuse me, Ryan."

Ryan remained near the water fountain, watching with a smile as the priest approached Colin Caitlin.

From the corner of his eye he saw Marilee join them, slipping her hand lovingly into the crook of her husband's elbow. He covered her hand with his, and she smiled up at him and whispered something.

Ryan turned away to respond to a greeting and was soon caught up in another conversation. But when Father Brotsky left them, Marilee brought her husband over to the group where Ryan was standing.

"Colin." He held out his hand. "Good to see you."

Colin returned the handshake firmly and grinned. "Ryan. It's good to have you back in the neighborhood. It even looks like we're going to be playing on a team together again."

"Colin has been trying to avoid Father Brotsky for weeks," said Marilee, patting his little pot affectionately. "It will be good for you, sweetheart."

Ryan said all the right things, answered their questions about his new position, but on another level he was more aware of the woman who had just come in through the swinging door from the kitchen. His sensitivity to Bree was a persistent thing, an irritant, there each time she entered with a pitcher of punch or left with a tray full of dirty cups.

A few times he and Bree had found themselves in the same group. They had both ignored the speculative looks directed their way, determined that conversation and laughter would come—or sound as though it came—effortlessly.

Bree put out a hand to snare the arm of a child running past the punch table. The child said something. She bent to answer, then swiped a cake off the table and presented it to the child with a conspiratorial grin.

She fit in here so well, he thought as he watched her move, an easy member of this community within a city. She still radiated the warmth and loving concern that had characterized her as a young girl. From this distance she might even have been twelve years younger. His honey Bree, that was what he'd called her. He'd forgotten the silly appellations. When she was sharp, his French Brie; when she was passionate, his heavy Breether.

In this gathering of friends they'd grown up with, he couldn't help the reflection that intruded so persistently: they could have been a part of it, could have had children by now, and a mortgage, and a station wagon.

He shrugged off the thought. At one time—when he'd been young and idealistic—he had thought the concept of hearth and home was a necessity in his life. Now a family was something he never missed. His job consumed great bites of his time and energy, and his co-workers were his family. A vacation was a trip to Bermuda with a beautiful woman. Taking the kiddies to the beach—even the idea was anathema to him.

Light feminine laughter brought Ryan back from his reverie. As he watched her talking with an older woman a sudden, inexplicably urgent need to escape this place came over him. He squelched the temptation to walk out without a further word to anyone.

These people, who he'd once known so well, were strangers to him. He lived in two worlds with two sets of characters, and he knew the world of his job far better. Having neither wife nor children nor a sense of community, he no longer fitted in.

For Bree, the afternoon was a triumph of determination over depression. Fully aware that her mother was watching her every move, Bree laughed and talked with old classmates, caught up on stories of their children, even deflected a pass from one of the two remaining unmarried men at the wedding. Ryan seemed to have no trouble ignoring her, while she had to guard her gaze, which seemed to stray in his direction every few seconds or so.

Though he talked and smiled, he was more disciplined this afternoon. His attention did wander a few times, and when it did there was something in his expression, something that was a remnant of the hardness she'd seen this morning.

When the reception was over she stayed to help clean up. And she wanted to talk to her mother. Well, not exactly talk... It would be easier now that Father Brotsky had taken Ryan off somewhere. She had to nip this dream of her mother's in the bud before Frances embarrassed them both further. And the way to do that was not by protest or lecture but by a clear demonstration of her indifference to Ryan O'Hara's return to Boston.

They were alone in the kitchen, Bree elbow-deep in dishwashing suds. She rinsed a coffee cup and set it on the drainer.

"It was a lovely wedding, don't you think?" Frances said, picking up the cup to dry it.

"Yes, lovely. Kathleen looked beautiful. And so do you, Mother. The dress fits you to a tee."

"I just love it, dear."

Bree had given Frances the royal-blue silk dress for her birthday. She'd known the color would be right; she'd gotten her blue eyes from Frances. And the rich blue also complimented her short white hair. But her mother wasn't any larger than a bird, and it was hard to find things small enough for her.

Frances's size belied her personality. A student waiting in the principal's outer office for disciplinary action had once called her mother a tough old broad. Bree smiled to herself. Frances had been delighted.

"I do hope they're going to be happy. Imagine, after all these years. Ryan seemed to enjoy seeing all his old friends again."

"I'm sure he did, Mother."

Gladys Sullivan came through the swinging doors with a last tray of cups and saucers. "This is all of them," she announced. "Two of the boys have taken out the trash. Are you sure I can't help you finish up?"

"No, Gladys," Frances said, reaching up to replace the cup in its storage cabinet. "We're almost through. Thank you for helping."

"I was happy to do it. Imagine, Kathleen and Craig after all these years." Gladys laughed softly. "Isn't it romantic? What about the flowers?" she asked. "Shall we have someone deliver them to the hospital?"

"Marilee is taking care of the flowers, and the leftovers, too."

Gladys left, and the two of them were once again alone.

Frances glanced at her daughter. "He looks well," she continued, as though the interruption had never occurred.

When her mother got hold of something she was as tenacious as a bulldog. Bree clamped down hard on her temper and ignored the remark. She placed the last punch cup in the rack to drain and rinsed the suds out of the sink before picking up a towel to dry her hands.

Lacking encouragement, Frances went on doggedly. "Well?" She laughed dryly. "That's an understatement if I ever made one. He looks gorgeous, doesn't he?"

This wasn't going at all as she'd expected. Bree's nerves were strung so tight she thought they would surely snap. All afternoon she had fielded questions, ignored not-so-subtle hints, declined invitations especially set up to include Ryan. Obviously her mother had been at work among their friends. She could imagine the conversation: "Isn't it lovely that Ryan's back in town? He and my Briana were so close. Do you remember?" A sigh. "My poor Bree, so alone now that she's a widow."

Carefully Bree folded the towel and replaced it on a bar under the sink to dry. "Mother." There was a warning in that one soft word, but Frances chose to ignore it.

"It's a shame he never married. Maybe you should—"

"Stay out of it!" Bree heard the snappishness in her voice. She paused for a minute to let things settle. She spoke slowly and distinctly, as though to a six-year-old. "Listen to me. There will never be anything between us again. Never. Ryan despises me. All your clever little hints and elaborate planning won't change that. So please, Mother, stay out of it."

"I'm sure he doesn't—"

"He does," interrupted Bree. "Just take it from me. He does. And he says you should know that as well as anyone. Oh, horsefeathers! I forgot the coffeepot."

Finally the hall was spotless, the dishes all dried and put away, the leftover refreshments and floral arrangements dispatched to the hospital, and Bree was giving the counter a last wipe.

Her mother had been strangely silent since Bree's outburst. She hesitated, then shrugged. She loved Frances, even if she was a busybody. Might as well try to mend fences as soon as possible. "I haven't any plans for this evening, Mother. Would you like to go someplace for dinner?"

Frances faced her daughter with a stricken look. "I, uh . . . well, I have accepted another invitation."

Bree was puzzled by the reaction but pleased that her mother had plans. Frances didn't get out enough. Maybe if she had more interests of her own she would not dwell on Bree's. "We'll do it another night, then."

Frances seemed to hesitate. She placed a hand on her daughter's arm. "Bree, I love you, dear. I'm sorry if I—"

"I love you, too, Mother." Bree smiled. Covering Frances's fingers with her own, she leaned over to kiss her mother's cheek. "All is forgiven. I promise."

"Are you ready, Frances?"

Bree spun around. She hadn't even heard Ryan come in.

He was still addressing her mother. "I thought we might try a new place I just heard about over near the bay. Father Brotsky and the Sullivans are going to meet us there."

"That sounds fine, Ryan. Just let me get my purse from the hall. I'll meet you outside."

Bree returned to her task, but inside she was seething. So he was taking her mother to dinner. Nothing wrong with that. Politeness might have suggested that he include her in the invitation, especially since they were a group. Not that she would have gone, but he could have made the gesture.

"Would you like to go with us, Bree?"

She changed her mind. She'd rather he hadn't bothered. "Thank you, Ryan. I have plans for this evening."

He gave her a long look, said a short goodbye and left.

Relieved that the ordeal of the afternoon was finished, she went home and took three aspirin for her headache.

Three hours later Ryan approached the bridge that connected South Boston to downtown. After dinner he'd dropped Frances off and gone back into town to see if there had been any developments in the murder case. He could have called, but he wasn't the least bit sleepy.

He let his mind wander over the events of the day. He'd seen some old friends, made some decisions. All in all, it hadn't been too bad a day.

The radio played softly as a background for his thoughts. Above the open T top the sky was clear.

As he drove along, his left elbow propped on the open window, his left hand gripping the windshield column and his right lightly guiding the steering wheel, nostalgia crept in again. The day hadn't been bad at all.

The meeting with Bree was behind him. After a couple of false starts, it seemed they had reached an understanding they both could live with.

He'd never forget the night he had first realized that Bree meant more to him than a pseudosister. He'd almost gotten himself killed. Looking back, he could see the humor in the incident, but he hadn't found it so funny at the time.

It had been a surprisingly mild night early in December, the last quarter of the last high school football game of his senior year—a sentimental occasion anyway, he had tried to tell himself when it had first happened. With only minutes before the final whistle, Catholic High was leading by a comfortable margin. Some of the seniors were starting to relax. A little horseplay, provided the team was winning, was almost a tradition.

He glanced over at the sidelines. The cheerleaders were going wild. Bree, in her little short skirt, had both hands over her head, fingers spread wide, bouncing around in a version of an Indian war dance.

He stared, stunned into immobility. She turned to grin at him, her eyes grew wide with alarm and—blam.

He hadn't even realized that the play had been called. A two-hundred-and-thirty-pound linebacker from the opposing team creamed him royally. Later, after the final whistle blew, she came up to him as he limped off the field. "Are you okay, Ryan?" she asked anxiously, her voice hoarse from yelling—and sexy as hell.

"Yeah," he managed to mutter, embarrassment warring with these disconcerting new feelings for a girl he'd always thought of as a pal. "But I may need a ride home." He never brought his car to the games, preferring to warm up by jogging the two miles to the school's stadium.

"Sure," she agreed readily. "I'll wait for you by the gate."

"No, the parking lot's dangerous," he said grimly. "It's too dark out there after everyone leaves. I'll meet you at the Pow-Wow." The Pow-Wow was a small café across the street that featured the best hamburgers in town and a jukebox. They always stayed open until midnight after the high school games.

She looked puzzled, as well she might. The parking lot wasn't all *that* dangerous, and he'd never been particularly concerned about her safety before, but she agreed. "Okay. See you in a little bit."

He took some ribbing about the block in the showers, but not as much as he'd have had to endure if they'd lost. When the coach saw his bruises he tried to get him to spend some time in the whirlpool. A soak in the hot water would have been appealing if he hadn't been under this strange compulsion to hurry across the street, to see Bree again, to find out if these feelings were an aberration. He mumbled some excuse about having to get home.

By the time he entered the café, his shoulder had begun to stiffen and he was limping. But the daze that muddled his brain had nothing whatsoever to do with his injuries. Bree was standing in a group near the jukebox. As he approached unnoticed, Jim Flannery—the guy she'd dated last summer—casually flung an arm across her shoulders and said something. His fingers dangled only inches from the heavy chenille letter on the front of her sweater.

Ryan suddenly discovered what people meant when they said they saw red. He wanted to march over there and flatten the jerk for his presumption. He didn't do it, of course, but he did manage to get her out of there on the double.

He politely opened the car door for her before rounding the hood and climbing in the passenger side. Her evident surprise prompted a rueful grin. She didn't have to say he was acting strangely; he knew it. He responded to her unspoken question. "Hey, let me be a gentleman for one night, huh?"

She chuckled as she backed out of the parking space. "I'm delighted. I'd never turn down an offer like that."

During the short drive they discussed the game. But when they arrived at his door he made no move to get out. He became silent.

"Ryan? Is something wrong."

"Bree..."

When he didn't go on, she turned sideways in her seat, her brow curved in a worried frown. "Are you hurt, Ryan? I noticed you were limping." Her hand covered his where it rested on his knee.

She was a caring person; she had touched him a thousand times in just such a way, but never before had her touch gone through him as this one did. "I know," he said quietly. "And no, I'm not hurt."

"That was a bad hit you took out there. What happened?"

He looked into her deep blue eyes and grew weak. He had no idea what he was saying, only that he wanted to keep her talking for a while so she wouldn't leave. "I was watching you."

"Me?" She laughed, the remnants of hoarseness in her voice scraping his nerves almost raw. "What was I doing? Making a fool of myself?"

"No. You were cute."

"Cute? *Cute?* Ryan O'Hara, haven't you learned yet that you don't call a woman 'cute'?" she admonished him with a teasing giggle. "Just for that, you chauvinist, get out of my car. I have to go home."

He met her grin and reached out to tweak her nose. "Yeah, I'd better, Ms. Feminist, before I say something I might really be sorry for." He opened the door and swung himself painfully out of the car.

"That sounds suspicious. What do you mean?"

He leaned down, his forearm on the roof, to look in at her. Such a bundle of femininity. He smiled tenderly. "I mean, Bree Regan, that despite all the hours spent naked in our wading pools when we were babies, I've only just now discovered you have breasts."

Her jaw went slack.

"Surprised? I was, too, or that lineman would never have nailed me."

Her mouth snapped shut, and she slipped the car into gear and stomped the accelerator. He barely had time to slam his door and step back before she was gone.

Ryan smiled at the memory. Lord, she was mad that night, he remembered. Her glorious Irish temper caught fire and blazed for weeks. It took him until Christmas just to get her to talk to him again.

But, he also remembered, by Valentine's Day he'd kissed her. Her mouth had tasted so sweet, so very sweet.

Suddenly, without warning, the image of her standing at the altar this afternoon, holding her modest bouquet, fumbling with the wedding ring, was so vivid he felt as though he could touch her. All the memories he'd fought, all the emotions he'd deliberately stored away years ago, came back in a rush to betray his control, as though they'd been just waiting there, ready to attack at the least crack. And he'd opened that crack himself. The memory of all that love— good God, so very much of it, and all wasted—came rushing in, too compelling to be denied.

He held out one hand and looked at it. It was shaking. He whipped the steering wheel to the right, pulling off onto a side street, and stopped the car. Folding his arms across the top of the wheel, he rested his chin on them for a minute, staring through the windshield, determined to get a solid hold on himself. Perhaps it was necessary to let all the emotions back in so he would recall the bad along with the good;

perhaps then they would be content to disperse and leave him in peace. He squeezed his eyes shut and dropped his forehead to his crossed arms. *Oh, Bree. Oh, God, Bree.*

She couldn't help her fear twelve years ago any more than he could help his bitterness today, but why hadn't he been able to keep the lid on his anger? He'd wanted to smooth things over between them, prepare them both, while at the same time he'd wanted to make his feelings perfectly clear.

"Let me see your driver's license, mister," growled a voice at his side.

Shaken abruptly out of his reverie, Ryan's head jerked around. "What?"

"Your license, buddy. You shouldn't pick a loading zone to sleep it off."

"And I'll take your badge number," Ryan demanded fiercely—and stupidly.

The young patrolman came to sharp attention. His hand hovered over his unsnapped holster. "Okay, mister. Out of the car," he ordered sharply.

Good sense returned, and Ryan complied without further complaint. Even over his chagrin at being caught doing something so dumb, he noted with satisfaction that the man was following proper procedure.

"Hands on the hood. Spread your legs. Don't move." The man reached carefully into Ryan's jacket pocket to relieve him of his wallet.

Ryan kept the position. He didn't say a word until he heard a muffled curse and a groan behind him. Poor kid, he thought, glancing over his shoulder. In the dim illumination from a streetlight a block away, he studied the young man's face. He couldn't possibly be older than twenty. His square jaw was flaming red, and he was beginning to perspire. Ryan recalled a few blunders he himself had made as a rookie patrolman.

"Mister—uh, Commissioner O'Hara, I'm…oh, hell…" Helplessly the young man held out the wallet and tried to remain at attention. "Patrolman Phillips, sir," he said as though reporting for duty.

Ryan smiled sympathetically, but he felt as if he were a hundred years old. "Don't worry about it, son," he said. "You did everything by the book. My mistake. I shouldn't have stopped there."

Phillips was fast recovering his equilibrium. "Thank you, sir. I was on furlough yesterday when you came in, sir. I should have recognized you from the picture in the paper, but the car sort of threw me, sir."

His beautiful baby wasn't the kind of vehicle usually chosen by policemen. For one thing, few could afford a Black Widow, as his little sports car was known. He wouldn't be able to make the payments, either, if he had responsibilities for anyone other than himself. "One 'sir' per paragraph is sufficient, Patrolman Phillips. As I said, you were doing your job. Now I suggest you get on with it."

"Yes, sir. Thank you, s—uh, Commissioner."

That'll teach me, thought Ryan as he climbed back into the car.

Chapter 3

The State Department was sending out its big guns, noted Bree as she listened to Mayor Quinlan introduce the man who had come to speak to them. John Carter, the undersecretary for Middle Eastern affairs, was a surprise, an unprepossessing man, younger than she'd expected. The applause that greeted his introduction was quietly polite.

Thirty or so people, the ones most closely involved with plans for the upcoming visit of the foreign minister of Karastonia, had gathered in the mayor's briefing room.

Bree kept her gaze fixed firmly on Carter. Had she shifted her eyes a quarter of an inch to the right she would have been faced with Ryan's profile, and she didn't want that.

A week had passed since the wedding and reception. She'd seen him once, on Tuesday, at another meeting, which had also concerned the minister's visit. But at other times he had been more in her thoughts than she'd imagined he would be, much more than was comfortable.

Now he sat in the row in front of her, only two seats down. When they had entered the room a few minutes ago he'd greeted her with a reserve she was determined to match. She hoped she could get through this afternoon without any personal contact.

He wore a tailored suit in a medium gray shadowed by a darker gray pinstripe. His tie, neatly knotted under a spotless white collar, was maroon with tiny navy-blue figures. Black tasseled loafers were polished to a bright shine. Her mother was right; he was gorgeous.

But his expression was grim. Not only the security for the visit but also the corpse in the Charles would be the reason. The picture on the front page of last Saturday's paper showed the scene of the crime and, one column away, a file photograph of the new police commissioner. The story also explained why he had seemed preoccupied at the wedding.

Follow-up stories each day had not revealed much additional information, but they had continued to receive front-page coverage. The banks of the Charles River were popular with Bostonians. Joggers ran there, children played, lovers walked and families picnicked there. In the summer, the Pops played in the nearby band shell. If there wasn't an early arrest, the people of the city would want to know the reason why.

She studied the lines of strain in his face, surprised to find herself reacting compassionately to his problems. He was assuming the leadership of a major city's police department, the youngest man ever appointed, with the accompanying pressure to prove himself. To be faced with a murder as horrible as the one last week, with its notoriety, would be a double burden on him.

Bree shook herself mentally. The room seemed small— any room she shared with him seemed small, she thought, shifting restively. She could deal with this situation so much more easily if they didn't have to work together. But they did, so she made a conscious effort to subdue her empathy. Ryan had barely spoken to her today. Why waste benevolent emotions on a man who neither needed nor wanted them?

For her own peace of mind, she'd rather he'd stayed in Texas. Ryan O'Hara in another city, in another state, on another coast, was a different matter from Ryan O'Hara right here in their hometown. Blindly she dropped her eyes to the pages in her lap.

At odd times she had found herself wondering whether or not he was romantically involved with anyone. Had he left a woman in Texas? And if so, would she be following him? No one who looked as good as Ryan would be alone for long, she reasoned, and she better get used to the idea. If there wasn't a woman in Texas, there would be one soon in Boston.

Bree ran the unattached women of the parish through her mind, dismissing each for one reason or another. She wondered whether, if he married, she would be able to meet him with any kind of aplomb at all. They had managed to present an amicable facade to the friends assembled for the wedding, but she knew she couldn't keep up appearances for long under those conditions. She might as well face the fact that she was much too sensitive to his presence.

During the meeting earlier this week, she and Ryan and the police lieutenant in charge of security for the minister's visit, Sam Dalton, had butted heads over a number of details. Ryan, it seemed, would have liked nothing better than to lock the minister in his hotel room for the duration of his stay.

Then the mayor's secretary had called unexpectedly this morning and asked them all to meet again at four o'clock, apologizing on Quinlan's behalf for the short notice.

It was Friday, she thought as she looked around, and bureaucrats didn't like their weekends cut into. Maybe this wouldn't take long.

From his tone of voice she could tell that the preliminaries were over. Carter was about to get to the point of his presentation. Thank God. She really wanted—needed—to get out of here.

"Ladies and gentlemen, again I apologize for the short notice of this meeting. Most of you have had some contact with people from my office." He held up a thick sheaf of papers. "From these written reports you sent to Washington, I can see that the city of Boston is well prepared for Minister Saber's visit." He dropped the papers and continued. "I'm here today not only to stress the importance of this visit but to let you know that my office will be alerted to give you any cooperation or assistance you might need. And I will be personally available, as well."

That was odd, thought Bree. She would have thought an undersecretary in the State Department would be content to delegate such duties.

"I have come personally to add to your problems with an official announcement," he said, grinning in response to the groan that went around the room. The smile disappeared; he was suddenly serious, and the attention of those in the room sharpened. "Only the mayor and Commissioner O'Hara had prior knowledge of this announcement. I apologize in advance for the problems the delay might cause you.

"I'm sure you have heard the speculation about the change in the government of Karastonia. The present king having no direct heirs, the country's ambassador to the United Nations will officially announce today to the General Assembly that, at the first of the year, the monarchy will come to an end. Karastonia will hold its first elections as a full-fledged democracy. You're intelligent people. I needn't tell you, I'm sure, of the importance of having a democratic ally in that part of the world. The foreign minister, who will arrive in the United States in less than three weeks, is the leading candidate to be the country's first elected president. The transitional period is expected to go smoothly. However, expectations are one thing, reality is another.

"There are forces at work in the area, as there always are," he said wryly, "that would do almost anything to stop the free elections. Or, not succeeding in that, to install their own candidate. In short, the security as well as the political importance of this visit cannot be stressed enough. The administration would have preferred that the minister come directly to Washington, but he is something of a history buff." He paused. "The man is fully aware of the responsibility he will be assuming if he's elected, and it is his desire to see the cities that spawned liberty in our own country—Boston, Philadelphia—before going to the capital."

Bree's gaze shifted to Mayor Quinlan, smiling slightly at the pride that shone in the man's eyes. He loved Boston and its history with a fervor that bordered on the fanatic.

Carter wound up his presentation. "If you have any questions, no matter how trivial they might sound, please feel free to ask."

Ryan stood. Bree had to look at him then and pretend to be interested in what he was saying.

For Carter's benefit, Ryan introduced Sam Dalton as the police officer in charge of security. Bree gratefully switched her attention as Dalton began to relate something about accommodating the personal bodyguards traveling with the foreign minister. Ryan continued to stand beside his subordinate as though standing with the man figuratively, as well. That would be Ryan's style.

The man from State had answered a question from Dalton and was now asking one of his own. "Commissioner O'Hara, since we talked on the telephone, have you had a chance to review all of the preparations for security during the visit? And are you satisfied?"

Ryan stood straight but relaxed and assured, in the familiar stance, his coat unbuttoned, one hand in his pocket. "Yes, sir," he said. "We'll be ready." That was it. No equivocation, no qualification, no excuses, just a man taking responsibility for his job.

How refreshing, thought Bree, more accustomed to working with people who always seemed to leave themselves a way out if any problem should arise. She couldn't help admiring him until he spoke again.

"I do have one remaining problem with the schedule, however," he added. "The walk along the Freedom Trail has always been a nightmare for security people. In the past, some visiting dignitaries have ridden in a limo instead of walking. I think that would be preferable in this situation."

Bree's pencil point dug into her notepad. She surged to her feet.

"Mrs. Fleming, do you have a comment?" said the mayor. He introduced her to Carter.

She glared at Ryan but directed her protest to the undersecretary. "Yes, sir. Commissioner O'Hara and I have already been through this. In light of your announcement I can understand his concern, and I will work with his office to find an answer, but the man chose to come to Boston for a reason, as you said, sir."

Professionalism warred with libido as Ryan watched Bree, trying with difficulty to keep his mind on her words and off the woman herself. She'd given him fits over this part of the minister's tour, and it had to be reconciled, but he couldn't keep his gaze from wandering over her slender body. A fashionably tailored royal-blue suit blurred the lines of her figure but emphasized the color of her eyes. Her black hair was firmly anchored in a chignon at her crown, but wispy pieces had escaped to tease her neck, her temples.

With an effort he tore his gaze away, looking to the dais to find that the mayor had been watching him watch Bree. A knowing smile curved Quinlan's thin lips.

Ryan allowed his mouth to relax as he met the mayor's smirk, but cautiously. Bree would be furious if she intercepted the exchange.

He glanced at her to find her eyes on him. She was still talking. "It's true that in the past some of the security people have insisted on the limo."

"Hold on—" Ryan said, straightening.

"Please." Bree held up her hand to quiet him until she was finished. Again she directed her statement to the man from State. "The minister is a devoted student of history. The Freedom Trail follows the most historically significant points in Boston, and it wanders a bit into places accessible only on foot, places like Public Gardens and the Common. Riding past in a closed limousine is not nearly as meaningful to the afficionado as actually following the trail."

"And not nearly as dangerous," put in Ryan.

"My office finalized the minister's schedule. Commissioner O'Hara was sent a copy by messenger immediately."

A muscle in his jaw jumped. "I tried to call you to discuss this. Your secretary told me you were out of town," he said, giving the impression that he didn't believe a word of it.

"I was away from the city on business." She had flown to New York with a client yesterday and returned at noon today. She hadn't left a number where she could be reached because there had been nothing pending that couldn't wait one day. But she hadn't anticipated the undersecretary's arrival; no one had.

The undersecretary looked speculatively from one of them to the other. He stroked his chin. "Surely this is something that can be worked out between the two of you. Perhaps a compromise? Part of the trip on foot and part in a limousine?"

He smiled at their reluctant nods and went on. "My primary concern and that of this administration is for the minister's visit to go smoothly. Boston is the first stop and can set the tone for the entire trip. We want to keep him safe—" he smiled at Ryan "—and we want him to have a good time." A second smile was directed toward Bree. "I need not remind you that since the Russians moved into Afghanistan our diplomatic ties to Karastonia are crucial."

His words served as a gentle admonition to them both. As they reseated themselves she noticed that the area above Ryan's collar was slightly red.

The mayor thanked the undersecretary, and the meeting was adjourned. As they filed out, Bree found herself wedged in behind Ryan. A woman Bree recognized as a representative of the governor's office turned aside, leaving a space. Bree tried to edge past him but felt her arm being gripped in a strong hand.

"Can we talk?" Ryan asked in an undertone.

"About the minister's visit?"

He hesitated. "Partly."

"Sam Dalton and I will work everything out. If you'll excuse me, I'm in a hurry."

"Damn it, Bree. Can't we act like the adults we are?" he muttered. "Time for a drink, that's all I'm asking."

"You know I don't drink." She recognized her words as the weak excuse they were.

"As you so recently reminded me, I don't know a damned thing about you," he bit out harshly, drawing a few eyes. He drew in a long breath and seemed once more to have himself under control. "A cup of coffee, then."

"Very well."

When they were seated in a booth in the small pub around the corner, Ryan ordered Scotch for himself and coffee for Bree. "Can we agree to compromise on the Freedom Trail?" he asked when the waitress moved away.

"Yes, of course we can."

He reached into his jacket pocket and pulled out a copy of her report. He spread the papers on the table between them and reached into his pocket for a pen. "Okay. Here's the route. If we pick up the trail here on Beacon Street at the State House and the archives..."

"Are you going to completely skip Boston Common? The trail begins there."

"It's forty-eight acres of public park, Bree," he protested. He studied the stubborn expression on her face for a minute, then relented. "Okay. I'll get together with Sam. We'll figure out something," he said wearily.

Ryan was willing to compromise, thought Bree; surely she could, too. She thought for a minute, a small frown of concentration wrinkling her brow. "What if we cut very short across the east corner? He'll have a good view from the hill there," she offered.

If Ryan was surprised by her willingness to adjust, he didn't show it. "And we can pray there aren't any political demonstrations going on that day, because that's where they'd be," Ryan said wryly, but he was smiling at her. He covered her hand with his in a brief salute. "Thanks, Bree. That will work well.... Then, when we leave the Boston Massacre site for Faneuil Hall..."

Her rational thoughts followed his ideas. She nodded or shook her head when she was supposed to, but her feelings were recovering from the brief touch. Her eyes roamed, noticing things she shouldn't have noticed. His large hand with its clean, short nails lay palm down, holding the map; light brown hair dusted his wrist; his fingers directed the pen in his other hand with confidence.

The waitress brought their drinks; he smiled with unnecessary warmth at the woman before returning his attention to the paper between them. Bree was stunned by her own reaction to the smile. Dear Lord, if she hadn't known better she'd have said she was jealous.

"Do you agree with these changes, then?" he said finally, looking up. He must have read something of her emotions in her face. "Now what's wrong?"

"Nothing. Really, nothing," she said hurriedly to cover her confusion. She decided not to mention the rather knowing masculine exchange she'd witnessed between Ryan and the mayor. She might have misinterpreted it. "I agree to the alterations, and I'll have the changes typed up. If that's all, I'd like to go."

"Finish your coffee."

"No, I don't want it." She started to slide out of the booth.

"Sit down," he ordered firmly, stopping her with a hand on her arm.

Her response was immediate and instinctive. She jerked her arm free, drawing as far away from him as possible. Just like a quaking virgin, she realized in disgust.

"For God's sake, calm down, Bree. I thought we'd settled this." He sighed and leaned against the padded booth, giving her the room she silently demanded. Hooking one elbow over the back of the booth, he held up his hands, palms out. The action opened his coat, stretched his shirt over his broad chest. "I don't know why you're acting like I have something contagious, but if we're going to work together effectively we have to deal with the situation between us. Now."

"I am calm," she said. He was right; this had to be dealt with, and emotionalism wouldn't help the situation. It was odd; she wasn't usually emotional. "You're the one who's been acting strange, Ryan. Thoughtful one minute, cold and hard the next. I know I'm to blame for twelve years ago," she said frankly. "But that's in the past and it must stay there."

"I agree."

"Now, when I'm trying to be polite—"

"I hadn't noticed," he interrupted dryly.

She took a long breath and controlled her irritation before she spoke again. "When I'm trying to be polite," she repeated slowly, "you're about as civil as . . . as . . ."

"As?" he encouraged with an arched brow.

"As cold cod," she finished, but without the sustaining anger the criticism was lame.

He chuckled and shook his head. "That's graphic."

She returned the smile with a cynicism she hadn't known she possessed. "It's childish," she admitted. "I don't know why I have this tendency to act so juvenile around you."

He raked the fingers of one hand through his sun-streaked hair, leaving it untidy, and slumped in the padded booth. "I'm not proud of the way I've been acting, either," he admitted. He tugged his tie free of its knot and opened the top button of his starched collar. Taking a long swallow of his drink, he fixed her with his iron-hard gaze. "It's difficult for me to feel friendly toward you. The reasons are so complicated that I doubt that I ever will."

She met his gaze levelly. "I know it's hard. We've seen each other three times since you've been home. Whenever I think we might have reached an understanding, I say or do something to set you off again. Ryan, maybe I deserve to, but I won't wear a hair shirt. If I made a terrible mistake twelve years ago, it's one I'll have to live with. I can understand if you can never forgive me, but if you can't, then stay away from me. Let me work with Sam." She shrugged. "Maybe if we didn't know each other so well . . ."

"Yeah." He hesitated before he went on. "The problem is that whatever it is that causes the sparks to fly between us is still there, just as strong as ever. I'm not sure how to handle it."

Bree inhaled sharply at his admission. She sat unmoving for a long minute, the room receding from around them, the sounds muted, as he held her gaze unrelentingly, waiting for a reaction.

"Sparks" was a perfect descriptive term for the electricity that seemed to pass from one of them to the other, the chemistry that reacted to the slightest provocation. But sparks suggested emotional involvement . . . and that could so easily lead to complications.

She'd had no idea he was facing the same problems she'd been fighting. "That's impossible," she said firmly, suddenly presented with a picture—his arms around her, his mouth on hers, his hands touching. . . .

"What are we going to do?" she added, then realized she'd just given herself away, confessed her own response. She felt the warmth that rose in her cheeks.

A flash of something silver in his eyes told her that he hadn't missed the slip and that it hadn't made him particularly happy. "So far the sparks seem to be manifesting themselves in animosity," he said evenly. "But that could change. It's something we have to think about. Ignoring it won't make it go away. I've tried all week long."

She sighed and traced the handle of her cup with one finger. She was surprised to see that the finger was steady. "I'm not interested, Ryan."

He spoke abruptly and sharply. "Neither am I, lady, believe me. Do you think I'm a masochist?" Then he sighed. It was a heavy sound. "There I go again."

She took a sip of coffee and tried to think rationally. The empathy she'd felt earlier reemerged. "You have enough to concern you right now without having to deal with feelings that shouldn't be there."

"You're telling me?" His gaze roamed over her face. After a minute he shook his head, laughing softly. "It's been a rough week."

She cupped the coffee mug in her hands and stared at him over its rim. "The murder case?"

There was an unvoiced question in his gray eyes. She knew what the question was. Could she talk about police work without becoming upset? She wasn't sure of the answer. "I heard that the man's body was…that you couldn't identify him," she said quietly.

"We don't have a single lead that's worth a damn."

"Nothing?"

"He was five-ten, a slightly built Semite Caucasian, olive complexion." Ryan stared into his drink as he went on. "He took care of himself, exercised regularly, and he had his appendix out when he was about ten. The rest of the coroner's report reads like an essay on possibilities. The poor bastard could be from Saudi Arabia or San Diego. Someone wanted to make damned sure we didn't get a quick ID."

The frustration built in him. She remembered exactly the same disturbance in her father when he'd been faced with a baffling case. Strangely, the recollection didn't hurt as much as it once would have. "No missing persons reports?" she asked, honestly interested.

"Not on anyone faintly resembling him."

"I noticed the papers are doing some heavy breathing down your neck."

"Yeah." He looked at her steadily with an expression that might have included a hint of approbation. She couldn't be sure. "It doesn't bother you to talk about this?" he asked.

She dropped her eyes under the force of that gaze. "I don't think—not so much anymore. Not since Dirk was killed." She swallowed hard, remembering that Ryan had once declared, "I could get killed crossing the street." And that was exactly what had happened to her husband.

"I hope you can follow my mother's example. She hasn't said, 'I told you so,'" she added in a moderate tone.

Ryan watched the moisture gather in her deep blue eyes; he watched her overcome the tears that threatened by sheer strength of will, and he respected her for the control it took. "No, I won't say that, Bree." He paused. "You loved him very much, didn't you?"

He wasn't sure how they'd arrived at this point—how, suddenly, his envy of the unknown man had come to be nearer the surface than it had been in years. He held his breath, waiting for her answer. If she said yes, it would be like pouring salt into wounds already opened and raw just from being around her; and they would hurt like hell before they began to heal again.

Yes, I loved Dirk, thought Bree. He was a good and decent man and everything I thought I wanted. He never set off firecrackers—or sparks. He didn't have the effect on me that you did, but he was tender and giving and honorable. That needed to be said. "Yes, I loved him."

Dropping his gaze to hide his expression from her, Ryan polished off the remaining Scotch in his glass. He'd thought he'd known pain. Now it launched through him with the power of an earthquake aftershock. Control was not easy to retain when he wanted to smash his glass, or his fist, against the wall. But he'd had twelve years—twelve long damned years—to learn it.

He'd finally been able to put Briana Regan out of his life, out of his mind. Rarely had she sneaked back in. Especially not since two years ago, when her very name had caused a major upheaval in his life.

There had been a woman, a woman he'd been very fond of. He'd heard of Dirk Fleming's death, but he'd told himself it had nothing to do with him. Then he'd been made by a fencing ring he'd been investigating undercover.

He'd been shot. In the gut, in the shoulder, in the thigh.

Days later he'd come to in the hospital, his fiancée holding his hand. But it hadn't been her name he had called in his delirium.

Ryan's long, thick lashes hid his expression from Bree. He seemed lost in faraway thoughts. "Have you ever thought about marriage?" Bree asked, then wondered why she'd brought up the subject. It was none of her business.

"I thought about it once. It didn't work out." Glancing at his watch, he set his glass down with a thump and picked up the check. Quickly he scanned the card and reached for his wallet. "I didn't realize it was so late. I have to be someplace at seven. I hope you'll excuse me." He took out a bill, tossed it on top of the check and rose.

Bree opened her mouth to tell him that she knew where he was going. Father Brotsky had bragged to everyone about drafting Ryan O'Hara for the church softball team.

"Of course." She closed her mouth without saying another word. Clearly he wanted to get away from her. Their emotions were at a dangerous point again. She couldn't help wondering if the subject of Dirk had lighted the fuse. Surely not.

This fragile truce they'd negotiated needed time to gel. That was all. Though the discussion had been necessary, it had left scars on both of them. Her question about marriage had probably brought on his need for distance. *It didn't work out.* She glanced at her watch. An hour from now he might be easier, more comfortable with himself and with her. "I have to be going, too. Thanks for the coffee, Ryan."

They left the pub together and parted at the corner with a casual goodbye.

Ryan jogged onto the field, anticipating a good workout. Physical activity, that was what he needed to release the pressure built up from another confrontation with Bree. He waved to Father Brotsky, who waved back from a seat in the deserted bleachers, and approached the cluster of men standing around home plate. Colin was there, thank goodness, he thought. Then he recognized two others, Ziggy and Fitz Delaney. Both were younger brothers of a friend of his, Stan Delaney. Much, much younger.

"Hey, Ryan. The good padre told us you were coming. Great to see you. We sure can use a man who can hit. That is, if you're as good as you used to be."

Ryan grinned and slapped Stan's kid brother on the back. "I haven't played softball in years, Ziggy. Father Brotsky talked me into it. But now that I see all you kids playing, I'm wondering if I should go home."

Ziggy grinned. "Just try it. Come on, I'll introduce you around."

Ryan liked them all, young to middle-aged—thank the Lord, there were some of those—businessmen, teachers, professionals. The team wasn't going to win a World Series, but they were enthusiastic. In a few minutes five men scattered into the infield and began to toss the ball around.

Three more headed for the outfield. "Hit them a few, Ryan," said Fitz, handing him a bat and ball.

Ryan crossed to the plate. Spreading his legs slightly, he dug his toes into the soft dirt. He lobbed the ball into the air. With one smooth movement his left hand joined his right around the handle of the bat, and he slashed at the ball on its way down.

He connected, his hands, forearms and shoulders absorbing the force of the hit. He swiveled on the balls of his feet, twisting on the follow-through, stretching and using muscles that hadn't been called upon in a long time. He'd taken up racquetball, he swam regularly, he jogged. But softball brought him something he'd missed. He laughed with the sheer enjoyment of being on a hot, dusty field on a summer night, using his body and his energy. God, it felt good.

"Way to go," said Fitz, pitching him another ball.

This time he sent one deep into center field and watched an accountant dive for it.

"I'll bet you're wishing that was my head," came a voice from behind him.

Startled, Ryan whirled, a frown drawing his dark, level brows together. He let the tip of the bat drop to rest on the ground.

Bree stood there, dressed in jeans that fit as though she'd been born in them and an untucked, oversize T-shirt that barely disguised her beautiful breasts. Most of her long black hair was tucked up under a baseball cap. She looked tiny and tomboyish and delectable enough to eat. "What are you doing here?"

She spread her hands in a self-deprecating gesture and grinned. "I'm your coach."

Suddenly Ryan became aware of calls from the players in the infield. "Hey, coach, you're late!" "Where you been, coach? Heavy date?"

"Coach? You? I thought Ziggy—"

She gave him a lopsided smile. "Didn't anyone bother to tell you? That's why I'm late. I thought I'd give you a chance to back out."

This was what she'd meant this afternoon when she'd said, "If you can't forgive, stay away from me." He was staring, but he couldn't seem to help it.

Ziggy had walked up in time to hear the comment. Laughing, he tugged at the bill of Bree's cap. "That's why we didn't tell him. Not all macho men are as open-minded as we are about having a girl coach."

Bree took a mock swing at him. "Get lost," she ordered. When he moved away she faced Ryan again, her hands on her hips, waiting.

Annoyed, unnerved, Ryan swallowed the laughter welling up in him. What a fiasco. He'd come to the field with the hope, no, with the full intention of working this woman out of his system with physical exercise.

What the hell, he decided, shaking his head helplessly. He'd never been one to throw caution aside, but now, as he felt his annoyance slowly give way, he opened up to the deep excitement waiting to take its place. The sparks were back, but he didn't feel hostile. No, he didn't feel hostile at all. He let the warmth flood into, around, through him. Though he'd tried to tell himself differently, he'd been fighting this awareness—hell, put the right name to it—this desire, from the moment she'd opened her front door to him. He was through fighting.

She'd said she wasn't interested, but he read other emotions in her eyes. And this time, whatever happened between them would be on *his* terms.

He took one purposeful step toward her. "Why didn't *you* tell me?" he asked in a low, intimate tone, allowing his smile to grow seductive.

"I'm not sure," Bree admitted, unsettled by his gaze roaming hungrily over her face, lingering longest on her lips, and by the sight of him in body-hugging jeans and a T-shirt that blatantly proclaimed the strength of his arms, his broad shoulders and his sex appeal. But she held her ground. "I'm a pretty good coach," she added.

"I'll just bet you are," he said softly.

"Well?" she prompted, herself again. "Are you going to join the team or not? We have a game tomorrow afternoon. I'll have to get you a uniform."

Ryan let his gaze slide down her body and up again, thoroughly enjoying the way she bristled in response. Slowly he grinned. "What position do I play, coach?"

Chapter 4

The next morning Ryan sat at his desk, elbow-deep in paperwork. He didn't mind the seven-day weeks, the uncountable hours, the occasional danger or the frustration; paperwork was the part of the job he hated. But it was a necessary part and had to be kept current, so he usually took care of it when most of the administrative offices, including his secretary's, were empty.

The room where he worked was at the top of the building, set there, he supposed, to insulate the commissioner from all the unpleasant elements that pervaded the lower floors. He didn't mind its location. There were always stairs and elevators, and the view was worth it.

He resisted the urge to swivel his chair toward the window. Instead he looked around the room itself. Except for a few personal items, he'd been satisfied to leave the room looking very much as it had when his predecessor had sat in this chair. The furnishings were simple but comfortable.

He'd hung a favorite print, Coheleach's *Snow Leopard*—the indolent pose of the powerful cat appealed to him—but he'd left the framed citations, scrolls and diplomas in their cartons. His secretary had unpacked his books and lined them in no particular order on the shelves that covered one wall of the office. He'd have to arrange them again to suit himself when he found the time.

Returning his attention to the papers in front of him, he grimaced. Time. He never had enough of it.

"Working on Saturday, commissioner?"

Glad of the interruption, Ryan leaned back in the swivel chair, stretching and flexing his sore muscles with the movement. After the softball practice, Bree had made the grumbling men run two miles. For a body that he hadn't had time to exercise since he'd left Texas, the workout had been unexpectedly strenuous.

He motioned for the chief of homicide detectives to come in. "Saturdays are never free, Maxwell, you know that. Paperwork. You're on duty this weekend?"

"No. I just came in for a couple of hours," answered Maxwell with a shrug. He sat in the straight leather-padded chair opposite Ryan. "I thought you might be here this morning." He held up a manila file folder. "The forensics report."

Ryan straightened, resting his forearms on the desk. "Let's have it."

Maxwell handed him the file. "There it is in scientific language."

Ryan laid the folder flat on his desk, opened it and began to shuffle through the lengthy report. "Can you boil it down for me?" he asked.

"The type of cotton used in the braided rope wasn't easy to trace. It is grown in only three places in the world. India, an island in the Caribbean and Karastonia."

Ryan's head came up. "Karastonia?" he said softly.

"Yeah. A coincidence?"

Ryan leaned back, oblivious to the squeak in his chair, and linked his hands behind his head. He gazed into the distance, a thoughtful expression in his eyes. "A man I greatly admired once said there aren't any coincidences in this business."

"A cop?"

"One of the best. Have you ever heard of Brian Regan?"

"Who hasn't? They called him Supercop, didn't they? Killed ten, twelve years ago? LOD?" Maxwell scowled.

In the mind of a policeman, "Line of Duty" conjured up a vivid image of a downed brother officer lying in his own blood. It could bring out the desire for revenge in the most dedicated peacemaker. Ryan nodded, carefully schooling his features against the other memories that accompanied any discussion of Brian Regan's death. "It was twelve years ago. Regan was the best, a born investigator. He had a nose for detecting."

Maxwell chuckled ruefully. "I wish I had two or three of the type right now. He didn't have a son, did he?"

"No, he had a daughter, but she hates police work."

The tone of his voice must have warned Maxwell, because he let the subject drop after a curious look. "Anyway, my little black book has produced nothing on the floater. A big fat zero. No one has reported him missing, no one has claimed the body, no one on the street has even heard a whisper of a motive for the killing."

"You trust these people?" Ryan knew that the confidential informants in Maxwell's black book were a necessary part of police work, but a good cop took what they said with a healthy dose of reservation. Their purposes were, at best, questionable—a favor, money, almost anything could buy their loyalty.

"Hell, no. Not any farther than I can see them. Sometimes not that far. But one of the women I talked to did come up with something that's probably unrelated but an interesting coincidence, especially in light of the forensics report."

"There's that word again. Let's have it."

"She heard that some group is planning to protest in front of the hotel when the foreign minister arrives. It's a political thing, probably unrelated, but the name of the country seems to be cropping up a lot lately."

"It does, doesn't it?" He glanced at the duty roster that lay on a corner of his desk, then crossed his arms on the desk and looked at the older man with a piercing gaze. "Austin, I know you'll be straight with me. And you can tell me to go to hell if you want to, but I'm working at a disadvantage here. I haven't had time to make judgments about all the personnel. Tell me, what do you think of Sam Dalton?"

"He's ambitious, capable, smart and young," answered Austin without hesitation.

Ryan nodded; he had recognized Dalton's ambition as soon as he'd arrived in Boston. Ambition wasn't undesirable. Sam Dalton seemed a nice enough guy, but as Austin had just confirmed, he was inexperienced. He had never had complete responsibility for an assignment of this magnitude. That worried Ryan somewhat.

"And he isn't a cowboy," Austin added. He shared Ryan's opinion of cowboys—men who thought of law enforcement as a cops-and-robbers game rather than serious work requiring a strong degree of discretion and prudence.

Relieved, Ryan grinned. "Thanks. That's what I needed to know."

"Dalton was appointed to head this security team by your predecessor, whom you and I both greatly admire, Ryan. I don't think he would have made the appointment if he hadn't believed in the man."

"I know. You needn't think I'll begin the job by immediately questioning his appointments. But this visit is almost on us. I needed information that isn't in the personnel files. Thanks for giving it to me."

Austin nodded. "Is Dalton on duty this weekend?"

"Yes, he is." Suddenly Ryan was galvanized into action. He swung his chair around, got to his feet and headed for the door. "Let's get him in on this."

Maxwell followed, bemused. O'Hara's predecessor would have sent for the man, which was more or less standard procedure. In contrast, Ryan went to him. Youth, he supposed. All that energy.

"Here he is now, Bree," Sam Dalton said, smiling as the two men entered his office.

In surprise, Ryan curbed his headlong rush into the room. Bree half turned in the chair and tilted her head to look up at him. Her eyes were clear and the color of Texas bluebonnets.

"Hi, Ryan," she said lightly, but the awareness of yesterday lay there between them. "I had to be in town this morning, so I brought over the revised schedule."

"That was quick work."

"Of course. I'm efficient." She gave him a slow smile, the same smile that she had given him last night when he'd asked her what position he would be playing, a smile that went straight to his midsection. That smile should be registered as a lethal weapon.

She was dressed casually, in beige slacks and a white silk blouse. Her hair was caught at the nape with a tortoiseshell clasp. He liked it loose and free, but it was better this way than twisted into that prim knot she sometimes wore. Her arms rested easily on the arms of the chair, her hands relaxed. Her legs were crossed at the knee, one high-heeled pump off her foot and dangling from her toes. She was obviously comfortable with Dalton. Ryan wondered why the idea annoyed him.

"Bree wants to know if we can arrange security for a department-store stop on the Thursday of the minister's visit. Jones and Doggett's is featuring products imported from Karastonia during that week."

Sam's words brought Ryan's attention to the present. "Has the store cleared it with the Karastonian consulate? Or the State Department?" he asked Bree.

"No. They wanted to check with us first to see if it could be done. They say Prince Charles and Princess Di promoted British goods during their trip to this country."

Ryan shook his head in disgust. "Excuse me, Bree, this is Austin Maxwell, Homicide. Austin, Bree Regan—Fleming. Her public relations firm is directing the minister's visit for the city."

Bree was hard put to concentrate on the introduction. She'd managed to hide her surprise at Ryan's unexpected appearance, but now he was near enough for her to get a whiff of his cologne, a fresh and slightly spicy scent that was having a heady effect on her. Disconcerted, she stuck out her hand. "How do you do, Lieutenant?"

"Mrs. Regan-Fleming." Austin nodded and accepted her extended hand.

It was a natural mistake, given the way Ryan introduced her. A lot of women used their maiden names and a hyphen before the names of their husbands. A lot of women never took their husband's name at all. "Bree, please," she said to keep from having to explain.

She bent to pick up a package at her feet and held it out to Ryan. "I have your softball uniform, Ryan. I was going to drop it off at your dad's."

Ryan hid a smile. Her voice was sort of soft. If she had realized how cozy and intimate the statement had sounded, she would have been appalled. He found that he was pleased she'd given that impression.

Sam Dalton, who had been so confident when they'd entered the room, now wore a look of disappointment. Austin Maxwell's expression was curious and thoughtful.

Ryan wasn't about to explain to either of them. "Thanks," he said, taking the package. He tossed it into the seat of the chair next to hers, then sat on the arm and looked at her, his mind functioning at about half speed.

Right now, he told himself, he had to keep this meeting professional. He had to keep it that way, despite his tendency to let his eyes wander to the curve of her lips. "Bree, about this Jones and Doggett thing, I think they've left it too late. They should have approached you months ago if they wanted to fit a promotion into the minister's schedule."

"They have a new marketing director over there, Ryan. The plans for this promotion got lost between the cracks with the changeover. I'm not making excuses for them. I'm just explaining." Now her voice was clear, firm and very businesslike.

"What if the minister doesn't approve of them using him as a huckster? How do you feel about it?"

She propped her elbows on the arms of the chair and threaded her fingers together. Making a steeple with her forefingers, she touched them to her lips as she considered.

He wished she wouldn't do that.

"That would have been his decision to make. But I agree that it's too late to make the arrangements, Ryan. I only said

I'd pass on the request. We'll be running our legs off, anyway. He arrives at two, there's the reception at three and the dinner cruise at five-thirty.'' Dropping her hands, she laughed. ''As it is, I'll probably have to change my clothes in the back seat of my car. I don't want to wear the poor man out before he gets to Philadelphia and Washington.''

Ryan hadn't realized that she was planning to be with the party during the entire visit. He was suddenly sober as he considered her involvement. The security force would be prepared; he knew that the minister's party would most likely be the safest place in the city during the visit. But he was worried for some strange, nebulous reason about Bree being so close to a man people protested against. Still, he could imagine her response if he mentioned the danger.

Unaware of his preoccupation, Bree stood. ''Lieutenant,'' she said, turning to Maxwell. ''Nice to have met you.'' She smiled warmly at Dalton. ''Sam, thanks for your help. I'll get out of here and let you get on with your work.''

Ryan made a quick decision. ''Why don't you stay for a minute? Then I'll walk you to your car.''

Her astonishment was only a pale thing compared to that on the faces of the other two men. She certainly didn't *need* walking to her car, and she doubted that any of these men were accustomed to discussing their business in front of an outsider. But her first reaction, the one that suggested she treat the offer with disdain, was tempered by curiosity about the case and about Ryan. What was he up to? After last night, she wasn't sure. She decided without much hesitation, to stay. ''All right,'' she said, and sat down again.

Ryan turned to Austin Maxwell. ''Why don't you show Sam the report and explain our suspicions?'' he suggested.

Maxwell didn't show by so much as the blink of an eye that this was an unusual procedure. Calmly he sat down and opened the file. ''The body discovered in the Charles a week

ago was weighted with a concrete block, Sam. But instead
of rope, the killer used torn strips of fabric, probably from
a shirt. Ryan and I noticed that the fabric was an unusual
type, loosely woven, with weak fibers. In spite of the fact
that the body hadn't been in the water more than twenty-
four hours, there had been a lot of raveling and breaking in
the strands. It took some time to trace, but Homicide finally received the lab report this morning. The type of cotton in these fibers is grown in only three places in the
world.'' His glance touched Bree briefly. ''One of them is
Karastonia.''

Bree kept a noncommittal expression on her face, but her
mind was racing, coming up with improbable theories, then
rejecting them. Surely the body in the river couldn't have
any bearing on the minister's visit. Could it?

Sam Dalton uttered an explicit word, then sent a glance
of apology to Bree.

''You see, Sam?'' said Ryan, indicating the file. ''Com-
bined with the dead man's body type and the upcoming
visit, the suspicion can't be dismissed that he may be connected to the minister.''

The younger man was clearly dismayed over this development. Ryan, knowing his qualifications, could almost
read his thoughts. Dalton had served well on many security
details but had never actually headed one. This was his big
chance for departmental recognition—if everything went
smoothly. And now there were complications he didn't
need. Sam was handling the news well.

''We can't prove a connection right now,'' Austin added.
''But another thing—an informant says that a group we
don't know anything about seems to be planning an organized protest.''

Sam frowned. This was his territory. ''What group?''

Austin shrugged, indicating that he didn't know. "I'll get that info to you as soon as I have more. I don't mind telling you, Sam, I'm worried as hell. There are too many coincidences. I've put the word out on the street and come up blank. My men have already contacted the FBI, as well as the State Department. So far we have no evidence that anyone connected either with the Karastonian embassy in Washington or with its consulates around the country has been reported missing."

The younger man gave a sigh of resignation. "And I'll get to work on identifying the protest group. Hell, the killer could have bought the cotton shirt from anywhere."

Ryan had straightened and was now wandering restlessly around the office, speaking in a deceptively mild tone. "We all hope that's the case. And that the protesters are just a bunch of disgruntled students wanting their say. But until we're certain we'll proceed on the assumption that this is a plot, that there is an assassin out there somewhere, that the unidentified man happened onto it. If I had my choice, I would postpone the minister's visit until this is cleared up. We all know that a determined killer can get through the tightest security." He came to a halt, facing them, and crossed his arms over his broad chest. "However, we all also know there isn't a prayer of postponement."

Bree had kept silent throughout the exchange. Now she had to bite her lip to keep from commenting.

"What is it, Bree?" asked Ryan.

He didn't miss a thing, thought Bree wryly. "Me?" she said innocently—or so she thought.

"You've been aching to say something."

"Just that all the planning for this visit hasn't been on our end, Ryan. The minister has set aside this block of time from a very busy schedule. It really can't be stopped."

Ryan pondered her words, seeing the truth in them. "You've been in on the planning of the visit from the first. You worked with the advance men and the consulate. Is there anything you can tell us?"

She thought back to ten days ago, recalling details of the meetings. "No. At least I don't think so," she said slowly. "There were six advance men, two for each city. Their plane landed here first, so I met all six but actually only worked with two of them. They were very efficient. Didn't you think so, Sam?" She got a nod of agreement and went on. "Very serious, and absolutely determined that every move the minister makes be thoroughly checked out." She shrugged. "That's perfectly natural."

"Could either of them have stayed on here without your knowledge?"

"No, I put them on their planes myself."

"Planes?"

"Yes. One of the men was joining the other four to fly directly home. The other one, a Mr. Pandal, was going to stay over for a while, visit relatives in Oregon and Washington and then rent a car to vacation in California."

"How long was he planning to stay?"

"I don't know. Several weeks, I think. There were no sinister undercurrents about those men, Ryan, I promise."

Ryan slid his hands into his pockets and nodded, the information cataloged in his mind though he couldn't see any importance in it. "Carter has to be informed of the developments," he said. "Will you call him, Sam, or shall I?"

"I'll call him," said Dalton.

"And I'll see if I can locate this Pandal. Maybe he can shed some light on our murder investigation," said Maxwell.

"Fine," said Ryan. "I'll be back in a few minutes," he told the men. "Bree?"

Bree got to her feet and said goodbye to the other two. She was silent as she followed him through the squad room. When they were in the hall and relatively alone, she said, "I'm not sure I understood what all that was about."

"You can figure most of it out. It's serious, Bree. I'm like Austin—worried as hell."

"This is going to sound so trivial that I'm embarrassed to ask. But are you going to be able to make the game this afternoon?"

"I'll be there. I have an idea the ID will be a long time coming," he predicted.

The halls of police headquarters were never deserted, but they had a weekend hollowness about them now. A woman in a tailored uniform approached them. Ryan nodded, and the woman greeted him respectfully.

As they moved aside to let her pass, Bree's shoulder brushed Ryan's chest. The contact was so fleeting as to be almost nil, but it didn't fail to stir her senses. Face it, she told herself. Ryan O'Hara still had the power to make her feel like the petal of a flower adrift on a turbulent sea, totally incapable of setting her own direction. The feeling scared her to death.

They had progressed only a short distance farther when he spoke again, this time abruptly, as though he hadn't meant to speak at all. "Would you have dinner with me tonight after the game?"

The invitation might be unwise, but she was stunned by how tempted she was to say yes. An acceptance wouldn't be smart. Fortunately, she had a perfectly plausible excuse. "The team always goes to Murphy's after the game for a beer and commiseration," she explained. "You'll have to come, too."

Ryan thought he heard regret in her tone. He felt his heart leap within his chest, but he kept his voice even. "Commiseration? Then Father Brotsky wasn't exaggerating when he said the team doesn't often win."

Her laughter was low and sexy and sent a responsive shimmy up his spine. Her high heels clicked on the hard floors; he could hear the faint sounds of her clothes moving as she walked. But he wouldn't allow himself to look at her.

"I was sure you'd been warned." She swung her eyes toward him then, and he had to meet her amused gaze. "We're not a total loss, but we never win against North End Baptist. I think they have a couple of ringers." She frowned.

Seeing the frown, Ryan smiled to himself. Bree had always been a competitor. If she went into something she went into it to win. But win fairly. She wouldn't appreciate ringers.

"A couple that I suspect," she went on. "One I'm sure of. Specter, the pitcher, is a ringer or I'll eat my hat." The frown cleared from her brow, and she smiled. "But all will be well now. Father Brotsky seems to think you'll save the team from an ignoble showing."

Ryan snorted. "I'm no savior. I hadn't picked up a bat in years until last night."

She grinned up at him. "You didn't do badly. Father Brotsky says you've brought new spirit to the team. He's betting on you."

"How about a side bet? We win, you go to dinner with me?"

Another silence. "It would only add to the talk in the neighborhood, Ryan," she said finally. And to the sparks, she thought. She could feel them right now.

She spoke slowly. Reluctantly, he thought. She'd come up with an excuse for not going out with him rather than use her other option, a flat no. Not yet, her tone implied. Or did it? Was he reading more into this than there was? Ever since yesterday, when he'd acknowledged his feelings of sexuality, the excitement had been with him, simmering, ready to come to a full boil. It was dangerous as hell, but he could no more have stopped it than he could have stopped the next words that came out, or their tone of anticipation. "Another night?"

"Perhaps," she said.

Her offhand answer didn't discourage him, because he could see the rapid pulse in her temple, recognize the expansion of her pupils for what it was. She'd acknowledged the excitement, too, the heaviness in the air between them.

During the time they'd been apart, things had changed, and so had they. He was no longer an agonized twenty-two-year-old. And he was discovering that Bree was no longer a fearful young woman. He didn't intend to let her hide this time. Desire might be a painful reality, but it was there. He'd faced it, and he'd make damn sure she did, as well.

And this time it would be on his terms, he vowed again. For now, he let the subject drop.

He'd accepted her refusal too easily, thought Bree as they arrived at the entrance to the building. "Well, I hope the uniform fits. I had to guess at the size." She dug into her deep shoulder bag for the keys to her car. "You don't need to walk any farther with me," she said as she came up with them in her hand.

He hesitated only long enough to bring her gaze to his. He wondered what she would do if he lowered his head, if he brushed her lips with his. He smiled. With one deliberate finger he traced the line of her jaw. He felt her shudder of response and held open the door to let her pass through. "I'll see you at four, coach."

The visitor's parking area where Bree had left her car was right outside. Ryan stood at the door. His gaze remained fixed on the empty space long after she had climbed into her conservative blue sedan and driven away.

Reentering the office a few minutes later, he met the questioning looks of Sam Dalton and Austin Maxwell.

"Softball, huh?" said Dalton, joking heartily, too heartily. "Is Bree the coach?"

A smile hovered around Maxwell's mouth.

"As a matter of fact, she is." Ryan said. "Back off" was what he wanted to tell Dalton, but he didn't have the right to say that.

"She is?" Dalton recovered quickly from his surprise. "Softball has sure changed since I was a boy. Maybe I should consider joining up."

Something disturbing twisted inside Ryan at the notion. He managed a smile but let his tone speak for him, making it clear that if the younger man pursued this he would have a struggle on his hands. "You don't qualify. It's a church team. Did you get in touch with Carter?" he asked, firmly putting the other topic beyond the limits of casual conversation.

Dalton answered. "Yes. State doesn't seem worried about the protests. They're just part of the system, they say. But he offered us extra men for the security team."

"Good," said Ryan. "We'll take him up on it. We need all the help we can get. What about your men, Austin? Did they come up with anything?"

"Nothing," said Maxwell. "Still no missing persons reports. Nothing suspicious among the expatriates. It'll take a while to track down Pandal."

Why? thought Ryan later when he'd returned to his own office. He steepled his fingers and stared at the wall opposite his desk. What was the motive? Not for the murder—a killer could have a dozen motives—but for the grisly method. Who had killed the poor bastard and dumped him, mutilated and unidentifiable, into the river?

The man's identity was significant, important enough for someone to take great pains that it not be revealed. Why? Why had no one missed this man? Where had he come from? What was he doing in Boston? Who the hell *was* he?

Ryan swiped at the sweat across his forehead with the back of his hand and replaced his cap. He settled his gaze on the batter and rammed his fist into his glove. An indescribable sixth sense, the same perceptive insight that served him effectively in police work, warned him that the game was about to burst into action.

Even before the man at the plate drew in his elbows, bringing the bat close to his body, before he bent slightly at the waist, Ryan was hunched forward. Ready even before the sound of wood meeting cowhide with a vicious crack reached his ears.

He took two running steps, scooped up the ball and fired it to first base for the third out . . . to the dismay of his sore muscles. One inning to go. The cheers from the bleachers registered only vaguely as he headed for the bench. He dropped his glove and took a seat a few feet away from where the coach was perched.

"Good job, O'Hara," she said, grinning.

He mumbled something irregular under his breath. When he'd agreed to play, he'd thought the softball team would be a good way to work out the tension of his job and keep him in shape. With Bree as coach it was having the opposite effect, and Lord, he was sore.

Ah, well, he just needed to work the kinks out. He was a great believer in fitness. He had to be; in his job a well-disciplined, healthy body was more important than the gun he carried. But he wasn't interested in joining a workout club. None of those fancy spas, where the social aspect often overrode the reason for being there, for him. He considered jogging the most boring pastime imaginable, but he jogged because it was easy. But softball used different muscles, and right now every one of them was protesting.

"Good catch, Ryan," said one of his teammates, taking the bench beside him.

"Thanks, Ron," said Ryan.

"This man's tough." As they watched the pitcher warm up, Ron began to discuss the history of this rivalry, describing the first game on last year's schedule. Their team had been beaten by a slim edge. Bree had been right about the pitcher. Specter had to be a ringer. If he hadn't played professionally in the past—probably in one of the minor leagues somewhere—Ryan would eat his hat, too.

"...and after that it was downhill all the way," said Ron.

Ryan was grateful for the game talk; it was something he could discuss without thinking too much. His mind was definitely elsewhere—not far away, just two seats down.

When he was in the field, Bree always seemed to be at the edge of his range of vision. He tried to ignore her, but unconsciously his eyes kept returning to the slender figure, like a homing device that was locked on to some supermagnetic target.

Now, though they sat several feet apart with a body between them, he could still smell her perfume. Incredibly, the scent masked all other smells, including that of nine sweaty men, and went through his bloodstream like fine brandy. Hell, he'd be better off playing racquetball or jogging.

Ron got up and went to the water bucket. Ryan turned his head so he could see Bree.

She was talking to Fitz, her body drawn up into an impossible position. Her spine was slightly curved, her jean-clad thighs held tight against her chest by arms wrapped around her knees, her left hand gripping her right wrist. The heels of her sneakers caught the edge of the bench. She looked so tiny, so feminine, there among the larger men.

But she was a capable coach—he'd realized that early in the game. She observed carefully, dictated reasonably and handled the players, both older and younger, with a combination of diplomacy, flattery and authority.

He let his head drop back and closed his eyes against the glare of the late-afternoon sun, but her image remained etched in his mind's eye. Even in her enthusiasm for the game, her gestures were unconsciously graceful.

I shouldn't even be here, he told himself wearily. *I should be at headquarters with Maxwell, working on the murder case, doing something, anything.*

But that was ridiculous, and he knew it. He had qualified men; his career had taken him past the point where he had to be out on the street talking to CIs. That was Maxwell's prerogative; Ryan's was to delegate, administrate, satisfy the mayor and the press that everything possible was being done.

The press. Wouldn't they have a field day with a picture of the commissioner of police playing softball while a killer ran loose in the city? Sometimes he missed the anonymity of walking a beat. *Who was the man?*

"Ryan, you're up next," Bree said, interrupting his reflections.

Ryan opened his eyes and automatically assigned the problem to a corner of his mind where, he knew, his subconscious would work on it. Sometimes it was the most effective way to solve a puzzle. He was accustomed to separating the parts of his life into detached cells; they were able to function efficiently apart from each other.

Bree was squatting in front of him, had her hand on his knee. The bright green baseball cap she wore to shade her eyes had Saints embroidered in white above the bill. Strands of hair had escaped their confinement to rest like dark ribbons on her neck. She'd eaten off her lipstick, her face was shiny. She looked adorable. He felt the muscles in his thigh respond spasmodically to her touch.

"Specter is getting tired," she was saying, indicating the pitcher with a nod of her head. "His fast balls are lower and his windup is a little sluggish."

He accepted her conclusion without question. Eyes narrowed against the sun, he studied the man who stood on the pitcher's mound, but his body was reacting to the warmth of her fingers on his leg. Who ever heard of a coach wearing perfume? And why had she refused to go out to dinner with him tonight if she wasn't closing the door completely?

The first batter was on first base. Ryan had no idea how the hell he had gotten there. The second man up was at home plate now.

Ryan stood, displacing Bree's hand with the movement. "Okay," he answered shortly.

She stepped back, wondering what had caused his irritation. She watched him scoop up the bat and move to the on-deck circle. He bent down to dust his hands with dirt, rubbing them together briskly. The action strained the stretchy material of the green-and-white uniform over his tight buttocks. She had never noticed how formfitting those uniform pants were. They didn't seem sexy to her—not on anyone else—but they were definitely sexy on Ryan's long, muscular legs.

All afternoon she'd been so distracted by his every move, by the symmetry of his body, by his balance and speed, that she could hardly keep her mind on the game. It was incongruous, she supposed, to think of a man as graceful, but he was.

She sat in the place he had vacated, gripping the edge of the bench on either side of her hips.

He straightened, and she was presented with his broad shoulders. The number 12 seemed small on his back. He swung the bat with a snap, warming up, and she let go of a sigh. His arms—if she lived forever she wouldn't forget their strength, their tenderness, as he'd held her. No matter how long ago, twelve years or a hundred and twelve years, the memory was as distinct as though it had been yesterday. It took some willpower, but she looked away from him, forcing herself to concentrate on the game.

Unbelievably, their team had a one-run lead, thanks to a triple with two men on base early in the game. The hit had surprised the hitter, Fitz, as much as it had surprised the other team. After a brief celebration, they had settled down to play ball. Only in the last inning had the men allowed the expectation of victory to creep into their expressions.

She knew how they felt. To some of them it didn't really matter; it was only a weekend church league. They played for the exercise and the camaraderie. But another one or two runs would give them some insurance.

Ryan had fielded well today, but he had yet to get a hit off this man. He'd walked twice and popped up to center field once. He was due. Then, if they could hold the other team for three more outs, the game would be over and they would have defeated North End Baptist for the first time ever.

Looking up into the bleachers, she saw what she'd known she would see. Father Brotsky was seated next to her mother, his hands folded in his lap; his thin lips were moving almost imperceptibly. She smiled to herself.

God had to be amazed by prayers directed heavenward from a softball field. His children should be offering up appeals for world peace or brotherly love. Instead they asked that the other team stumble, bobble and blunder. She crossed the fingers of both hands.

Ryan approached home plate, pausing to tap the dirt from his cleats, stepped into the batter's box, took a couple of practice swings and fixed the pitcher with an implacable gaze that brought a grin to Bree's face.

Specter stared back at Ryan, meeting the determination in his eyes with a smile of unrelenting arrogance. He spit on the ground and began his windup.

Whether the gesture was delivered as a sign of contempt or bravado Ryan didn't know. Or care. It made him mad as hell. He took the first pitch. It was low, as Bree had warned, but he got the wood on it. The way he felt, he would have taken the pitch if it had been in the dirt. There was a loud, satisfying whack, and he grinned as he watched the ball sail out over the head of the center fielder, who turned to chase it. *You won't get that one, buddy. It's outa here!*

There was something to be said for anger, he decided as he rounded the bases, jubilant. The Saints' supporters were screaming wildly on the sidelines; even Father Brotsky was on his feet.

His teammates were waiting at home plate to congratulate him. Bree stood back from the others, laughing exultantly. He could have sworn she was ready to throw her arms around his neck. But she didn't; she simply congratulated him along with the rest of them.

His excitement was completely out of proportion to the accomplishment, he tried to tell himself; but he hadn't hit a home run since high school, and the grin on his face wouldn't be denied.

The last inning was an anticlimax. The other team seemed to have been demoralized by the home run, and they submitted three easy outs in three times at bat. After the game Fitz came up to pound him on the back again. "We usually go over to Murphy's for a beer after a game, Ryan," he said, taking it for granted that Ryan would join them.

Ryan didn't tell him he'd already been invited. "I'll see you there," he said.

Chapter 5

Ryan took an inordinate amount of time showering after the game. He called headquarters, wondering if he was looking for an excuse to avoid Murphy's. Surely not. His terms, he reminded himself.

He was informed by the officer on duty that there was nothing pressing that required the commissioner's presence. The officer's response implied that the whole city was awash in brotherly love, that the cops on the beat were there for a sociable outing.

Ryan knew the man's reassurances were for his benefit. He'd done the same thing more than one time when he'd been on duty. *Keep the commissioner happy; we'll take care of anything that comes up.* Obviously word of Ryan's philosophy hadn't spread throughout the department yet. Another week ought to do it. If not, he'd have to send around a memo.

Boston was like any other major city in the U.S. Its people were for the most part basically honest, hardworking and law-abiding. But as in any other city, there was the small gray underbelly of greed and deceit, treachery and suspicion, which created the criminal element.

He inquired as to the presence of Lieutenant Maxwell and was told the lieutenant was at home. Austin wouldn't have left if there'd been anything on the murder. He said a polite good-night to the duty officer and hung up.

When he arrived at the neighborhood tavern, the long table at the back of the room was full of players, their wives and girlfriends and a few others who had been at the game. They were flushed with the satisfaction of victory, and their byplay was boisterous as they replayed, commented and congratulated each other. Bree was right in the center of the melee. Instead of joining them immediately, he took a stool at the bar.

"Hi, Murph. I'll have light beer."

"How ya doin, Ryan?" The burly man behind the mahogany expanse reached for a mug and held it under the draft dispenser. "I hear you played a great game. Wish I could have seen you take that home run off Specter."

"We were already leading, Murph. Fitz got a triple in the second inning." Resting his elbows on the bar before him, he reached for the handle of the mug. Before he could lift it, another hand was there.

He turned his head to look sideways over his shoulder, watching with a small smile as Bree raised the frosty glass to her lips and took a long swallow. She slapped the mug back down on the counter and gave him a wide grin.

He swiveled to face her, meeting her smile. "Buy you a drink, lady?"

Murphy laughed.

"Thanks, I don't drink."

Ryan lifted a brow. "So you've been telling me."

"A Coke, please, Murph." She shrugged casually and wedged into the space between the stool where he sat and the one next to him. "Oh, I indulge once in a while, when there's something to celebrate. And that home run was something. Ryan, that was the *most* exciting thing that's happened to me in my entire coaching career."

They were shoulder to shoulder, Ryan sitting, Bree standing, grinning at each other. The scene was reminiscent of many others when they'd been younger and had less to concern them. They'd stood or sat with their noses almost touching, sharing a happy moment. She'd gotten rid of the cap and now her hair curled wildly around her shoulders. He fought the urge to bend the few inches it would take to close the distance between their mouths. He wanted, with an urgency that left him weak, to run his tongue across those naked lips, those shining white teeth. "Your entire career, huh? And how long has this illustrious career lasted?" he forced himself to ask mildly.

They used to be like this together, thought Bree. But his amused indulgence used to drive her up the wall. Now that she had a woman's confidence in herself, she found it rather sweet. A frosty mug of cola appeared in front of her. "Thanks, Murph," she said, sobering as she went on to explain how she had gotten the coaching job. "Just two years. I had only been back in Boston a few months when Father Brotsky came down with a really bad case of the flu."

"And you were drafted to fill in. Do I have to ask who volunteered you?"

She shook her head ruefully. "Frances Q. Cheerleader. Who else? She thought I needed something else besides work to occupy my time."

"Frances Q. Cheerleader was doing her best today," said Ryan. Their eyes tangled. They both remembered that her father had started the naming of Frances. "Frances, quit being a worrywart,'' he would say. Finally he shortened it to Frances Q. Whatever The Current Complaint. "Father Brotsky was really sick, huh?"

"It took him a long time to shake the bug." She looked up into his eyes. "He's still the real coach, of course. I just do all the running around he used to do."

"That's not true. You're a terrific coach."

"Thank you, sir." A teasing light appeared in her blue eyes. "I find that ordering around a bunch of men who are bigger than I am fills me with deep satisfaction." The light faded slightly when her thoughts returned to the priest. "Your home run gave him a thrill this afternoon."

Ryan smiled. "I saw him after the game."

"He wanted to come here with us, but..." She paused, letting her voice trail off. "He's getting old, Ryan."

"I know." They were thoughtful for a minute. The priest-principal had been an integral part of their lives for a long time. But he'd seemed old when they'd been kids.

She lifted her chin, determined to dispel the somber mood. "If he were here he would say, 'Let's not get serious. It's a night to celebrate. A toast to the Saints and their triumph over the ringer!'" She raised her glass.

Ryan chuckled at her mimickry, but there was a lingering sadness in her eyes that he longed to expunge. He touched his glass to hers, and they both drank to the victory. "It certainly is a night to celebrate. *This* old man can still cut it, how about that?"

"You're not old," she informed him. "Because if you were old, I would be old."

"I can't argue with your reasoning. And you look about fourteen." He let his gaze trail across her face. She was very still. "But tell that to my hamstrings," he finished, his smile a little strained.

"Poor Ryan," she said softly. "I hope you have some liniment at home." An image flashed across the screen of her memory. A bruised shoulder—she couldn't recall the cause—her fingers massaging the pungent liquid into his tanned skin.

When he spoke, his voice dropped to an intimate level and she knew his thoughts paralleled hers. "I jogged to the field. Can you drop me off at home?"

Bree grasped the handle of her mug but didn't raise it to drink, just moved it around, drawing a haphazard circle in the condensation it left on the bar. Ryan's question brought more memories rushing back. He'd always jogged to the field before a game to warm up. And she'd often taken him home afterward. And they'd usually ended up in each other's arms. Too *many* memories. She squared her shoulders. "Ryan, I *told* you—"

"Bree," he said quietly, interrupting. "I've done a lot of thinking since last night. We can't escape the memories. They're there. But they happened to two other people, in another lifetime. Can't we put those people where they belong, in the history books, and begin from here? No strings, no entanglements. Just go out together occasionally and see what develops?"

Bree wasn't surprised that he'd come up with a logical suggestion. It was decision time, and she was unable to think of an answer to give him, mesmerized as she was by the smoky depths of his eyes. "I don't know, Ryan," she told him candidly. "I just don't know."

In a swift change of mood, Ryan touched her hair, pulling lightly on a strand. "Besides, I've promised myself I was going to kiss you before this night is over." He hid his smile at her reaction—immediate, ruffled, totally predictable. Before she could question the presumptuous statement, he continued, "You owe me."

Her brows rose. "I owe you?" she asked, separating the mild words precisely. "Where on earth did you get such an idea?"

"From you." His voice took on that slow Texas drawl, and Bree realized that she'd responded to the challenge exactly as he'd thought she would.

"When I hit the home run? You were waiting at home plate, ready to throw yourself into my arms. You wanted to kiss me then." His gray eyes were suspiciously innocent, but the corner of his mustache twitched. "Didn't you?"

Bree couldn't deny it, so she didn't say anything. Someone called a question from the table at the back, reminding her of their surroundings. "Okay, I'll give you a ride home. As for the kiss, you'll have to hit me another home run." She picked up her cola and turned away. Ryan wrapped his hand around her upper arm, stopping her, but released her before she could demand that he do so. He held her in place with nothing more than that strong gaze.

"Shall we join the others?" she suggested, shaking her head in silent denial. She wasn't going to get into this right now.

With a nod and a small smile that she didn't trust one bit, Ryan slid off the stool to accompany her.

She wasn't aware of the hand that hovered near her back until they were halfway there. Suddenly his broad palm was resting firmly against her spine, heating her skin through her clothes. Casually Bree put up a hand to dislodge it, but her fingers were immediately caught and entwined in his.

"Ryan," she breathed, twisting to free herself.

He bent to whisper in her ear. "You have the sexiest fanny in Boston."

"Ryan!" Her admonition was too loud, she realized as soon as the word was out of her mouth. Conversation came to a halt. They were the object of several interested stares.

Some of the people at the table had known Ryan and her in high school. The ones who had not had undoubtedly been filled in by now about their previous relationship.

Colin cleared his throat and glanced down at his watch. "It's seven o'clock already. We've got to go. My mother has the kids, and I promised Marilee a big night out."

Marilee, under her husband's arm, made a face. "Dinner at McDonald's."

There was a general shuffling of chairs and gathering up of assorted duffel and sports bags.

"I didn't realize it was so late."

"Great game, Ryan."

"See you next week, coach."

The group dispersed quickly.

Bree and Ryan joined the exodus more slowly. She led the way out of the tavern and across the street to her car. He held her door and circled the hood. Tossing his bag in the back, he climbed in beside her.

She drove in silence for a few minutes. When they were almost to his house, she spoke. "Why did you do that? I thought you said we'd wait to see what develops."

He didn't pretend to misunderstand or to hide his amusement. "I paid you a compliment," he said, turning to lay his arm along the back of the seat behind her head.

"A compliment?" she inquired dryly. His position made her slightly uncomfortable.

"On your—derriere."

"Fanny was what you said, O'Hara. Fanny," she scolded. "Were you trying for a shock effect?" she asked primly.

Ryan couldn't contain his laughter any longer. Unrestrained, it came rolling out of him. "Sorry. I've had a *great* night."

"'Hail the conquering hero,' huh?"

Most of the laughter trailed away eventually, but a wide smile remained. He sniffed and rubbed a hand down his face. "Something like that," he admitted.

Bree fought off the impulse to join in and laugh with him. Ryan O'Hara in this confident, happy mood was a dangerous hazard to her libido.

"Are you shocked by the use of the word 'fanny'?" he asked finally over the remnants of his laughter.

"Of course not." She wasn't. What had shocked her was his qualification of the word. *She* knew she didn't have the sexiest one in Boston, but her heart had begun to thud lightly at the flattery nonetheless. She brought the car to a stop in front of his father's house, but she didn't turn off the ignition. Her fingertips beat out a tattoo on the steering wheel.

"What about that kiss?"

"Another home run and I'll think about it. Get out, Ryan." Her lips twitched.

He sighed with exaggerated disappointment. "I made a mistake. I suppose I should have stuck to the conventional kind of compliment." He edged across the seat, reached out to turn off the ignition.

She was forced to look at him then.

He lifted his hands to frame her face. Leisurely he studied her, each lovely feature, the clean curve of her brow, her high, elegant cheekbones, her eyes, her lips. Her lips, moist and slightly parted. His meticulous inspection, though still slightly playful, was tender.

"How's this? You're a beautiful woman. I'm attracted. I want to spend some time with you. I'm impressed with this new Bree, the one who plans state visits with one hand while coaching a softball team with the other. I want to get to know her better." He smoothed her brows one at a time with his thumbs. "I should have talked about your beautiful azure gaze, your hair that smells heavenly and makes a man want to bury his hands in it, your mouth—oh, lady, that mouth defies any kind of compliment a man could conceive.''

Spoken in his low voice, with unmistakable desire, his words had her trembling. She wished he'd stuck to the playful mood. ''Good Lord, when you decide to correct a mistake you don't fool around, do you?'' she breathed.

After a split second he laughed again, but this time his laughter was low and husky and sexy.

However lightly she might have taken his declaration, many questions remained in her mind. Could she agree to his request without letting her emotions become involved? Could she live with the fact of his job? She wouldn't have the answers to those questions until it was too late to reverse her decision. But, she realized suddenly as she watched his eyes change from smoke to silver, the decision had been made already.

Bree didn't, couldn't, pull away from the unfamiliar body so close to hers. He was stronger, thicker, taller than he'd been at twenty. From the spot where his left thigh touched her right, warmth radiated, and a kind of electricity that set her nerve ends singing. Her sex life with Dirk had been satisfying. He had been kind and caring. Ryan would be more demanding, and more exciting.

Maybe she'd been headed in this direction from the moment she'd seen him through the peephole in her front door. She sighed and dropped her eyes to his shirtfront as though she might find some great wisdom there, the right words to let him know that she felt the same pull but that she also had some deep reservations. Finally she settled on honesty. ''It would be foolish to lie to myself—or you, Ryan.'' She raised her eyes. ''You were right when you said I was self-protective. I've been afraid—there've been so many changes in my life. I don't want any more," she said. "But I can't walk away from you this time. I don't know what will come of it. I certainly don't intend to hop right into bed with you just to satisfy a few physical urges."

"You look so sad when you say that," he observed carefully. "Bree, I don't want to hurt you. I don't even want to change your life except to make a small space for me to fit into. Revenge isn't on my agenda." He hesitated. "Neither are marriage and commitment."

"For me, either," she admitted. His hands were warm and callused on her cheeks. Unbidden, her own came up to rest on them. She couldn't even hide her needs from him; she knew they were there in her eyes. They were a woman's needs, but she'd been able to circumvent them in the past. Only this man could make her admit them now.

A wonderful feeling of anticipation began to blossom within her, and she sighed. Her gaze roamed over his features, ending up at his mouth. Memories of other kisses were suddenly very clear to her, but they were the kisses of different people, as he had said. She was about to find out what it would feel like to kiss this new, more mature Ryan. She smiled to herself—the man with the mustache.

The expectancy built relentlessly, steadily, until her heart was pounding under its force. "Ryan." Had she spoken aloud? Or had his name simply settled there on her lips like a sweet taste, like the kiss she had discovered she wanted? She caught her breath, waiting for the flavor of him on her lips. "Ryan?" she murmured again, distracted.

Suddenly two things happened at once. He tilted her head, bestowed a kiss on her brow and released her, and the distinctive sound of a paging device reached her ears. She wasn't sure which had come first.

"You're right, honey," he said. "I can't take a kiss just because I think you owe me. You have to give it freely. And I want more than just one kiss from you."

His scruples chose a hell of a time to surface, thought Bree as she battled her way free of the mist that still seemed to surround her.

He opened the door of the car. The light came on, illuminating his expression. She searched his features but found nothing revealed there. She might as well have been still sitting in the dark. He took out the pager and flipped a switch, quieting the harsh sound.

She turned away from him to grip the steering wheel, irritated now—with him, but more with herself for her disappointment.

He reached over the seat to grab his bag. "Just remember, Bree, I want you, but I also want to get to know you. We're going to be together a lot. And I don't give a damn about neighborhood gossip. If I want to touch you, if you want to touch me, I won't hide that from our friends. Hell, let them speculate."

He waited a long time for his answer. "All right," she said finally, her composure in place again.

"And the rest? Do we have a deal to put our past behind us?"

"We have a deal, commissioner."

Ryan sank lower in his swivel chair. Pinching his bottom lip between his fingers, he stared at the office phone. He'd just hung up after talking to Maxwell and now he had to call Bree. It was Monday afternoon. He hadn't seen her since Saturday, but they'd talked a couple of times. About nothing, really. He'd asked her why she'd let her hair grow—not that he didn't like it, he'd assured her. He just wondered.

She'd said she looked too young with those short curls around her face.

Now, when they were becoming comfortable on the first plateau in this relationship, he was going to have to do something that might just blow their whole understanding to dust. Again he had to discuss the extent of her participation in the minister's visit. He'd decided the discussion would be best held over dinner.

Pride was a funny emotion. Often it kept you from doing things that were totally necessary, in fact crucial. His pride reminded him that he'd been on the receiving end of Bree's rejection before. In a very big way.

Suddenly, making this first formal request of her—going out to dinner—seemed a hurdle. He couldn't explain it to himself.

Accompanying the minister was part of her job. He knew what her response would be when he asked her to stay out of the entourage; she'd tell him to get lost. He couldn't blame her. She'd tell him that more important people than she were going to be present—the mayor, the governor—and what right did he have to ask this of her?

His only argument was that her presence was not necessary. Taking into account Carter's announcement, the body in the Charles, the fibers and now this new development, he'd asked the mayor to cut the group to the bone. A smaller group would be easier to move around, easier to monitor.

Ryan surged up from his chair and paced the circumference of the room. He came back to his desk and stood staring down at the telephone. Finally he reached for it.

"Dinner?" said Bree. She held the receiver away from her ear and stared. It was about time.

"Yeah, dinner. Can you make it? I realize that it's late. You probably have plans. . . ."

"No. I have no plans."

"Well?"

"Thank you, Ryan. I'd like to have dinner with you."

He felt just as he'd felt when he'd first discovered that the little girl down the block had become a woman. As if he'd been kicked in the stomach. As if he wanted to turn time back to five minutes ago, when he hadn't had such dangerous knowledge.

"Is Jimmy's okay?" Silently he cursed his choice. Jimmy's was the place he'd taken her on their first date. Couldn't he have been more original than that, for Pete's sake?

"Jimmy's is fine."

"I'll pick you up at seven."

Bree rummaged in her closet, keeping one eye on the clock. Of all days for her to run late at the office, she groaned. Gigolo sat on the bed and watched as she chose and discarded several outfits.

She pulled out a green silk. "Too dressy, don't you think?" she asked the cat.

He ignored her and began to wash.

Finally she was dressed in a calf-length skirt and a not-quite-off-the-shoulder blouse of creamy white handkerchief linen trimmed with Battenburg lace. A broad sash in pastel madras was knotted in front, defining her narrow waist. Her dark hair had been piled carelessly upon her head, leaving strands to curl gently on her neck. She studied herself in the pier mirror. No, the look was much too romantic. She had just untied the sash when the doorbell rang.

She ran down the stairs and answered the door. The sash still trailed from her hand. He looked bigger and more appealing than ever in a linen jacket a shade lighter than his eyes and navy trousers. His shirt was a soft white knit polo. "I'm running late."

He smiled down at her bare feet and at the brightly colored piece of fabric she held. "Don't worry about it. Need some help with that?"

"No, thanks," she assured him. She rewrapped the sash around her waist and tied it haphazardly, as though she hadn't spent a full ten minutes on the same job before. "I'm ready except for my shoes."

They were almost out the door when she remembered the cat. She pursed her lips to whistle, as though she were summoning a dog. The cat came sauntering down the stairs.

"Bree, that may be the ugliest, meanest-looking cat in the world. What's his name?" he asked, giving the malevolent creature plenty of room to precede him out the door.

"That just goes to show looks aren't everything. His name is Gigolo. Gig for short. Don't you like cats?" she asked guilelessly. Gig didn't like men.

"I don't mind them if they're friendly," he answered evasively.

Ryan's car was low-slung, black and risky-looking. Like the man. Bree had to crouch clumsily to get inside. "Ouch," she said as she bumped her knee. A breeze of an inhibiting feeling cooled the tops of her shoulders. It felt rather like entering a bullet. She shivered, deciding she preferred her faithful sedan.

Ryan eased in sideways, as effortlessly as if he were sliding between satin sheets. "Are you cold?" he asked, seeing her shiver.

Considering the nighttime temperature was close to eighty, she supposed the question was a rhetorical one. "No. I'm just surprised at your car."

Leaning forward to insert the key in the ignition, he glanced at her over his shoulder. He smiled that slow, sexy smile and raised a brow. "I've developed a few vices. Fast cars is one of them."

Bree settled her hands neatly in her lap to stop herself from asking the obvious follow-up question. "It's very nice." She realized from her own tone that she sounded as prim as she'd been at seventeen. On the drive to the restaurant she made an effort to correct that, keeping up her end of a light conversation.

The restaurant didn't take reservations and, even on a Wednesday night, was crowded. The hostess said they would have a half-hour wait.

Ryan turned an inquiring smile to Bree. "How about it? Do you want to try someplace else?"

"I don't mind waiting," Bree said.

Ryan gave his name to the hostess. "We'll be outside."

They walked along the wharf. In the summer Jimmy's was always this popular. Less well-known than the famous Anthony's, Jimmy's was equally desirable, both to tourists who knew of it and to native Bostonians.

They wandered away from the crowd of tourists toward a less crowded area of the pier. The silhouette of the city ringed the harbor before them. It was quiet here, except for their footsteps and the background noises of the water-front. The soft sound of a well-tuned motor drew her eyes to the lights of a police cruiser patrolling slowly around the harbor. The water from its wake broke against the pilings.

Ryan raised one foot to the lower rung of the guard rail and rested his forearm on his knee. He looked out over the water and inhaled the myriad scents of the harbor. "Smell that. Even Galveston Harbor doesn't smell like Boston."

Bree backed up to the rail and crossed her arms. "Are you glad you made the change? You'd been in Houston for a long time. It must have begun to feel like home."

"In a way it had, but I'm glad to get back to where the seasons change."

"And to where your parents are close."

"I guess so. Dad hasn't changed. He's set in his ways. I'm beginning to get on his nerves. And Mother just goes along with him. I've got to find a place of my own before they get back."

She hadn't known Ryan's parents were out of town. "Get back?"

"They went to California."

Ryan's older sisters both lived in California with their families. "I can't imagine you staying very long with them," she said, thinking of his parents. They were not difficult to like, but Ryan's father had been older when Ryan was born. They'd never gotten used to having a son the same age as one of their grandchildren and had more or less left him to grow up by himself. She knew that at times it hurt him. That was one reason he'd been so close to her parents. "Have you decided yet where you want to live?"

Ryan loved his parents, he supposed, but he would never understand them. "Believe me, the sooner I find something, the better for all of us. Maybe after the minister's visit I'll have time to start looking."

"It's a shame you aren't more compatible."

"We've never gotten along. You know that. The only thing I ever did that either of them approved of was to get engaged to you." He straightened and put out a hand for hers. "Come on, let's walk."

Bree didn't hesitate, though it felt funny to have her hand held. They walked for a while, slowly, in no hurry, toward the far end of the pier, the deserted end. Light and noise were at their backs. Darkness enfolded them; water surrounded them. Stars blinked directly above, vying for their notice. "It's a beautiful night," she said softly, not wanting to disturb the peace.

Ryan came to a halt. She had taken a step or two beyond him, but their fingers linked them still. Turning, she retraced her steps until they were even again. He kept tugging until they stood face-to-face, only inches apart. She looked up at him, expectation tightening the breath in her throat. She waited.

He touched her bare shoulder first; a brushing caress like a feather trailed over her skin. Sliding his free hand around her narrow waist, he spread his fingers, warm and possessive, on her back. Inches separated their bodies, but she could feel him breathing; she could almost feel the beat of his heart against her breast.

Slowly Ryan lowered his head. His lips brushed hers with the lightest of touches. He squeezed his eyes shut, almost overwhelmed by the emotions that churned through him. The kiss was like a dream he'd long ago forgotten how to dream. His hand, fingers spread wide, seemed frozen to her back. He couldn't remove it. He lifted his head. Their gazes locked in confusion for an endless second.

The Klaxon sounded its regular moan, startling them both, breaking into the moment. Bree looked back over her shoulder and laughed, but the sound was unsteady even to her ears. When she faced him again he was waiting to cover her mouth with his, and this time his passion was unleashed with a ferocity that dazed her. Opening his legs slightly, he held her off balance, gently urging her to lean against him.

She was suddenly aware of every plane of his solid body. Her breasts were crushed against his chest, her hips arched toward him. She lifted her arms, vaguely telling herself that she needed to hold on, but when her fingers plowed into his thick hair to bring his head closer, she no longer excused herself. The intensity of her response was a shock to her. She wanted, needed, to hear the sound that emerged from deep within him, that hungry, almost desperate groan. Desire washed over her in waves.

His name, spoken in a feminine voice from over the loudspeaker, brought them back to earth.

Ryan's arms tightened spasmodically around her as though he would have given anything to ignore the summons. Finally he loosened his hold. "Damned poor timing," he drawled unsteadily, giving her tender mouth a last kiss.

"Yes," she whispered, laying her head in the perfect spot between a man's shoulder and chin. She smiled—the mustache had been soft and tantalizing.

They didn't speak as they retraced their steps, but Ryan kept her under his arm in a possessive hold. Bree could still feel the imprint of his body, of his mouth on hers. The scent of his cologne filled her nostrils. Her senses seemed alive, open, receptive, as they had never been before.

The kiss had left a stunning imprint on them both. They were halfway through the clam chowder before they were able to talk rationally again.

The candle in its fat mug flickered fitfully between them as they ate and talked and laughed softly.

The friendly waitress cleared their plates. "Would you like dessert?"

Ryan smiled at Bree, who was delicately blotting her lips with her napkin. "If I remember correctly, it used to be your favorite part of the meal. Do you still have a sweet tooth?"

"I haven't outgrown it yet." She grinned at him. "I'll have the strawberry cheesecake, please, and coffee," she told the woman.

"And you, sir?"

"Just coffee for me."

He watched with pleasure as Bree devoured her dessert. "Such a delicate-looking little thing. Who would believe you eat like an elephant?"

Bree hesitated with her fork halfway to her mouth to shoot him a telling look. She completed the motion, finishing off the last bite of cheesecake, and put down her fork. A tiny bit of strawberry glaze was left on her lip.

Ryan's gaze grew dark as he watched her. She rescued the tiny bit with a flick of her tongue. It was an unconscious act, but its effect on him was instantaneous. He felt the surge of desire and shifted in his chair to ease the tightness in his loins. Dear God, he was reacting like a randy kid.

A muted imprecation drew Bree's eyes to his face. "What's the matter?" she asked.

"Nothing." Before he could say anything else—and he didn't know what the hell he was going to say—the waitress approached their table again. "Everything okay here?" she asked.

"Fine," said Ryan evenly. "May we have our check, please?"

Something in his face must have warned the woman that he was no longer in the mood for casual chatter, because she presented the check immediately. He scanned it. Taking a credit card from his wallet, he placed it on top of the check. The waitress picked them up and left. When the woman returned he slashed his signature along the bottom, adding a generous tip. "Ready?" he asked Bree.

The air was cooler when they left the restaurant; that helped in his struggle to regain control of the sudden, uncontrolled craving to bury himself deep in her. He'd wanted her before, but tonight, now— He shook his head, breathing deeply of the fresh air.

"The dinner was delicious, Ryan. Thank you. I haven't been to Jimmy's in years."

"We came here on our first date, and on prom night," he reminded her. And wondered why he'd brought up another romantic memory.

"We did, didn't we?" A sigh escaped her; a smile curved her lips. "All those elaborate preparations. I was on the dance committee; we probably could have tied a bow around the moon with all the crepe paper we used to decorate."

"I rented a tux and bought you orchids. God, they were gaudy."

"I thought they were beautiful," she said defensively. "Orchids were the ultimate corsage among senior women, you know. I searched for weeks to find just the right gown to do them justice, since they were so popular and I knew that's what you'd select for me."

He took her hand again, linking their fingers. Their footsteps echoed hollowly against the wooden pier. "We were so sure of ourselves. We knew exactly where we were headed."

The conversation evoked more bittersweet memories. *And where are we headed now?* Ryan wondered.

Chapter 6

They were nearing her street when Bree asked, "Ryan, was there another reason for this invitation? I got the feeling that you've had something else on your mind besides just buying me dinner." She turned as far as the seat belt would allow to watch his profile.

The constraint in him was so sudden, so obvious, that she felt a moment's dread. "You always did read me too well. Yes, I do have something I'd like to discuss with you."

"Okay, shoot."

He waited until he had turned onto her street, parked in front of her house. "I don't want you to be a part of Foreign Minister Saber's entourage," he said quietly.

"What!" But he had stepped out of the car and slammed the door. He came around to her side to help her out. She repeated the word. "What?"

They faced each other on the sidewalk in front of her house. Moonlight painted a cap of silver on her hair and made her shoulders look like creamy velvet. He couldn't think about that. "The major part of your work will be done before the minister arrives, Bree. Except for the formal meals, I've asked the mayor to cut the group to a minimum."

"For heaven's sake, why? You told Carter that you'd be ready."

A muscle in his jaw jerked. "Something else has come up. Austin found out today. One of the minister's advance men, the one you told us about, Dimitri Pandal, is missing."

"Oh, no," breathed Bree, stunned by the news. She was standing beside the white fence that bordered her lawn. Needing to hold on to something, she wrapped her fingers tightly around one of the picket caps and asked the question she didn't want to ask. "You don't think that Pandal is the one, the body of the man in the Charles, do you?"

Ryan shrugged, but the gesture was not a casual dismissal of the situation. "We can't say positively. The identification is still going to take some time. My instincts tell me yes." There were no fingerprints to compare. The only thing they had was a portion of dental work. But he didn't tell Bree that.

"He was a nice man, Ryan, easy to work with and very efficient. He'd never been to the United States before and was so excited about seeing some of the country."

Her distress was evident. He hoped that fact would help him convince her to go along with his plans. He wanted to hold her, to reassure her. Instead he opened the gate for her to pass through. "He was supposed to be back in Karastonia yesterday. He didn't show."

"Maybe he was delayed somehow." She paused. "I still don't understand what this has to do with me."

Plunging his hands into his trouser pockets, he matched his footsteps to her shorter stride. "Bree, we have an unidentifiable corpse tied to a concrete block with a piece of material woven from fibers grown in only three places in the world, a group of crazies that we have no information on planning to cause a stir during Saber's visit to this country and now a missing advance man.''

"'In this business there are no coincidences,'" she said softly. "That's what Dad always said."

They had reached the steps to the porch. He stopped at the bottom while she took two steps up. "Exactly. So will you stay out of it?"

She turned to look down at him. "Of course not." Knowing the pressure he was under, she tried reasonable argument. "You're asking out of personal consideration, not because of official need, Ryan. Dad wouldn't have approved of that, either."

"It is official need, Bree. The group is most vulnerable when it's moving. We *need* to keep it small, one lead car, one chase car and two limos."

She shook her head, her face taking on a determined expression. "Fine, I'll ride in the chase car. The mayor *needs* me to be there. I may have done all the planning for the visit, but plans have a way of going awry if there isn't someone available at all times to implement them."

"I've already talked to the mayor."

"You've talked— How could you do such a thing?" she asked, angrily planting her fists on her hips. A light came on in the house next door. She made an effort to keep her voice low. It wouldn't do for the neighbors to hear her shrieking like Kate the shrew from her own front porch.

Ryan felt himself being pulled in different directions. On one hand, this wasn't a girl he was dealing with here. Bree was a woman and a professional. He understood and even applauded her usefulness; on the other, he selfishly wanted her out of the line of fire—if there was a line of fire. And in the back of his mind, there were other questions, more nebulous, that caused him to feel a certain amount of guilt. Did he have the right to even try to talk her out of participating? Was he not using the same tactics she'd used on him twelve years ago?

"I have a feeling about this," he said finally, unhappy about admitting his reservations. "And I'm worried for you." He'd said the wrong thing. He knew it as soon as the words were out of his mouth. He shouldn't have admitted his concern for her personally.

Bree shot him a furious glare, but it didn't ease her own sense of foreboding. She knew that law enforcement was as much an art as a science. Ryan had had the sense to trust his instincts all along. She hadn't quite believed in his concerns for the minister. Until now. Well, she had responsibilities, too. Planning this visit was a professional coup for her fledgling business. He wasn't going to take the opportunity away from her without a fight.

"Would you like to come in for coffee?" Bree asked. She kept her expression guarded and her temper under control as she unlocked the front door.

Surprised by the invitation, Ryan raised a brow. "Sure, thanks."

She left her purse on a small table in the hall and led the way to the kitchen. She filled a glass carafe with water from the sink and proceeded to make the coffee. He stood there watching her, stirring up uncomfortable feelings she tried to dispel with meaningless conversation while searching for the right argument.

"Have a seat if you like, or we can sit on the porch." The last came out a question as she turned from her task to look at him.

"The kitchen is fine," said Ryan, watching her warily.

He had an idea the glider on her porch would be a little too romantic for the conversation they were about to have.

He would have preferred the porch himself, he thought, watching her movements appreciatively. The bare-shouldered dress was romantic, the way the bright sash defined her small waist was romantic, and the hair escaping from her loose topknot to tickle her neck was romantic. But her pretty back was as stiff as a board. Pulling out one of the ladder-back chairs, he sat down.

While the coffee was brewing, Bree reached for a towel to dry her hands, taking her time over the task, thinking hard. From the minute he had said, "I'm worried for you," she'd known she had to make him understand that her presence as a part of the official party was necessary.

The noise from the electric coffee maker filled the long, stretched-out silence. At last she tossed the towel aside and joined him at the table, taking the seat across from him. She took a deep preparatory breath. "Ryan, I don't want anyone, ever, to be worried for me. You and I both know that no matter how much you want to you can't guarantee the safety of anyone. It's a lesson I learned the hardest way. I thought my father was indestructible. When he died I drew into myself. For a long time I refused to take a single chance. I wouldn't let anyone else near me. Then I thought that Dirk would live forever because he wasn't a policeman." She gave a wry smile and propped her cheek on one hand. The other lay flat on the table between them. "I've changed. I had to, to cope with Dirk's death."

Ryan covered her hand with one of his. She sat still for his lengthy study. At last he spoke. "You don't have to do this, Bree," he said simply. "In fact, it isn't easy for me to hear."

"I know. You hated me for too long," she said softly.

His fingers tightened. "I never hated you, Bree," he said quietly.

She gave him a skeptical glance.

"Hate is a useless emotion. I felt a lot of things, but I never hated you," he repeated, looking directly into her eyes.

His palm was warm, his fingers sure. This was a moment she'd known would come; she was about to hear things she didn't want to hear. But she owed him the opportunity to say them. Shaking off the temptation to leave the subject there, she turned her hand until they were palm to palm and curled her fingers around his. "What did you feel?"

He was clearly as reluctant to share these feelings as she was to hear them. "We seem to have gotten off the subject. I don't know what good it can do to rehash all this now."

"We could clear the air," she suggested. "It's been pretty clouded for a number of years. I'm no more anxious than you are to open all this up, Ryan, but if we're going to deal with the desire between us..."

It was a dangerous offer. She was inviting him to unburden himself of resentments that he'd had under control for years. He didn't release her hand. When he spoke it was as though he were talking about another person, but the strain of his memory was there, as well. "I felt helpless," he said. "There was nothing of substance I could fight. I couldn't throw you over my shoulder and disappear. All I could do was try to reason with you. But you wouldn't listen. It was as though you had closed off a part of your mind—the part that contained all the warmth and love. I vowed then I would never feel helpless again."

His voice had taken on the hard edge of steel. His eyes were the cold gray of the sky before it thunders.

"I felt the same way," she said suddenly, interrupting. "After I moved to New York and once I had recovered from the awful pain of Daddy's death, I felt as though I had lost a critical part of myself. I loved you so much and I felt so guilty for hurting you, but I couldn't see an alternative, Ryan. Do you remember what you said to me?"

If he was surprised by her directness, he didn't show it by more than a raised eyebrow. "I said a lot of things. I even remember begging."

And that was where a great part of his resentment lay, she realized, as she had known it would. She had not only broken his heart, she had damaged his masculine pride. And she knew with a certainty that he had never talked about this with anyone before. He had had no one to talk to.

She tightened her fingers on his. "You asked me what I thought it would do to your love if you had to give up your ambition. I thought a lot about that question. Aside from my own motives, it was reason enough to break our engagement."

He gave a dry laugh. "So you were able to rationalize your guilt away. How comfortable for you. I wasn't able to get over it so easily."

She closed her eyes. "Ryan, it was twelve years ago. *Twelve years.*"

"It was yesterday to me."

Though she'd asked for it, Bree couldn't believe she was hearing this. There was nothing to read from his expression. She had to depend on his words, and they didn't make sense. She shook her head. "We were young."

"We were twenty-two and engaged."

"And after all this time you've never forgiven me," she whispered.

"You want it all?" he demanded.

She nodded.

Suddenly the pain broke through his carefully maintained demeanor. His mouth twisted with it, sending an answering agony through her. "You were *mine*. And you married someone else, damn it. It's hard as hell for me to forget that some other man was your husband, some other man touched you.''

That was a lie, she realized instantly. No other man had ever touched her, not the way Ryan had. But this was something between them that he could never forget or forgive. His bitter words cut deep. Her eyes were dry, but tears were there behind them, ready to break free. He still gripped one hand, and the other shook as she dragged it through her hair and fought to keep her voice steady. "You were right, we should never have gotten into this," she said.

Ryan saw the trembling hand, heard the slight crack in her voice and felt like a heel. He struggled to regain the control that the pain and the anger had swept away. He didn't want to hurt her. He had never wanted to hurt her.

After a long minute he spoke again in a soft and thoughtful tone. "Maybe we should have." His pulse was quiet now. He was tired but somehow more at peace with himself than he'd been since the moment he'd seen her. "Maybe the telling was long overdue. We want each other, Bree. Maybe this had to be said first."

Bree watched his pupils expand, effectively darkening his eyes, and felt the warm charge from his fingers creep up her arm. Slowly she withdrew from his grasp. "Maybe."

Or maybe the conversation marked the end of it all. The kiss they had shared on the pier was forgotten. She was exhausted, but she made a concerted effort to keep the emotion from her expression as she rose and crossed to the counter. There was still the matter of the minister's visit to be dealt with before she could end the evening. The coffeepot was silent now. "What about Saber's visit?" she asked.

Ryan accepted her withdrawal. He linked his fingers and leaned forward.

Before he could speak, she went on. "I am still self-protective; to an extent I probably always will be. But I have learned that I can handle the basic risks in life with a certain maturity." He watched her reach into the cabinet, take down mugs and pour coffee into them. When she was once again seated across from him she looked into his eyes, her own wide with sincere appeal. "Please don't make me argue with you over the visit, Ryan. You could probably convince the mayor that my presence is superfluous—although I'm not sure you could convince Mrs. Quinlan, the mayor's wife. Making sure everything goes smoothly is part of my job."

All her careful planning for this visit wouldn't mean a thing if something went wrong and she wasn't there to deal with it. Her professional name would be mud. The personal feelings, the passion between them, couldn't be allowed to dominate this situation. It needed to be handled with a clear head and a strong hand.

"Bree, I can't guarantee anything. I meant it when I said we need to keep the party small. But I'll think about it."

"Damn it, Ryan, there isn't anything to think about." She slapped the table between them. "Who is going to handle the problems that might arise? Let me give you a few examples. What if the chauffeurs' union decides to go on strike Saturday morning? Who will find substitutes? Who's going to print and distribute the daily press releases? Who makes sure the minister is taken to the television station on time and introduced to the right people?"

His eyes narrowed. "You can do that without being a part of the entourage," he said stubbornly.

"Oh, yeah? What if one of the minister's aides is allergic to Boston water? Who's going to make sure he has bottled water in his glass when he sits down to lunch at the New England Aquarium?" As though she couldn't control the energy surging through her, she rose and began to pace. "Carter said he wanted Saber to have a good time. What if one of the limos has engine trouble? What if two of them do? He won't have much fun sitting in the hot sun waiting for a replacement. You could put him in a police car, but I know who to call for an immediate replacement, not one an hour later. I know how to solve those problems, Ryan. Just as you have your job to do, I have mine. And I won't let you take that away from me. I'm a part of the official party, and I'll go to the mayor myself if I have to."

Ryan sighed. "All right. I'll talk to Dalton about it."

Whirling to face him, Bree planted her hands on her hips. "That's a damned cop-out and you know it. You're the one who will make the final decision."

His features hardened. "Not without consulting the man delegated with the responsibility. I don't work that way. We'll leave it until tomorrow."

She muttered a word he didn't hear. He decided it was just as well. The volatile atmosphere between them wasn't solely the result of the argument or of her explanation. They were alone, it was late, and he couldn't help thinking that somewhere in this house was a bed. He made an effort to dispel the tension. "Do you have some cream for this coffee?"

She looked at him as though she had no idea what he was talking about. "Sure," she said finally with a dry laugh.

They didn't linger over the coffee. She walked with Ryan to the door. When he bent his head to kiss her good-night, she turned her face to the side.

"Blackmail, Bree?" he questioned.

She didn't even take the trouble to honor the accusation with an answer.

"You responded very sweetly to the kiss we shared earlier," he pointed out succinctly. He hesitated again. "Bree?"

Having avoided his gaze for as long as possible, she looked up at him. "Yes?"

"Can't we separate our business connections from our private lives?"

"I doubt it, Ryan. After all, that's why we aren't married." She couldn't keep all the bitterness out of her voice.

The following afternoon, Bree left the downtown office building and decided to walk the couple of blocks to her office. She needed to do some thinking about the appointment she had just concluded.

In the public relations business, big money was to be made by working to help political candidates get elected to office. She had avoided such work in the past for several reasons, not the least of which were the traveling, the demanding schedule of a political campaign, the total commitment.

She had just been offered a healthy retainer just to do some preliminary surveys for a woman who was considering a run for governor of the commonwealth. She knew as well as the prospective candidate did that if she did the surveys she would be in for the duration.

Work like that demanded full-time devotion, and she simply wasn't ready to give it personally. Her other clients would suffer—or go someplace else. But she had been thinking for a while about hiring a political consultant.

When she reached her office her secretary, Louise Crenshaw, handed her a fistful of pink slips.

"Most of them are from Mrs. Quinlan. She seems upset about something, but she wouldn't leave a message."

Bree didn't have to wonder what had upset the mayor's wife. "Get her on the phone for me, please, Louise." She glanced down at the small gold watch on her wrist. "Then go home," she ordered pleasantly. "It's well past six."

She was sitting at her desk, leafing through the slips, discarding those from Mrs. Quinlan, when her secretary informed her the mayor's wife was on the line.

"Bree, dear, I've been trying to call you all day," she said rather petulantly, as though she had been deliberately deferred.

Bree smiled. She had worked well with Mrs. Quinlan in the past, but the mayor's lady wasn't known for her patience. "I'm sorry if you've had difficulty reaching me. I've been out of the office."

"I understand that there is some effort to remove you from the minister's party."

"Well, yes, but I think I've taken care of it."

"What a relief. I was sure my information was an error. But now I'm afraid, my dear, that I'm about to put another glitch into all your careful planning."

On a number of occasions Bree had learned that the tiniest deviation from their preparations was a major glitch to the mayor's wife. "What's the problem, Mrs. Quinlan?"

"The dining room in this old barn is leaking like a sieve. During the hard rain we had Sunday night a piece of the ceiling landed in the soup tureen. The carpenters tell me we can't possibly have all the repair work and painting done by the time the minister arrives. We'll have to relocate the last night's dinner."

Bree's mind had already latched on to the problem, dealing with the consequences and sending out suggestions. There was the dining room in the city offices downtown, but it was too sterile for a formal dinner. Besides, the party was lunching there one day. She hated to repeat herself.

She had learned from her research that the minister preferred small dinners when possible. She and Mrs. Quinlan had agreed that the ambience that last night should be homelike, to send him on his way with an impression of the warmth and charm of the beautiful house on Beacon Hill and of the city itself. His next stop was Philadelphia, then Washington, and he would be subjected to enough pomp and ceremony in both places.

On the other hand, the city offices would already have been checked out by the security detail.

Mrs. Quinlan spoke again. "Marjorie Landon would give her eye teeth for us to use her house. It's large enough and it's nearby. But she's such a snob, I just hate to give her the satisfaction."

Bree bit back a laugh. "May I think about it tonight?" she asked.

Louise stuck her head through the open door, a raised brow indicating her reluctance to leave. Bree waved her off.

"Of course, dear," Mrs. Quinlan was saying. "But we only have eight days. I'll think, too. Maybe we can come up with an acceptable alternative. One of the Eliots? Maybe the 'Browns,'" she said, using the code word for a famous branch of the Rockefeller family that lived across the river in Cambridge. "No, I believe I heard someone say they're going to be in Europe for a family wedding."

"I'll call you tomorrow, Mrs. Quinlan."

"All right. Goodbye, dear."

Bree's hand was still on the receiver when the phone rang again. "Hello?"

"Why didn't you tell us about the change in the schedule, Bree?" barked Ryan. "Sam Dalton's office is supposed to be informed immediately. Can you tell me why we had to hear it from the mayor himself?"

"I just this moment found out," she barked back. "I've cleared my work for next week during the visit, but I do have other clients, you know. Oh, hell. Why am I explaining myself to you?"

"You tell me."

She massaged her temples with the fingers of one hand and attempted to speak reasonably. "Look, Ryan, I've been out of the office all day. I had messages from Mrs. Quinlan waiting on my desk. She's very upset. This is an important dinner."

"I see," he said grudgingly. "Well, where have you decided to hold this important dinner?"

His sarcastic tone made her furious. "You make it sound like a meal is a frivolous afterthought. The minister does have to eat while he's here, Ryan," she snapped, matching his sarcasm. "Though I suppose tough cops can exist on a few nails, all of us are not such supermen that we can forgo sustenance."

There was a long silence. Then she heard him chuckle. "You think I'm tough, huh?" His voice had changed, chiding, urging an amused response.

But Bree was not so easily appeased. She kept quiet.

He sighed audibly and returned to the subject. "Have you and Mrs. Quinlan decided on another location?"

"No. We were discussing it, though."

"Would you consider a suggestion from a nail-eating cop?"

She smiled, though it was against her will, and picked up a pencil. "Of course."

"What about Elmwood? The minister will be touring the campus the last afternoon, anyway, so the security would be in place."

An image of the Harvard president's home rose to Bree's mind. The three story yellow-and-white federalist mansion, set on tidy manicured grounds and surrounded by huge old trees, would be a beautiful setting for such a dinner. She quickly ran over the possibilities, searching for drawbacks.

She could find none. "Ryan, that's a wonderful idea. I'll call Mrs. Quinlan right now and put it to her."

"Okay. And Bree—?"

"Yes?"

"I'm sorry I snapped at you."

"I'm sorry, too. I don't like surprises in my job any more than you do."

"I know." Ryan paused, doodling on the desk calendar before him. He placed the point of his pen on a date. Next Saturday. "You looked beautiful last night, by the way. I'm not sure I remembered to tell you."

"Thank you." Was that her voice? That husky tone? She cleared her throat. "Mrs. Quinlan had something else on her mind, Ryan. You're still trying to keep me away from the minister's party, aren't you?" She leaned back in her chair, swiveling it slightly back and forth. "What was it you said? That I could coach a softball team with one hand and plan a state visit with the other? You wanted to get to know this new Bree. And then at the first sign of trouble you start treating me like the old Bree."

"We'll talk about it. Do you still want me to pick you up Thursday for dinner at your mother's?" he asked.

Drat. She'd forgotten the invitation, which she was sure she'd accepted in a moment of complete insanity. "Why not? I'd rather ride with you than have to explain to Frances Q. why we came separately."

He laughed. "Thanks a lot."

Chapter 7

Invitations had been filtering in from old friends, some casual, some very specific. "We'd like you to come to dinner. We've invited Ryan, too. He's offered to pick you up." "We have four tickets to Fenway Park on Sunday. You and Ryan used to love baseball." The community, with a little help from her mother and Father Brotsky, had done its work well. So well that it was almost comical, and finally Ryan and Bree, though there was still a strain on their professional relationship, succumbed to the humor of their personal predicament.

She had declined all the invitations to dinner, but she hesitated over the baseball tickets. Sunday's game was a sellout. She could wait until tonight and tell him about them when he picked her up for dinner at her mother's. But, refusing to ask herself why, she finally decided to call him. She had to look up the number for police headquarters and go through a battery of people to get through.

"Ryan, this is Bree."

"Hi, honey."

Honey?

"I was just thinking about you. Are we still on for tonight?"

"Yes, I guess so." She hated that expression. "I'm calling because Marilee and Colin have four tickets to the Red Sox game Sunday. They've invited you and I—" that sounded better than "us" "—to join them."

"It would be a crime to turn down an invitation to a Red Sox game," he told her after the slightest hesitation. "What kind of example would it set if the police commissioner committed a crime?"

Relaxing, she laughed, responding to the humor in his voice. "I thought you'd like that one."

"You've had others? Me, too." The hesitation lasted longer this time. "The problem with these people is they don't understand you."

"Really?" His voice had taken on the lazy Texas drawl that sent shivers of anticipation across her shoulders and a warning down her spine. Ryan talking Texas was dangerous. "And you do?" she questioned dryly.

"Mmm. Better after Monday night."

He was referring not to the conversation in her kitchen but to the kiss on the pier. She knew that as surely as she knew her name was Briana Regan. Fleming, she corrected. She'd learned that much about the mature Ryan O'Hara. When he was about to make an outrageous statement he reverted to the drawl and dropped his baritone to a full bass. "Ryan," she said with a cautious glance at the open door to her secretary's office, "I'm at work."

"So am I. And you, Briana Regan, were playing hell with my concentration even before you called." The drawl was so thick now that cold molasses would have run all over it. "I keep replayin' that kiss over and over, Bree, rememberin' how good your body felt shaped against mine.''

"O'Hara, you are shameless. I'm going to hang up."

"I want to make love to you, honey, and you want me, too, don't you?''

Very slowly, very carefully, she replaced the receiver in its cradle. When Louise came in a few minutes later she found Bree with her hand on the telephone. She had to speak twice before her boss responded.

Ryan was thirty minutes late. Bree let the curtain fall over the front window, paced the length of the living room and back and resisted the temptation to check the street again for his car. She had been late getting home from the office. With the minister's visit only a week away, she had been pushing herself to get everything else out of the way so she would be free for those four days. And she had just found out today that she had to be in New York again sometime next week.

She looked at her watch for the umpteenth time since seven-thirty. She had foregone the right to worry about Ryan O'Hara twelve years ago. Even so she worried, rationalizing that she would have worried had he not been a policeman.

She straightened a picture over the fireplace and rewound the mantel clock, which now sounded like a carpenter's hammer in the stillness. The house was so quiet. At last she spun away from the mantel and went to the telephone. She could at least apologize to her mother for the delay.

She had just begun to dial when the doorbell rang. Her shoulders relaxed. Until then she hadn't even realized they were braced. And she wouldn't let herself dwell on what they were braced against. She took a long breath and let it out, putting a determinedly casual smile on her face.

"Hi," she said lightly. "Come in. I just need to get my purse. I left it upstairs."

Ryan stood there with his hands at his sides, a concerned expression on his face. "I'm sorry I'm late."

Bree made some kind of noncommittal noise and hurried up the stairs to her bedroom. She took one precious minute to lean against the dresser, letting the relief wash over her. This was what she couldn't take, what she had known all those years ago she couldn't live with.

She looked around her bedroom, which had definitely been decorated without masculine influence. Here she had indulged her need for something feminine and fussy. The colors ran the spectrum of pink, ranging, from blush to rose, as though to reinforce the conclusion that she didn't need a man in her life. And now Ryan was making deep inroads into her emotions.

He waited by the door, eyeing her alertly, but made no comment as he reached for the knob. Then he changed his mind. Instead of the doorknob, he took her elbow and turned her gently to face him. "Hi."

She pretended to be mystified. "Hi. Shouldn't we go?"

"When you take off that stiff face. I said I'm sorry for being late." His words were delivered gently. He knew she'd worried, and the last thing he wanted to do now was to cause her to worry. She would never agree to any kind of a relationship if he did. And oh, he wanted her. The desire grew stronger with every passing hour.

Her blue eyes looked as though someone had scattered flecks of twenty-four-karat gold dust in them.

"You weren't that late," she answered blithely. "But we will be if we stay here any longer."

He brushed a knuckle across her cheek. "You look absolutely beautiful. I like your dress." The dress was a scarlet sheath, sleeveless and straight—or it would have been straight if she hadn't been inside it. "All day I've looked forward to being with you tonight."

His words flustered her. "Why, thank you, Ryan. I've looked forward to tonight, too," she answered.

"Then why did you hang up on me?"

She dropped her eyes under the force of his gaze. "Because I didn't have an answer to your question," she murmured. "I still don't."

"Then I'll have to do some convincing. Later."

At his words she stopped breathing. Convincing? Did she need convincing? She had been making her own decisions for a long time now. She'd been under a lot of pressure, from her friends and her mother, pressure at work, pressure about the minister's visit. This pressure from Ryan was the last straw. She either had to succumb or erupt. "That's it." She slung her purse down on the hall table. "I'm not going. You make my apologies to my mother."

His fingers tightened. "Hey, what's happening here?"

"If I need to be convinced, then it's not the right thing for me. Write me off, Ryan, as a bad experience. I'm not going to bed with you. I'm basically a private person and I don't like being the object of speculation, not even from you. I'm not going to spend any more of my time trying to field your innuendo and my mother's maneuvering. Can you imagine what would happen if your car stayed past midnight in front of my house? She'd be over here the next morning with a shotgun."

He released her shoulders to draw her gently into his arms. To his surprise, she didn't resist. "Do you think I haven't been subjected to the same kinds of pressure?"

He was too near. His scent was too potent. She couldn't think clearly. But her body seemed to be doing her thinking for her. She relaxed against him, enjoying the warmth, the strength of the arms that held her. "Have you?" she murmured. "I'm sorry. I'd hate it for you as much as me."

"Would you like to know how I handle it?"

She nodded, scratching her cheek against the linen of his jacket. Her arms slid around his waist. She didn't stop to ask herself why. She did it simply because it felt good. She felt his lips in her hair.

"I tell myself that it's our business, yours and mine. I try to balance my desire for you—and I do want you, very badly—with my decisions about my own life. And I feel pity for all those people who have so little to occupy themselves that they have time to meddle."

She leaned back in his arms to look up at him. Though his tone was gentle, the muscle in his freshly shaved jaw was tense. "Even my mother?"

The mustache tilted up to the right. "Your mother most of all. Because she knows more about us than anyone. She knows that you're not interested in marrying again, and she knows my feelings on the same subject. But she's still hoping for a romantic ending—lovers united after years of separation. When the curtain went down, Romeo and Juliet weren't dead after all. It was a big mistake."

Again her cheek found a resting place against his broad chest. "She would think like that," agreed Bree.

His hands moved over her back, his fingers pressing into the tense muscles below her shoulder blades, smoothing them with a moderately firm massage. She felt the tension ease, felt the sigh that gathered in her lungs.

"You want to know what else I've thought?"

A smile was beginning to form on her lips. "Most definitely. Your thoughts are very interesting tonight."

"I think we should turn the tables, find her a nice man. She needs something to occupy her time when she isn't working."

Bree laughed out loud at that, and the laughter was a welcome relief. She released him, bringing one hand around to lay it against his face. "Thank you, Ryan."

He placed his hand over hers, holding it there for a minute. Then he turned his head to leave a kiss within her palm. "Anytime," he said in a low voice. "Just don't ever tell me to write you off again. Because I don't intend to do that. You're a beautiful, desirable woman that I want very much to take to bed."

"Shall we go?" she asked unsteadily.

The gleaming metal of the sleek Black Widow had just been washed and polished to a bright shine. "You washed her. I'm impressed," she noted when they were in the car.

The powerful motor growled into life. "Isn't she looking good tonight?"

"Why do men refer to their cars as she?"

Ryan thought for a minute. Then a wicked smile flashed from beneath his mustache. "You don't want to know," he said.

"I wonder if Mother's having anyone else for dinner," she said, deciding from the suggestion in his smile to drop it there.

"She told me she'd asked Father Brotsky, but she didn't mention anyone else."

"Nor to me," she admitted. Her mother had been thrilled when Bree had told her she would ride over with Ryan, but she had quieted somewhat when her daughter had threatened never to come back if she started hinting.

The dinner was almost an anticlimax. The evening passed without incident, which in itself was a surprise. Frances was the perfect hostess, so perfect that it must have taken a tremendous amount of self-control. She moved and spoke so slowly and carefully all evening that it was almost painful to watch. Not once did she hand out advice. Nothing more controversial than the weather was discussed.

Father Brotsky seemed totally at a loss. He kept asking if Frances felt well. And Bree and Ryan broke up laughing as soon as they were in the car again.

"I can't believe her," gasped Bree. "Surely that wasn't *my* mother."

"Maybe you should put her in charge of the minister's dinner. The department of protocol couldn't find fault with her tonight," Ryan laughingly agreed. Conversation between them continued in a light vein all the way home. He was relieved. When he'd called Frances today to warn her not to try any of her tricks, she'd been strangely quiet.

He drew in parallel to the curb in front of Bree's house and got out of the car.

A bit dry mouthed, Bree waited while he rounded the hood to open her door. When they reached the porch, he was going to kiss her again. She would ask him inside. And where did they go from there? She wasn't sure. But she was sure what he expected.

Just as she stepped out of the car his beeper went off. His pleasant expression disappeared as suddenly as a puff of smoke. "Damn!" he exploded, slamming the door behind her.

"Ryan!" she admonished with a smile, indicating the car. "Aren't you afraid she will object to such rough handling?"

Unamused, he shot her a glance and continued in a more controlled tone. "I've got to get a phone installed in this car. May I use yours?"

"Of course." As they mounted the steps, she rummaged in her purse for her key ring. "Here. This one."

Ryan took the key and quickly opened the door. He left the ring dangling in the lock and headed directly for the phone.

Bree watched him with a small smile curving her lips. Just so had she watched her father respond many times to a call from headquarters, his mind completely on the task that awaited him. Like Ryan, he had kept the parts of his life separate. When duty called, he had responded instantly.

Frowning, she asked herself if she was becoming accustomed to going around with a cop, if she was even beginning to feel a strange kind of pride. No, definitely not. She worked the key free and dropped it back in her purse.

"I'll be there in ten minutes."

Grinning, he turned to her, unable to hide another kind of pleasure. "We've got a break in the Beacon Hill robberies. Some idiot just tried to fence a dozen bearer bonds to one of our undercover men. He's singing like a bird about the others involved. I want to be there for the questioning. Do you mind?"

"Of course not," she replied immediately. "Congratulations."

"It isn't my success. The robbery detail did all the work."

But the suspicion that the apparently unconnected robberies might be the work of an organized gang had been his. He'd mentioned the problem to her over dinner on Monday. The plan for the undercover fence was his. Ryan was anything but an uninvolved commissioner.

He slid his hand around the back of her neck and brought her to him for a kiss that was all too brief. "Tomorrow," he said firmly.

"We have softball practice," she reminded him.

"Maybe it will rain."

She hesitated. "We could come back here afterward. Would you like to test my cooking?"

He nodded, a smile curving his mustache. "I'd love to test your cooking," he said huskily. "By the way, I've been invited to the Maxwells next Tuesday. You've met Austin. His wife, Natalie, is a terrific lady. He was on the force with me in Houston, and we've visited back and forth since. They, ah, asked me to bring someone. I think you would enjoy them."

Bree caught her lower lip between her teeth to hide her grin at his hesitancy. *They were going to fix you up with a friend, more likely.* Poor Ryan, he was getting it from all sides.

Still, submitting to the speculation of friends and relatives was one thing, submitting to speculation by his colleagues was another. She withdrew from the pull of his hand, hedging. "I don't know, Ryan. Minister Saber arrives on Thursday. There will probably be a hundred last-minute things to do."

Ryan clamped down on the temptation to argue with her. He knew exactly where her thoughts were leading. She was going to try to pin him down on the visit. He sure as hell didn't want to get into *that* discussion right now. "We'll talk about it tomorrow." He left.

Bree opened her mouth to remind him that they were supposed to talk about it tonight. Then she realized that he was impatient to leave. This wasn't the time to press the issue. She sighed as she watched him jog down her front walk. There was *never* enough time.

Bree turned off the alarm and lay back on the pillows for a minute without feeling a smidgen of guilt. Morning wasn't her best time, but today she had no early appointments, so she could take her time dressing. She loved days like this.

She was still floating somewhere between sleep and wakefulness when the telephone rang. She groped for the receiver without opening her eyes. "No," she said into it.

"How do you know the answer when I haven't asked the question yet?"

Bree turned on her side, cradling the receiver between her ear and the pillow. She smiled. "I'm still in bed. Any question asked when I'm still in bed deserves a negative answer," she murmured, her voice husky with sleep.

"Oh, lady, I wish you hadn't told me that," Ryan said softly. After a long pause, he went on. "I can see I'm going to have to come up with some creative questions."

Bree chuckled. "What's going on? Where are you?"

"I'm at headquarters. Have you looked outside?"

"Of course not."

"Well, Sleeping Beauty, it's raining. According to the weatherman it's going to rain all weekend." He sounded content at the prospect.

"That's nice for the flowers."

Ryan laughed. "And the tomatoes," he added. "But not for the Saints or the Sox."

Bree finally opened her eyes. She turned half onto her back and looked toward the strip of dull gray light under the window shade. "No practice," she said.

"And probably no game tomorrow."

Bree tried to decide whether she was disappointed or not. "Are you still coming for dinner?" she asked before making up her mind.

"Of course," he said immediately. "What time?"

She decided she wasn't disappointed. She was going to go with her feelings, not her reason, for once. And if her feelings led her to make love with him, there would be no regrets. She found that she wanted—with a wanting that left her weak—to explore this new dimension of an old love.

They'd have time, plenty of time; and they would be alone. "About seven." Then she remembered. "Or whenever you get here."

"If I'm running late I'll call you."

Ryan's heart was racing when he hung up the phone. He made an effort to erase the picture of Bree curled up in bed, still warm from sleep. Would she be in a thin, sexy nightgown or did she sleep nude? Was she saying what she seemed to be saying? How in the name of hell was he going to get through the next twelve hours?

Bree replaced the receiver. Twelve hours. How on earth was she ever going to be ready? Her mind filled with thoughts of the menu, shopping, housecleaning and Ryan. She had several appointments set up for this afternoon. She jumped out of bed and headed for the shower.

At 10:00 a.m., Bree swiveled her chair, turning her back on a potential client who wanted her to propose a way of restoring his restaurant's reputation after an outbreak of salmonella had closed him down. She stared out her office window through the rain and wondered what Ryan was doing. Was he as impatient as she for the day to be ended?

She turned back to the short, skinny man, who looked lost in her client's chair. "Have you taken steps to see that the conditions that led to the poisoning have been corrected, Mr. Vernon?"

The man looked at her as though she'd lost her mind. "Whaddaya think I've been talking about for the last half hour, lady?"

Ryan stood at the wide window in his office, hands thrust in his pockets, only half listening to the man behind him

rave on and on. He'd been informed that the situation was
delicate and had to be smoothed over by the commissioner
himself.

The man was in town for a convention. He was a cousin
to a congressional representative from Idaho—or was it
Iowa?—who served on a committee with Boston's congressional representative. His cigar was stinking up Ryan's office.

The rain blurred the skyline, but he could still pick out the
building where Bree had her offices. Was she as impatient
as he was for seven o'clock to come?

He turned back to survey the man across the desk. Mid-
forties and fighting it, Ryan decided. Good-looking, he
supposed, in an oily sort of way. He successfully hid a grin
as he interrupted the flow of complaints. "Mr. Jackson, I
believe the officer on duty explained to you that there is no
law on the books that would allow us to arrest a man for
impersonating a woman."

"But I spent three hundred and forty dollars on the son
of a bitch. Took her . . . him . . . to dinner at the Hampshire
House, drinks, dancing—" the man shuddered, and Ryan
felt a certain sympathy "—the whole bit. I didn't find out
who he was—what he was—until we got back to my hotel."

"You had no inkling?" asked Ryan, finding that hard to
believe. He found it even harder to believe that the man was
here. If he'd made a fool of himself over a female imper-
sonator, he certainly wouldn't report it to the police.

The man leaned forward, speaking confidentially, man to
man. "Commissioner, you wouldn't have believed her—
him. The most gorgeous pair of . . ."

Ryan tuned him out. Should he take Bree flowers? Wine?

At six forty-five Bree gave the chicken breasts a last bast-
ing with the delicate sauce and turned the oven setting to

low. The savory smell that filled the kitchen mocked her. She should have had steak. Ryan was definitely the steak type. Well, it was too late now. She picked up a cheese tray and a bottle of wine nestled in an ice bucket and headed for the living room.

She put the ice bucket on a serving cart beside two crystal wine goblets, squared the tray on the glass-topped coffee table and fanned out a supply of small paper cocktail napkins. She took a napkin, mopped up a drop of water that had spilled and looked around.

Where should they sit? Her sofa was a raw wood frame, low to the floor, covered with a modified Japanese *futon*. She loved it, but Ryan, with his long legs, would probably find it uncomfortable. He could sit in the one upholstered chair by the fireplace; she could sit on the sofa. She tried them both out to make sure they were sittable.

At seven o'clock Ryan rang the doorbell. Bree jumped, startled. She hadn't heard the car. She hurried to the door, paused to take a calming breath and smooth her hair and reached for the knob. She still had the wadded-up napkin in her hand. Jamming it into the pocket of her white skirt, she opened the door with her other hand.

He stood there looking as handsome as any man on earth. He wore dark jeans and a white cotton sweater over a yellow shirt. He held a bottle of wine by its neck in a throttling grip. "Come in," she invited. "You're right on time."

"I've been sitting on your front porch for ten minutes," he announced grudgingly. "In the glider."

Bree stared at him in astonishment. "On my—" She shook her head. "But it's raining."

"Not on the porch. At least not much."

"Why didn't you come in?"

"Hell, I don't know." His hair was damp, from his shower or from the rain, she didn't know which. He combed his fingers through the thick strands, sending a mist of tiny droplets into the air. "About four o'clock this afternoon I decided this day was never going to end. Then, when I got here, I was ten minutes early. I guess I'm nervous."

Ryan O'Hara nervous? The laugh began as a small sound in the back of Bree's throat. She let her head fall back until she was staring at the ceiling.

The honesty in his statement brought back an appreciation for this man, who was not a game player. He'd always said exactly what he was thinking. And so had she.

Without warning they became Bree and Ryan again, not Mrs. Fleming and the commissioner. "I've been—" she gulped, but the laughter would not be denied, "—been trying out the chairs." She shut her eyes helplessly, then opened them again.

"Trying out the chairs?"

She nodded. Damp, his hair was darker, even the sun-streaked strands altered to a color that suggested that Midas might have scattered coins there. "To see which one would be the most comfortable for you."

A grin stretched the mustache wide across his handsome face. He started to laugh, too, until a sudden clap of thunder interrupted.

Bree reached for his arm and brought him through the door, unexpectedly rising on tiptoe to kiss his cheek and inhale his spicy after-shave. Then she closed the door behind them, muting but not shutting out the sound of the rain. "I guess I'm a little nervous, too," she admitted softly.

Ryan would have reached for her after the kiss, but her admission was unanticipated and disconcerting. "Something smells good."

"It's chicken. I realized after I started cooking that you might have preferred steak."

"I love chicken." *I would love shoe leather.* He handed her the wine.

She took it in her arms, hugging the bottle to her breast, and wondered why she couldn't stop smiling. "Thank you. It looks delicious. Better than mine. I'll get a corkscrew."

Ryan's mouth curved. She hadn't even looked at the bottle. "You're going to have some wine?"

She nodded.

Touching her cheek with his knuckles, he asked in a voice that was not his own, "Does that mean this is a night for celebrating?"

Bree's breathing stopped. The tender gesture didn't warm her; it set her blood on fire. Distracted, she handed him the bottle of wine.

He wasn't sure what she wanted him to do with it, so without taking his eyes from hers he groped behind him to set it on the hall table. She laid her hands on his chest and tipped back her head. He had no trouble deciphering that move. As he settled his hands at her waist, pulling her to him, he gave a slight moan. "Oh, Bree." He covered her parted lips, feasting hungrily on their softness, taking large mock bites, tasting, wetting them with his tongue, seeking a response. "Your mouth is so sweet."

Her tongue answered his demand without hesitation.

"Hon—honey," he murmured, catching his breath when she wrapped her arms around his neck, closing what little space remained between them. "I'm not misunderstanding you, am I? We are going to make love?"

"I thought tonight would never, *never*, come," she whispered into his mouth.

He needed no more answer than that. The hands at her waist lifted her, holding her face-to-face with him, fixing her with a zinc-colored gaze. He gave her one more chance. "You've cooked—"

Bree smiled tenderly at him. At the smile his eyes changed to charcoal dark, half hidden by his lashes. With her held to his solid, hard-muscled body like this, his yearning for fulfillment was hot against her thighs. Her own longing burst within her, equaling or surpassing his, leaving her weak and strong with it, hot and cold.

Passion and desire were torrid, flowing through them both. There was not the slightest need to wait, to put a civilized front on something they both wanted so much. "Dinner will keep. No longer, Ryan," she whispered, holding his gaze. "Let's not wait any longer."

Ryan's heart threatened to thrash its way out of his chest. He swung her up into his arms and mounted the stairs, staggering slightly as he reached the top, not because of her weight—that was nothing—but because Bree was planting little kisses along his jawline that had him reeling with desire. He elbowed his way into a bedroom—was it hers?— hell, he didn't care. He had waited years—an eternity—for this.

Through the fog that was his need for her, he realized he had to get control of himself. Had to slow down. If not, he was going to ruin everything. He dropped the arm under her knees, letting her feet find the floor. The friction set up by the slithering of their clothes didn't help. He held her tightly against him for a moment, burying his face in her neck, struggling with a hunger that threatened to overwhelm him. "Bree," he whispered into her hair. "I don't want to go too fast."

The quietly spoken words were intimate, warm. "You won't," she said, smoothing the hair at his nape.

"Has it been a long time for you?"

She had to think for a minute before she understood what he meant. "Two years."

Ryan's head came up to search her features, which were barely defined in the soft light from the hall. Very cautiously he searched his mind for the right words. "You mean you, ah...haven't..."

"Not since..." She couldn't bring herself to bring her husband's name into this conversation.

Ryan felt his emotions swell to fill his chest. The control he'd sought was suddenly there. "Then we'll take it very slowly. That's the way I want it to be with you." He sat on the edge of the bed and gently tugged until she was sitting on his knee, her legs between his legs, his arms around her in a loose circle. "No sex? Bree, that's unhealthy," he teased unsteadily.

Bree rolled her eyes playfully, content for the moment to follow his lead. "Oh, Ryan, I can't believe you'd repeat the oldest one in the books. The poor love-starved widow needs her physical release?" She laid her head on his shoulder.

He smiled and began to pull the pins loose from her hair, carefully collecting them in his palm. "You've heard it before, huh?"

"Besides, it's medically incorrect. Look at the nuns and the, ahhh...priests." He had lifted a strand of fallen hair to his lips. Hair was nerveless, so why did she feel the kiss all through her body?

Ryan looked at the soft, dark curls spilling through his fingers. "You're no nun, Bree," he said softly. He held his hand over the bedside table and dropped the pins. They made small pinging sounds as they fell, barely audible over the slash of rain on the roof.

Bree lifted her arms to sweep the mass off her neck but found his hand there first, doing wonderful things to the hollows at her throat. He dipped his head, seeking the sensitive spot where jaw and neck and ear meet. His breath was warm as his tongue reached out to taste. With restless urgency she twisted her face to meet his, declaring her need without words. His mouth covered her lips, his tongue busy on its path of discovery, as though the world could go to hell, he was going to explore every angle of her mouth. She sighed her gratitude.

The buttons of her blouse were dispatched one by one. He raised his head to follow the path of his fingers as they traced the scalloped edges of her bra. Suddenly he grasped her elbows, brought her to her feet in front of him. He dragged her shirt back and the thin straps off her shoulders, baring her tender breasts to his hands, his mouth.

"Oh, Ryan," she murmured huskily, cradling his head against her. But this was unsatisfying. The movement of her arms was restricted by all her clothing. She whimpered slightly in frustration.

"Did I hurt you?" Ryan asked immediately, hoarsely.

"No, no. It's just—" She didn't say anything more. She didn't have to. She stepped back. Holding his gaze with hers, she let the blouse fall to the floor. She reached behind her to the hook of her bra.

Slowly Ryan got to his feet. Facing her, he grabbed the hem of his cotton sweater and whipped it over his head. His knit shirt followed.

Bree's gaze dropped to his chest and the hair that grew there in profusion, narrowing to a silky line as it reached past his navel toward his low-slung belt. When he took off his loafers and reached for his belt buckle, she swallowed. He unsnapped, unzipped and disposed of the rest of his clothes with one movement and straightened, magnificent in his nakedness. His arousal rose, full and breath-threatening, from the apex of his muscular thighs.

Her skirt was a wraparound style. It took only the loosening of one tie to remove it. But her sandals had straps with tiny buckles. Reluctantly she tore her eyes from his and started to bend, but he stopped her. "Let me."

On one knee before her, he unbuckled the first shoe, his big hand a warm bracelet around her ankle. Then, his hands trembling slightly, he slid her panties down her legs. Holding on to him for balance, she ran her fingers across his broad shoulders. Satin over steel. As he rose, his hands measured the length of her thighs over the swell of her hips to her waist. His eyes followed the path of his hands until they rested at the outer curves of her breasts. By the time he was standing, her knees were as weak as gravy.

"You are so beautiful," he whispered.

Bree knew her hips were too full to be really fashionable, her breasts adequate but too small to be really sexy. Still if in Ryan's eyes she was beautiful, she felt so.

They faced each other, only inches separating them. He took a half step, letting his hardness kiss her flat belly. And then they were in each other's arms, hungry mouths seeking, restless hands exploring. He spread his legs; she stepped between them, arching as he bent over her.

Finally, turning as one, they moved to the bed and sank onto the soft down comforter. Ryan tried to hold his weight off her, but Bree curled her arms around his neck, pulling him down. She wanted to feel his weight, the glorious warmth of his body, from her head to her toes.

Gently Ryan's hand covered the soft, dark delta between her thighs. He murmured her name on a moan as his hard arousal replaced his hand, nudging insistently at the entrance to her femininity.

They both gasped as he filled her completely, deep and hard against the entrance to her womb. He paused, catching his breath. His face filled her vision, his features painted lightly with a film of perspiration, drawn with desire. Then he began to move, slowly at first, then faster, stirring each of her nerve endings to delight.

Her eyes grew wide as she arched against his thrust. This wasn't the shallow passion of youth. This was deeper, more profound, than anything she'd ever felt before. That was her last conscious thought as she was swept up in the storm of shuddering completion.

Later they were lounging on Bree's sofa, he on his back, his arm around her, she on her side, pressed against his length, the *futon* making a comfortable nest for them both. An old movie played softly on the television, they sipped the wine Ryan had brought and nibbled on brownies, and during the commercials they kissed—long, hungry, totally satisfying kisses that tasted of wine and chocolate.

Ryan had on his jeans; Bree, his yellow knit shirt. It barely covered her fanny, he noted as he looked down her back.

He pulled the shirt up until she was bare and rubbed gently at the base of her spine, his fingers doing delightful things there. "Do you know what this is called?" said Bree sleepily.

Intent on the interesting contrast of his dark fingers against skin that had never seen the sunshine, he didn't answer.

"Hey." She raised her head to prop her chin on his chest and grinned, fully aware of where his mind was focused. "I'm talking to you. Pay attention."

"Yes, ma'am." He tightened his arm and lifted her closer. "Sure, I know what this is called." His lips sought and found the corner of her mouth where the tiny indentation played. "Necking."

"No, I don't mean that. I mean this." She waved an arm. "Staying at home, relaxing, watching a movie on TV, having something to eat and drink—it's called 'cocooning.'"

Ryan smiled. "Really?"

She returned his smile. "I swear."

"Where did the term come from?" he asked as he combed her hair away from her face. He held her head in his hands.

"I don't remember. Probably from some cheap, lazy fellow who didn't want to go out to eat one night. But I don't care. I like it anyway. It has a nice comfortable sound."

"Ummm... Especially on a rainy night. Now if it were winter, we could have a fire." His eyes gleamed devilishly. "You wouldn't want to turn the air conditioning up and—"

"Are you kidding? Do you know what my bill would be next month? Besides, I don't have any firewood."

Ryan let his head rest on one of the down-stuffed pillows and closed his eyes. With Bree wrapped in his arms like this, he couldn't think of a place in the world he'd rather be at this moment. "Remind me to get you a load next fall. Someone on the force usually wants to earn extra cash. Then we'll cocoon again on the first cold day."

He missed the flash of doubt that dimmed Bree's eyes for a second. Such planning for the future surprised her, and despite the wonderful lovemaking they had just shared, she wasn't altogether comfortable with it. But she put it out of her mind for now. "What time is it?" she asked.

Ryan groaned and flipped over onto his side, taking her with him. When they were nose-to-nose, he kissed her. "It's late." He lifted his arm and squinted past her shoulder at his watch. "Twelve-thirty. I don't suppose you'd let me spend the night?" he asked hopefully.

Bree put a finger to his lips. "No," she answered softly. "But you can come back for breakfast." A smile mitigated her refusal.

"It's a date." Ryan kissed her fingers. "And if it rains again tomorrow, we'll find a movie and make out in the back row."

"Good Lord, Ryan. Aren't we a little old for that?"

"I don't want you to think I'm one of those cheap, lazy fellows who won't ever take you anywhere. I left my shoes upstairs." He untangled their limbs and got to his feet, though not without some difficulty. "That thing's a trap, Bree," he said, helping her up.

"All the better to cocoon in...on..." she informed him as she jiggled a bit on one foot and caught his shoulder to get her balance.

He laughed, but suddenly he wasn't feeling jocular. Turning her toward him, he hooked his fingers together behind her back. The small impression played at the corner of her lip for a minute while she tried to decide on the proper adverb, and then it was gone. Her fingers remained on his shoulder. She'd first noticed the scar when they'd come downstairs into the lighted rooms. She'd stared at it for a long time, but she hadn't commented.

Now she did. "This is where you were shot."

"Yes," he answered. He could have elaborated then, but he chose not to. He tried to tell himself he was being staunch and dismissive, but in reality he was dreading her reaction.

Bree fingered the ugly edges of the wound. She could almost feel the blood beneath her fingers. The visions she'd had of him lying on the pavement somewhere, barely conscious and hurting, the blood pumping, draining his strong body of strength and life, returned in a rush of fear and grief. She'd wanted to go to him; of course, she couldn't.

She wanted to talk to someone who would reassure her; of course, she didn't.

She called the hospital every day and felt overwhelming guilt for doing so. Her husband had been dead for less than three months.

She opened her mouth to tell him about the calls and decided against it. "I was so relieved when I heard you'd been released from the hospital."

He looped an arm across her back and turned her toward the stairs. "I was relieved to get out of that place," he said negligently. "You wouldn't have believed those nurses." When she would have accompanied him up the stairs, he stopped her with a hand on her shoulder and a tender smile. "You'd better not. If we both go up there there's no telling when I'd leave."

He took the stairs two at a time and was back in seconds, pulling on the cotton sweater as he descended.

"Your shirt," she remembered suddenly.

"I'll get it tomorrow," he said. He pulled her to him for a last, lingering kiss. When he finally lifted his head he was breathing heavily, and so was she. "What time?" he asked.

"Eight?"

"I'll be here."

After he'd left, Bree sank onto the bottom step of the staircase and stared blindly at the door, seeing instead the picture of Ryan, injured and bleeding. She folded her arms across her knees and buried her face there.

Finally, wearily, she roused herself. What had she been thinking of? She never got up that early on Saturday morning.

Bree was almost relieved when she had a call from a client early the next morning, the same man she was to accompany to New York. He told her that he needed her there

Monday. She agreed but suggested that she go Sunday night instead. He was pleased by her eagerness.

She was torn. With the impending visit she didn't want to be out of town, but she admitted to herself that she needed some time away from Ryan. Far away, in another city, in another state.

They had a leisurely breakfast and went into town to wander through the Faneuil Hall marketplace until the theaters opened. They saw a double feature—Bree would never recall what the movies were—picked up a pizza and came back to her house.

The next morning he watched her pack, his expression guarded and unsmiling. By Sunday afternoon the skies had cleared, and they met the Caitlins at Fenway Park. They yelled themselves hoarse for the Red Sox, but after they had said goodbye to Marilee and Colin they became silent, almost reserved, with each other. Ryan drove her to the airport. She had wanted to take her car, but he insisted.

As she buckled her seat belt she sighed, relieved to be free of the heightened intensity involved in simply being around him.

But by Tuesday afternoon, when he met her plane, she was absurdly glad to see him again.

Chapter 8

The Maxwells' home, a refurbished Victorian town house, was near the Charles River in the area known as Back Bay. Its formality and elegance—the elegance of a bygone age—charmed Bree on sight. She wondered at the appropriateness of her slacks, but Ryan reassured her. He'd shown up at her door wearing jeans, boots and one of those Western shirts that closed with pearl-headed snaps. She found to her delight that he was right. The formality ended at the door.

Dressed in baggy Bermuda-length shorts and a tailored camp shirt, Natalie Maxwell was a tall blonde with arresting features, not beautiful, but striking in a sophisticated way. She was much younger than Bree had expected, having met Austin Maxwell, who was over forty. The smile on her lips was reflected in her warm brown eyes as she responded to Ryan's introduction. "Come in, Bree. We're delighted that you could have dinner with us."

Behind Natalie, descending the staircase a two-footed hop at a time, was a miniature version of the woman, probably under six years old. "Ryan!" squealed the child. "Mama told me you were coming." She made a beeline for him, and he swung her up into his arms.

"Howdy, squirt."

"Howdy, pardner," drawled the child, wrapping her arms around his neck and giving him a loud kiss. "I wore my cowboy shirt, too."

"You sure did, didn't you? Does that make us twins?"

"Yes. We're twins," she declared, pleased.

Natalie looked on fondly, and Bree smiled at the child's eagerness.

Ryan turned with the child in his arms. "Bree, may I present Amanda Maxwell?" he asked formally. "Squirt, this is Bree."

Bree had always gotten along well with children, so she was surprised when the little girl eyed her with obvious distaste. "Is she another one of your wo—umph?"

Natalie slapped a muffling hand over the child's mouth and swept her out of Ryan's arms before she could complete her question, but Bree had a pretty good idea what the designation would have been. She didn't protest when Ryan entwined his fingers with hers and grinned.

"I don't believe that innocent look for a minute, so you can just wipe it off your face," she murmured.

"Come on out to the deck," Natalie invited hastily. "Austin's cooking tonight." She led the way down a long hall to a back entrance. To the child she whispered audibly, "You promised to be good, Amanda. Are you going to keep your promise or am I going to have to put you to bed early?"

Amanda nodded, her eyes wide above her mother's hand.

Bree laughed. Natalie's expression as she looked over her shoulder reflected her thanks. "Bree, you've met my husband, Austin," she said as they stepped outside.

"Yes, it's nice to see you again." Bree shook hands with the man, who seemed rather reserved in contrast to his wife. She recalled that he had been quiet the day they'd met in Sam Dalton's office, too.

"Can I get you a drink?" he asked, indicating a white wrought-iron cart that seemed to hold everything a guest could possibly want.

"We'll serve ourselves, darling," said Natalie as she set Amanda on her feet. The child scampered away. "You keep an eye on the steaks. And Ryan, you keep an eye on Austin to make sure he doesn't overcook them."

The modern deck, where they stood, had been added onto the back of the house, above ground level, giving them a view of the river. Several steps down was a small fenced lawn, shaded by a large maple tree and dominated by a sandbox and a swing set. A picnic table was set with colorful linen beneath the tree.

"Your home is lovely," Bree commented to Natalie when they were seated with drinks in their hands. The men hovered over the barbecue grill.

"It's much more house than we need." Natalie made a face. "But I do have to do a certain amount of formal entertaining as part of my job."

"Ryan tells me that you moved here from Houston to take a promotion."

"That's right. I was offered a vice presidency with the company that necessitated the move. Austin was wonderful about leaving Houston. Of course, the parents on both sides were horrified that a man would postpone his career plans for his wife."

"I think it shows a rare understanding. You're very lucky." Her gaze was drawn to the men but lingered longest on the tall figure standing next to Austin Maxwell.

Natalie's eyes followed hers to rest on her husband. "Yes, I definitely am," she said softly. Her gaze returned to Bree, twinkling mischievously. "Besides, I make more money than he does, and he likes that fine. We both prefer not to have to live on a cop's salary."

Bree chuckled. "You certainly couldn't afford this house on one."

"You're telling me. We tried it for a while." Natalie sighed and shook her head. "When we were first married and I was trying to get pregnant, I took a leave of absence for a year." She shifted in her chair. "Tell me about yourself, Bree. You have a media consulting firm?"

As Bree began to explain about her own job, the two women regarded each other carefully. The polite conversation served as an overlay while each wondered if there might be friendship here. Encouraged, Bree began to feel at ease, and Natalie seemed equally comfortable with her.

They were distracted by childish laughter. Amanda, quite obviously preferring the company of men, danced around Ryan's long legs. He reached down to lift her into his arms, nuzzling under her chin with his mustache. Bree felt a lump form in her throat. He would have made a good father. She shook off the sudden feelings of regret.

Natalie read Bree's thoughts precisely. "Ryan is great with kids. He's a favorite of Amanda's," she explained. "And she doesn't get to see as much of her father as either of them would like."

"As the daughter of a policeman I can certainly appreciate that," Bree said truthfully. She sipped her Coke, lifting her head to smile when Austin approached the drinks cart.

He pulled the tab off a can of beer. "You're the daughter of Brian Regan, aren't you?"

"Yes." She wrinkled her brow in confusion. "Did you know my father? No," she said, answering her own question. "Of course you didn't."

"No, I'm sorry to say. But he's a legend in the department. I certainly know of him." He laughed quietly and took a deep swallow of his beer. "I once asked Ryan if Regan had a son. I sure did want him on my force. You wouldn't be interested in going into police work, would you?"

The tableau froze to be forever printed on the surface of Bree's mind as her gaze flew to meet Ryan's. He was as still as a rock, waiting for her answer, or rather the way she would give it. Bree felt his rigidity from a good ten feet away. She suddenly wanted to reassure him, but she couldn't think of a way, not without making a point of the issue between them. And that issue was private.

She forced herself to withdraw her gaze and turned to Austin with a calm smile. "No, but thanks anyway," she said evenly. "If my business goes under it's nice to know I have an alternative career choice."

She felt Ryan relax . . . slowly.

Amanda had come over to crawl up on her mother's lap. "I'm hungry," she muttered.

"Me, too. Hey, fellows, how much longer before those steaks are ready?"

They all pitched in to get dinner on the picnic table under the tree and sat down to hungrily devour the steaks, baked potatoes and salad. Bree found that she fitted easily into the familiar friendship of the other adults. Amanda hadn't made up her mind yet. They had reached the dessert course, a wonderfully light lemon mousse, when the telephone rang.

Austin groaned. "Once!" He cast his eyes heavenward. "Just once, can't you let me finish a meal?"

The others laughed. Natalie looked at her watch and gave her husband's hand a reassuring pat. "Maybe it's just a magazine solicitation; they always call at dinnertime, too."

But it wasn't, of course. Austin returned in a few minutes with a sober but excited expression on his face. "The dental records have finally arrived from Karastonia. Pathology is working on them now."

Ryan gave Bree a guilty glance. This was the third time in so many dates that he'd had to end the evening before he'd planned to. Would she understand? "Bree" he began hastily.

"Go," she interrupted. "Just leave me your car."

"My car?"

She giggled; it was a most un-Breelike sound. "Yeah, cowboy. I finally get to drive that car. Or you can take me home and come all the way back to town. That shouldn't take more than, oh, thirty to forty-five minutes. Maybe an hour."

He groaned and caught her hand, hauling her to her feet. "Okay, you win. But you'd better take good care of her," he warned with a mock growl. "Come on. Walk me to the garage."

They didn't get that far. Austin went upstairs for something, and Ryan stopped in the living room, bringing her into his arms. "I'll come by your house when we finish, okay?" he asked hesitantly, as though he were waiting for her to refuse.

She didn't waver. "Okay. I'll be waiting for you."

His head dipped, his mouth slanted over hers, the tip of his tongue traced a lazy line under her upper lip. Then they were together, mouth to hungry mouth, the world around them reeling on its axis. Slowly Ryan released her lips and rested his forehead on hers. His breath came fast. She realized Austin was coming down the stairs behind them. "Be careful," he whispered, and was gone.

"I understand that you and Ryan were engaged at one time," said Natalie later. The dishes had been cleared, Amanda had been put to bed and the two women were once again settled into chairs looking out over the river.

She certainly was not one to tiptoe around a subject, thought Bree with grudging admiration. "Many years ago," she conceded.

"I'm glad he brought you here tonight. I had some pre-conceived notions about you and I'm glad to find that I was mistaken."

"About me?" Bree was surprised. "Ryan talked about me?"

Natalie waved a dismissive hand. "Not much, and never by name," she assured Bree. "Just an occasional mention of a woman in his past. I always wondered why he wasn't interested in a permanent relationship. Believe me, I trotted out the most eligible women in Houston, and any one of them would have gladly lassoed Ryan O'Hara."

"Not you, too," laughed Bree. "Since my husband's death, my mother's become a dedicated matchmaker. Poor Ryan. I can certainly sympathize."

Natalie defended herself. "He didn't seem to mind. In fact, he almost got married one time—to a very good friend of mine."

Bree didn't know what to say so she didn't say anything. But her thoughts were atumble. *I came close one time,* he'd said when she'd asked him why he was still single.

"I'm sorry, Bree," Natalie apologized quietly. "That was uncalled-for. They probably weren't suited, anyway." She sighed. "They broke up right after he was shot. I suppose she couldn't handle the danger in his job."

The words struck at Bree like blows. Dear God! Twice. To have such a thing happen twice. She shook her head, feeling his pain and her own guilt. No wonder he was adamant about not wanting a commitment.

Not noticing her reaction, Natalie went on. "I suppose it's the nature of the happily married beast to want to arrange the same for people they care about. I hope you'll forgive me—and your mother, too."

"You're forgiven." Bree smiled to let her know she meant the words, but her heart wasn't in it. Natalie certainly noticed this time.

When the blonde gave her an inquiring look, she added, "My mother, I'm not so sure about."

Ryan finally arrived at 1:00 a.m., cursing vehemently as he stalked through the door Bree held open. "I didn't put a scratch on it—her," she proclaimed.

"What?" he asked blankly. "Oh, the car? Never mind that. It's the damned bureaucracy in Washington. I've been trying for two hours to reach Carter. 'Mr. Carter is attending a reception at the Turkish embassy and can't be reached.'"

Ryan mimicked a falsetto voice with a scathing accuracy that had Bree grinning. But the grin faded fast when she realized what the statement meant. "Then the body was—"

He nodded grimly in answer to the incomplete question. "The minister's advance man, Pandal." He thrust his fingers through his thick hair in a gesture of frustration. His hand remained to massage the tight muscles at the back of his neck. "She finally promised to get in touch with Carter and relay my message. I gave them my number and yours. I hope you don't mind."

"Of course not," she said dismissively. "Did you explain how important this was?"

He shot her a look.

"Of course you did," she answered for him. "Well, what do we do now? Coffee?"

Bree led the way to the kitchen, walking with an unconscious grace that finally pierced Ryan's frustration. She had dressed, or undressed, for bed. She wore a rose-colored gown and matching robe. He watched the subtle sway of her hips beneath the flowing fabric and felt a powerful urge to take her, right there on the floor, losing himself in her softness. He'd said that she still had the sexiest tush in Boston. But that wasn't entirely accurate. When she'd been a girl, she had been sexy to a young man. Now she had the rounded hips of a woman, and they drove a man wild.

"I made this coffee about eleven-thirty. I hope it's still drinkable."

He had to clear his throat before he could answer. "I'm sure it will be fine," he murmured, coming up behind her to wrap his arms around her waist. He bent his head to nuzzle at her ear. "You smell good."

"Thanks." She turned in his arms, the coffee forgotten. "Ryan, what do we do now?"

She wasn't referring to them, that was for sure. He sighed and released her. "We wait for a phone call or until the bureaucrats open their offices at nine, whichever comes first. We're going to have to have extra manpower from them, but I want the men coordinated under our orders. I hate to make the security force so obvious, but I can't see a way out of it. Even so, a determined assassin will be hard to stop. We can protect the minister if we're allowed to do it our way. About that walk on the Freedom Trail . . ."

He had expected a knee-jerk reaction. After all, this was the woman with bulldog tendencies. To his astonishment, she didn't protest. "Yes, I can see that the walk would pose problems. We'll have to do all of it by car."

"You don't mind?" he asked, his surprise evident in his voice, his raised brows.

"Certainly I mind," she tossed back. "But I'm smart enough to realize that there's a murderer out there."

Ryan smiled. "Ideally we should postpone the visit until we catch the man who did it. Realistically I still know there isn't a chance of that."

He pinned her against the counter, his hands roaming restlessly over the smooth fabric of her robe. The cat appeared from somewhere, but Ryan didn't spare him a glance. "My car's been parked in front of your house for several hours now, Mrs. Fleming."

She was fingering the pearl-topped snaps on his shirt.

With a gentle hand he pushed back a long curl that had fallen forward over her shoulder, baring the lovely line of her throat. The collar of her robe was satin, slick to the touch. His finger delved inside to stroke the side of her neck. "I guess I should go."

"I guess you should." She dipped her chin, keeping her eyes on the pearl snaps. "I saw something in a movie once that I've always wanted to do." She raised her eyes. "Do you mind?" she asked, carefully polite.

"Whatever you want to do, honey," he said, distracted by his exploration.

With a smile that completely belied her intentions, Bree wrapped her fingers around the open edges of his shirt, her knuckles meeting over his collarbone, lifted her elbows and ripped! The snaps popped noisily, and he felt the sudden chill on his flesh.

He was too stunned to react for a minute. His hand made a fist in the fabric of her robe, and he used it to haul her onto her toes. "I saw the same movie," he said, delighted with her slight show of aggressiveness.

"Good. Then you know what comes next," she said, laughing huskily, her fingers lost in the thick hair on his chest.

The foreign minister of Karastonia, Nicholas Theodor Saber, was a good-looking man, taller than Bree had expected, taller by several inches than the compatriots who accompanied him off the plane. He was dressed with Western conservatism, in a dark suit, white dress shirt and rep tie.

Bree knew his age to be forty-two, but even though his dark hair was liberally salt-and-peppered, he looked younger. He had been educated for the most part in his own country, where the educational system was excellent, but he had also taken an honors graduate degree at the London School of Economics.

A distant cousin of the king, Saber might conceivably have made a case for ascendancy to the throne. But his mother had been English and had imbued him with a respect for democratic government. He would probably be elected his country's first president anyway. There were no other conspicuous contenders at this time.

All these things ran through Bree's mind as she watched him follow the mayor to the bank of microphones that had been set up on the tarmac in front of the small crowd. He stood quietly to one side as the mayor stepped up to the podium to officially welcome him to the United States. He responded briefly and with equal formality. His voice was deep, his accent upper-class British.

Then, as she watched, several things seemed to happen at once. The wind picked an errant lock of his hair and mussed the perfect grooming. He turned to face the cameras and they caught their first glimpse of the hint of humor in his eyes, eyes that were as black as the wing of a raven in the noonday sun. He smiled and a masculine dimple in his cheek found life. With long fingers he tucked his unanchored tie between the lapels of his suit jacket and gave a self-deprecating shrug; the movement was faintly reminiscent of the young John Fitzgerald Kennedy.

The rhythm of the motor-driven cameras of the press increased noticeably, a woman behind her sighed, and Bree felt her heart hit her toes. She remembered something else about the minister from Karastonia. He was a widower.

Unless she was greatly mistaken, and she feared she was not, the man at the microphones was about to become the newest darling of the American press. Such a complication would greatly hinder not only her job but Ryan's, as well.

She was proven right almost instantly. As soon as the small ceremony was complete, the reporters, probably second-stringers who had grumbled at the assignment, began to shout, hurling questions at Saber like firecrackers. The mayor's aide said something in an aside, and both the minister and the mayor nodded. The security force cleared a path to the waiting limousine. Not until they were both tucked safely inside did Bree allow herself a breath.

Bree and Ryan met again at the doorway of Faneuil Hall, where there was a small reception. A tour of the city and state offices were to follow, and dinner would top off the evening. "Can you believe this?" Ryan muttered sotto voce as they took their places in the receiving line. Under cover of the bodies around them, he reached for her hand. The crowd had grown to an astonishing size just in the short time it had taken to drive in from Logan Airport. Word travels fast, thought Bree wryly.

"We don't have enough to worry about and Prince Charles walks off the plane," he added.

"I'd thought more in terms of John Kennedy," she whispered back.

"Rolled into one," he agreed. "Did you see the protest group outside?"

Before she could question him about that, she spied the mayor's wife, who had evidently been watching for her. Mrs. Quinlan waved frantically.

"Everybody and his brother will want an invitation to a dinner or luncheon or reception now," she predicted.

"We'll have to clear them."

"I know, I'll get Sam a list as quickly as possible. See you later," she whispered. His fingers tightened briefly before letting go.

Mrs. Quinlan drew Bree aside. "Good Lord, you didn't tell me he could charm the birds off the trees, nor that he was going to be so devastatingly handsome."

"Charisma," pronounced Bree with a smile. "It doesn't show up in pictures, Mrs. Quinlan."

"Well, you can imagine what's happened."

"Requests for invitations?"

Mrs. Quinlan nodded. "From some of my husband's biggest contributors. We've got to let some of them come to something, Bree. The mayor's next campaign will be political hash if we don't."

Bree fought against the urge to laugh. Mrs. Quinlan was deadly serious. The media called her the politician in the family. "Let me have a list as soon as you can. I'll see what I can do."

"Thanks. Now if we can get close, I'll introduce you." The women began to edge their way through the crowd. Ryan was talking quietly to the minister and the mayor. "Look at them. It ought to be against the law for two such good-looking men to be in the same room."

"Three," corrected Bree diplomatically.

Mrs. Quinlan studied her husband for a minute. She grinned at Bree. "You know, I believe you're right. Sometimes we become so close to the forest we can't see the trees.'' She sighed. ''It's a shame that Ryan won't be here long enough to be the party's next candidate for mayor.''

Bree felt her heart stop for a second. When it resumed its pace, the rhythm was heavier. ''What do you mean? Is Ryan leaving Boston?'' And he hadn't told her?

''Heavens, no. Not right away, anyway. I just meant that someday he will.''

''Why should he do that?'' asked Bree. ''Boston is his home.''

''My dear, surely you know how widely he is respected in his field. He'll end up in Washington eventually. Maybe head of the FBI.''

Bree had known that Ryan enjoyed an excellent reputation for police work. Everything about him had been written up in the papers when his appointment had been announced. But she hadn't thought about his leaving. The prospect left a hollow feeling in the pit of her stomach.

As she approached the two men, she paused. The minister turned at the movement, his polite demeanor warming at the sight of a beautiful woman.

Ryan turned at the same moment and missed the expression. Automatically he held out an arm to her, and automatically she moved to stand beside him. It was an intimate, proprietary gesture that was not lost on any of the three people who saw it, the mayor, his lady or the minister, who gave her a small smile of regret.

The mayor recovered first. ''May I present Briana Fleming, who is a public relations consultant? She has been in charge of the arrangements for your visit.''

''Ms. Fleming.''

''Minister Saber. Welcome to the United States.''

"Thank you. It is a pleasure to be here. I'm looking forward to my visit, all the more so since discovering you planned it for me."

Bree had never had anyone kiss her hand before, and she was enchanted by the gesture.

Ryan, on the other hand, was not. But he carefully schooled his features to ignore the contact. He had already notified those present, by action, that Briana Fleming was his. His? That was an uncharacteristically possessive word for him to use. He didn't want to put strings on her. Did he?

The minister had turned again to him. "Commissioner O'Hara, I hope there will be an opportunity for us to talk privately."

"Certainly, Minister Saber. I'm at your disposal."

"Perhaps we might take a few minutes now?" He looked at the mayor. "If we have the time?" he asked.

"Go right ahead," said Quinlan.

"This way, sir," said Ryan. He led the way to an anteroom behind the stage.

With the closing of the door behind them, the minister shed the image of the charismatic leader, and an angry man emerged. The anger was directed inward, however, and was tempered by sorrow. "I was informed only minutes before my plane took off that you had successfully identified a murdered man in your city as one of my advance men." He waited, tense, for Ryan's answer.

"That's correct, sir. We have confirmed the identification utilizing dental records we received from your country. I cannot tell you how much I regret this tragedy," he said sincerely.

The minister spun on his heel and paced the length of the room. "Damn it!" he erupted. "Talk to me, Commissioner O'Hara. Tell me what happened. And why the hell wasn't I notified?"

"The body was found in the Charles River almost four weeks ago. Identification was difficult because—" Ryan hesitated, understanding the guilt that sat heavily on the man's shoulders "—because the body had been deliberately mutilated. I was under the impression that the State Department was in contact with the aide who reported the man missing."

Saber's hands clenched into fists. "If they were, I never heard of it."

Someone's head will roll over this, thought Ryan, wondering if it would be his. "From what we can piece together, sir, the man, Pandal, returned from California to Boston without notifying anyone in your embassy of his movements. He was probably killed the same day he arrived."

The minister swung away, but not before Ryan had seen the agony that distorted his features. "You were close." It was not a question.

"Pandal was like my right arm. He was also my brother-in-law."

"I'm very sorry," Ryan said quietly.

"I have to thank you for determining the identification. At least now his body can be sent home for burial."

"I believe it has already been arranged, Excellency. And I assure you that the security forces assigned to protect you personally have been increased."

He gave a dismissive wave. "We both know, Commissioner O'Hara, that if an assassin is determined enough no force will stop him," he observed sadly. "But I refuse to curtail my duties to cater to the whim of a murderer."

Ryan's features assembled into a mask. He couldn't argue with the reasoning or with a statement they both knew to be the truth. "We will find Pandal's killer, Minister Saber."

The determination in his tone convinced the minister. "Thank you." His face eased into a half smile of friendship. He extended his hand. Ryan met the strong grip. "I have no doubt that you will give it your best effort, Commissioner O'Hara. If there is any information I can provide to aid in your search, I hope you will inform me."

Ryan hesitated for a minute. It was not quite a dismissal, and he decided to push the older man. "Thank you. The lieutenant who is in charge of the investigation will have some questions, as well. In the meantime, there is something you can do to aid in providing for your own protection."

"Oh? And what is that?"

"You saw the protest group outside when you entered the building?"

"Who could have missed them? But protest is one of the prices of freedom."

This time it was Ryan's turn to wave dismissively. "I won't argue that. And we are monitoring their every move. But I would ask that you not deviate from your schedule or make any unrehearsed moves, sir. We are prepared to keep you safe under those conditions."

The minister's brow rose. "I'm not sure I understand. I hadn't planned on running off."

"May I speak frankly?"

"Please do."

"There is a certain amount of, glamour...about you, sir. The media here in the United States is rather enthusiastic. To put it bluntly, Minister Saber, the reporters are going to be on you in droves."

After a long minute the minister spoke, a hint of amusement back in his voice. "Very well, commissioner. You have my word." The man looked at Ryan for a long minute. "What is your first name, Commissioner O'Hara?"

"Ryan, sir."

"May I use it?" Before Ryan could respond to the startling request, he went on, "And will you call me Saber? It is my family name. I have a feeling we are going to know each other well before this visit is over."

Saber had asked that Ryan be included in the official party whenever convenient. The commissioner of police was a political appointee and was often included in official functions; in fact, it was often compulsory. But drinking champagne to the tune of a string quartet was not Ryan's idea of a good time. He'd rather be on the line with his men.

Tonight it was the harbor cruise. One of the mayor's friends had brought his yacht from Nag's Head to take the party sight-seeing. They would have dinner on board.

And tonight Maxwell was questioning the leaders of the protest group, hoping to come up with a suspect in the murder case.

As the crew was casting off, Ryan caught up with Bree at the stern. "I'm glad you're planning to eat today." She tempered her acerbity with a smile. He planted himself close beside and slightly behind her. On a boat this size there was no necessity to spread your feet for balance. They looked back at the dock, at the sun sitting low over the horizon of skyscrapers.

The boat picked up speed. On the nautical staff an American flag was immediately caught by the wind, and a strand of Bree's hair whipped across her cheek, into her mouth.

Ryan's broad shoulders shielded her from the sight of the others as he reached up to brush it back. "Just toss me a few nails. I'll be okay," he growled, the masculine slash visible in his cheek.

Bree looked up at him, yearning to touch that spot. She had to settle for touching his hand where it lay beside hers on the rail. Just a touch, but it brought a smile to his face and softened his expression. She realized that the hard-edged look she'd noticed that first day was seldom evident now. At least not when she was around.

"You look fantastic," he told her. Her calf-length sleeveless dress was of a rich teal blue, a color that darkened the shade of her eyes, giving them a mysterious glitter that was infinitely arresting. The neckline dipped discreetly but enticingly. A matching shawl was knotted loosely between her breasts. The hem of the dress and the edge of the shawl were trimmed with a wide fringe, providing a fragile shield and tempting glimpses of her legs and shoulders.

He put out a finger to separate two strands that dangled on her upper arm. The skin beneath was as silky and soft as it promised. "I like your outfit. I've always been a sucker for fringe."

"Thank you." The effects of his light touch threatened to steal her composure. She tried to smile, but it was difficult when all her baser instincts tempted her to do more inappropriate things. She moistened her lips and tried again.

He tensed. "Please don't lick your lips like that."

"I'm sorry," she murmured. This magnetism between them hadn't diminished at all with their lovemaking. She would have thought the intensity would have eased somewhat by now. Instead, their desire seemed to grow stronger, more concentrated and more unsettling with each encounter.

"I've got to speak to Quinlan," he muttered. He covered her lips with his in a soft, hurried kiss and headed for the bow.

Bree looked around to see who might have observed the kiss. No one was paying particular attention to her.

She began to circulate, and she must have said the right things to the right people. But she was moving inside a foggy bubble of her own. Everyone outside seemed lifeless and one-dimensional, the only exception being Ryan. Bree mentally shook herself. This had to stop. Her step quickened with resolve. She had a job to do and she'd better do it.

With a practiced eye she checked the condition of the waiters hired for the evening to supplement the boat's staff. Mess jackets and dark trousers were perfectly pressed; hair was neatly combed; smiles were in place. They passed the hot hors d'oeuvres and the chilled champagne smoothly while the luxurious yacht moved along the edge of Boston harbor. A string quartet played from under a sky-blue awning amidships.

If genteel laughter, smiles and easy conversation were any indication, the guests were having a wonderful time. She had planned all this; she should be relishing her triumph. But she felt strangely removed from it all.

Dinner was announced at eight and the group moved inside. The dining room aboard the yacht seated eighteen, but they had opened a folding partition that separated it from the main saloon and extended the table to seat an additional ten people. Spotless white linen, delicate crystal and china, Georgian silver, all glowed in the warmth of candlelight. Southern red lilies and heavy-headed dahlias were arranged in casual profusion and lent their scents to the delicious aromas of the food.

The civilized hum of the motors was audible, but she had decided against moving the quartet inside during dinner, opting instead to let the guests enjoy quiet conversation. Later, when the stars had come out and the moon had risen above the horizon, there would be music again on the deck for those who might wish to dance.

At dinner she was seated below the salt, as they used to say, and had to watch Ryan charm a councilman's wife. He caught her gaze once, when she was careless. He gave her a slow, deliberate wink that brought blood rushing to her head. She made up her mind then and there that she wouldn't insist he go home tonight. As he'd said, it was their business. She would like nothing more than to curl up in his arms and sleep.

"Bree, dear, this evening has been perfect," said Mrs. Quinlan. The boat had reached the dock and was discharging its replete passengers. The minister, accompanied by the governor, had been first off and most flattering in his praise of the evening.

"It was kind of the mayor's friend to lend us his boat," she answered.

Mrs. Quinlan patted her hand. "It was clever of you to think of suggesting it. Get a good night's rest, dear. Tomorrow's another big day. See you in the morning."

"Good night, Mrs. Quinlan."

"Yes, dear, get a good night's rest," said a voice at her ear.

She kept her eyes to the front, muttering out of the side of her mouth. "Wretch."

A hand settled at her waist. "I didn't even get to dance with you," he complained. "Are you through now? Can we leave?"

"I just have to give the waiters their checks. Then I can go. Do you want to meet me at home?"

A quizzical look flew across his features for a minute. "No, I'll wait for you. Then I have to make a short stop at headquarters to speak to Austin." He hesitated for the briefest of seconds. "Why don't you ride with me? I'll bring you back for your car in the morning."

Her hesitation was longer. "All right," she said.

Their minds on the night to come, they both made an effort to talk about anything else during the ride to headquarters.

"The evening was a roaring success, from everything I heard."

"Thanks. I'm relieved that everything went well this first night, but I won't be able to relax completely until the visit is over."

"Come in with me," he suggested as he pulled his car into the space reserved for him. She accompanied him to Maxwell's office.

Austin looked as though he'd been combing his hair with his fingers. Parts of it stood straight up.

"How did it go?" asked Ryan, referring to the questioning.

"Nothing. We came up blank. The official leader of the protest group, Malina, is a student, a smooth character but too young to be effectual. If he's involved in the killing it's on the edges. I don't think he's the perpetrator. But we'll keep a watch on him. He may be the one who telephoned in about the threat."

"A telephone threat?" Bree hadn't known there had been one.

"Not a threat, a tip about one," Maxwell answered. "Someone called in to say that these protesters were making threats. It could have been one of my informants, but no one is taking the credit—or blame—for it."

"Does this Malina have a girlfriend?" asked Ryan.

"Melissa Gardner. BC student, too. Lives at home. We have a watch on her parents' house."

"What about the other man your CI told you about?"

"Yeah. We don't have a name. Malina pretended not to know anything about a second-in-command." He sighed and leaned back in his chair. "How is the minister taking it?"

"Badly. Pandal was his brother-in-law and evidently a close friend, as well."

Bree hadn't known that. Silently she listened as the two men continued to speak in the police brand of verbal short-hand, which conveyed the greatest amount of information in the shortest possible time.

At last Ryan stood, preparing to leave. "Go home, Austin. It's late. There's nothing more you can do here to-night."

"I have this odd impression there's something missing, but I can't put my finger on it."

"I know the feeling," said Ryan. "What about the ex-port-import shop on Newbury Street?"

Bree's attention was caught by that. She had arranged for the minister to make a brief stop there on his way to the air-port Sunday morning. The shop was owned by a man from Karastonia, and the stop was for a private hello.

"It's clean. The owner is a friend of the royal family, the son of the palace gardener, grew up with the minister. Emi-grated in '80. He employs thirteen people, most of them older relatives of his. He brings in some goods from Ka-rastonia but mainly ships U.S. goods back home. He's been very helpful, deplores the group that is protesting."

Ryan nodded. "Doesn't seem to be anything there. Did he know the victim?"

"Vaguely, he said."

Chapter 9

I, ah...feel I must warn you. I'm—*Ry*an—dangerous when I'm teased."

They lay, legs entwined, on the crisp, faintly scented sheets of her bed. The light from the hallway threw her body into sharp relief.

"You are, huh?" Ryan touched her, felt her tremble beneath his fingertips. He savored each touch, each response, slowly, deliberately; they had all night. Lazily he lifted her arm, raising it above her head. Her hand rested on the pillow. Taking his time, he ran his fingers along the profile of her hip to the feminine dip at her waist.

"You're driving me crazy," she warned again.

"Shhh." He curved his back, caught one rosy nipple in his mouth, caressing it languidly until it rose to a hard nub. Then he turned his attention to her other breast.

The pull of his lips was the catalyst to her passionate response. "No more," she cried, pushing at his shoulders.

"Wha—" Ryan suddenly found himself flat on his back with a long-haired vixen astride him, looming above him, her arms stiff on each side of his head.

"Now," she said firmly, with only a hint of desperation in her voice, "you're in for it, cowboy."

He smiled. "Be my guest," he offered in a husky murmur, content to let her take the lead for a few seconds. He was delighted with this side of her, free and open with the passion that hid beneath the surface of her composure. He'd suspected all along it was there, and he certainly wouldn't want to squelch any creativity.

Then he gasped. "Ah, God, Bree. I didn't mean—" His fingers dug into the soft flesh of her hips as she mounted him and began to move in a slow, seductive rhythm. Her hair fell in a scented curtain around them. In the dim light he could see her beautiful face, now intently aggressive, and the sight provoked the wildest response Ryan had ever experienced.

He completely lost control, bucking under her sensual movements. He heard his own voice murmuring thick, dark words of encouragement, but he didn't know it was his.

This was passion in its purest, most unadulterated sense. She caught her breath, threw her head back. The cords in her neck stood out. He felt his body alter, break and reform, heard himself fight for breath. And then he was ripped apart.

She collapsed on top of him, gasping. Her body, which had been agile and quick and strong, now felt like a boneless little bundle of softness. His arms, like bands of steel, held her there.

The combination of heat and cool was exhilarating, infusing Bree with the certainty that she would never run out of mountain. She could ski forever down this slope, the crisp wind rushing to meet her head-on, chilling her face, her neck, all the front of her. But her back was warm, protected from the chill by a wonderful blanket of heat that encompassed her from her feet to her head.

An unpleasant ringing intruded on Bree's dream. She knew it was a dream, a glorious, delirious hallucination. The mountain became a cliff, but she wasn't afraid. Just as she had known the mountain would never end, she knew she could fly, soaring beneath the ice-blue sky, over the shadowed crags and crevasses, reaching up to brush the fleecy clouds with her fingertips. She didn't want the dream to end.

The ringing persisted, dumping her suddenly and unpleasantly into full consciousness. She slapped at the alarm clock without result. Frowning, she opened one eye—barely. Through the screen of her lashes she saw the red numerals of the digital clock shift from 6:01 to 6:02. The warmth against her back was Ryan.

She shot up in bed, clutching the sheet to her breasts. "Oh my gosh! Wake up, Ryan. We've overslept."

The large body next to her rolled over and continued rolling and muttering curses until his feet hit the floor. The telephone let go with another ring, and she snatched it up.

"Bree, it's Louise. I can't begin to tell you how sorry I am."

Bree stifled a groan at the words and kept her voice steady. "What's happened, Louise?"

"Jimmy has something. He's running a high fever and is hoarse. I hope it's just a bug, but I have a feeling it might be his tonsillitis again. And here we are in the middle of this minister's visit. The office—"

"Louise, don't worry about the office." She knew the cautionary words were useless. The office was Louise's other child, and she took great pride in its successful operation.

She would never have called if her son weren't really ill. "I'll get a temporary."

"I've already called the agency," Louise answered. She elaborated on the provisions she'd made for the office to function halfway efficiently without her.

"I should have known that." Bree smiled to herself. By the time she'd finished the conversation and hung up the telephone, Ryan had thrust himself into his clothes.

"Trouble?" he asked, borrowing her brush to tame his hair.

She turned to respond, but instantly she was caught by the sight of the large, powerful figure at her delicate nineteenth-century dressing table. He spread his legs to straddle the small taboret—thank goodness he didn't try to sit on it—and stooped in order to see himself in the oval mirror. The action strained the fabric of his trousers across his slim hips. God, he was so male! He looked at once totally out of place in the deliberately feminine room and yet totally suited to it. She wondered why she'd never realized that to be truly feminine a room required the contrast of masculinity.

He met her eyes in the mirror and raised an inquiring brow.

"What? Oh, no...well, yes," she said, frowning at her own convoluted response.

He smiled tenderly at her reflection.

She gestured, then let her hand fall limply into her lap. "My secretary has to be out. She wanted to tell me she had called the temporary help service we use."

Ryan put down the brush and crossed to sit beside her on the bed. He reached for her hand and tugged slightly. "I understand. All you need this week is another crisis."

Bree scooted forward to let her head rest for just a minute on his strong shoulder. "It's not really a crisis. I just hate for things to hit me when I'm not completely awake."

He wrapped her in his strong arms to lift her, covers and all, onto his lap. It was comforting to be there. He smoothed back the dark tumble of her hair.

The frown cleared, and she snuggled closer. "This is the way I'd rather wake up."

He adjusted his arm across her back, slid his hand under the sheet until his fingers found and gently stroked the side of her breast. "Me, too. With time to kiss and touch and make love." His lips rested briefly, carefully, on hers. "And talk about good things. Like last night."

She smiled against his wrinkled shirt, reveling in his caress.

"Tomorrow," he growled softly into her hair. "Tomorrow we'll wake up early and have breakfast together. We've never done that."

The promise, huskily delivered, reverberated through his chest, into her ear, into her mind, provoking anticipation of the night to come and the appealing domesticity of the scene he described. But first there was the day to get through, and she'd rather walk on fire than leave his arms right now. Peace had settled within her, and she was aware of an odd sort of togetherness between them that they hadn't shared before. It warmed her strangely and puzzled her. She wished she had the time to examine the feelings.

She might as well have spoken the thought aloud.

He lifted his head. Catching her face in his big hand, he raised it until their eyes met. "I wish we could spend today together, just the two of us. What was the word? Cocooning?" he murmured, stroking his thumb across her lower lip.

She summoned the energy to smile. "The minister waits," she pronounced, and touched his cheek. "Today we walk— 'scuse me, drive—the Freedom Trail."

He caught her fingers before she could withdraw, held them against his cheek. The skin on the back of her hand was like satin beneath his fingers, reminding him of the other places on her body that were smooth and soft. Still swollen with sleep, her eyes were exceptionally blue this morning, the color of a summer sky. He wavered for only a heartbeat. "Sam Dalton will be supervising that."

"You won't be there?"

His pulse kicked in response to the disappointment in her voice. "Honey, I have other things to do." He didn't tell her how he'd agonized over the decision. What he really wanted was to glue himself to her side—and Saber's—until this dangerous episode was finished. But he had to trust someone else.

As he'd said, he had other responsibilities. The murder case to work on, for one. And the speech to write for the new recruits beginning Monday at the police academy, and the meeting with Vice concerning the invasion by the hookers and pushers of the new waterfront hotel, and his presentation to the council next week for a salary increase. That was important. Hell, his men didn't make as much as the bus drivers. And last night there had been another attack of vandalism that had totally destroyed a vehicle parked on Commonwealth Avenue.

Violence of any kind, even against an inanimate object like a car, was bad news. He had to go over the reports to see if he agreed with the street detail that there was a pattern developing. If so, they'd have to increase patrols there. Which meant taking them from somewhere else.

And all he wanted to do right now was to bury himself in this beautiful woman. "Gotta go." He eased her off his lap and stood. "I could use a couple more hours of sleep."

Bree watched him lift his arms over his head, stretching his long body. The movement pulled his shirt partway out of his trousers, baring a patch of skin on the left side of his stomach. She started to avert her eyes in self-defense, but then she stopped, staring. "What's that?" she murmured, touching the bare skin.

Ryan bit back a curse. He hadn't tried to hide his other scars from her, but he hadn't pointed them out, either. At night, in the low light of her room, they hadn't been obvious, but this morning, with sunlight streaming in, they were hard to miss.

He lowered his arms and his shirt covered Bree's hand. She could no longer see, but she could feel the hard ridge of flesh. "I wasn't only shot in the shoulder, Bree. You must have known that," he said quietly.

She withdrew her hand instantly, as though the touch scalded her fingers. Of course, if she'd thought she would have known that you didn't spend weeks in the hospital with a shoulder wound. But she'd elected not to think, not to ask. "Were there more?" she asked calmly.

"Just one," he answered, suddenly amused. He took her hand and placed it on the inside of his thigh, high on his leg. She felt the heat through the fabric of his trousers. "This gave me more cause for alarm than either of the others."

What began as a chuckle at his droll words became a choked sound.

He cupped her chin, forcing her to look at him. "It was over two years ago, Bree. Forget it."

She met his eyes, eyes that were dark gray with determination that this be put behind them. And she nodded, her thoughts willingly diverted from the scars by the tender smile beneath his mustache.

"Good girl."

As she watched, he automatically tucked the shirt back in. She recalled her father's fetish for neatness. He'd told her once that it was one way of commanding respect. And a police officer needed all the respect he could get. Apparently, even in wrinkled clothing, the discipline persisted.

"I have to stop by Dad's to shower and shave."

Bree was always disturbed when he referred to the house where he'd grown up as "Dad's house." She would have said, "I have to go home" as naturally as she called the woman who lived there "Mother."

But Ryan obviously didn't think of it that way. When he talked about finding a place to live, he made it clear that he was indifferent to where he lived and what he lived in. He never spent much time there. "A house is a house and a bed is a bed," he'd said. She couldn't imagine a place of residence not being important. Her home was her refuge, her place to rest and find solace when the world intruded too closely, to rejuvenate her body and her mind.

It was all a part of his apparent reluctance to put permanency into his life. She couldn't blame him for that; it was she who had first robbed him of the prospect. When they had been engaged he had been just the opposite. Lacking affection and warmth in his parents' house, he'd craved a home filled with love and laughter and children. "We'll have to start off small, honey," he'd said many times. "But we'll always have a place of our own."

"Dad's house."

Determinedly she reached for her robe and pulled it on. When it was tied around her she stood to face him, smiling thoughtfully as she slid one finger between the buttons of his shirt to stroke the wiry hair of his chest. "And dress in something very conservative, I hope. Otherwise you might be the one that's mobbed by the media today. There's something very sexy about a wrinkled shirt."

"You're flirting with me," he accused with a smile. Catching her wrist, he firmly withdrew her hand. "Much more of that and I won't go at all." Linking their fingers, he took her with him through the door, along the upstairs hall, to the banister.

"If I don't see you before, I'll be at the dinner tonight," he said, releasing her hand and taking the first step down, away from her. Even with the height advantage he had to dip his head to bestow a last quick kiss on her lips.

But the kiss was delivered as an afterthought.

With a small smile she watched him jog lightly, surely, down the stairs and snare his jacket from the newel post, knowing his thoughts were on the day to come. Already she had been relegated to another section of his mind. When the day was over, he would once again turn his attention to her.

"Ryan!" she said suddenly.

He looked back.

"My car is in town."

He frowned. "Sorry, honey. I forgot. How long will it take you to get ready?"

"Thirty minutes?"

He was already out the door. "I'll be back for you."

It seemed so easy for Ryan to compartmentalize his life.

In the deep silence of the house she heard his car start and realized she had been standing there as though she had all the time in the world. Whirling, she hurried back into her room, dropped the robe and headed for the shower.

The hot spray stung her mind to full awareness. She scrubbed her body vigorously, until the tingling sensation assured her that the rest of her was awake and ready. By the time she draped a lemon-yellow scarf beneath the lapels of her smoke-colored suit, her energy level had returned to normal.

She sat at the dressing table and, with the ease of practice, twisted her hair into a long rope and wound it into a loose circle on her crown. Anchoring the mass with pins, she was unexpectedly faced with the memory of Ryan removing them.

She clipped large silver disks on her earlobes. And remembered Ryan's persistent nibbling at that sensitive spot. For a moment she closed her eyes, experiencing again the feel of his strong fingers holding her head, the taste of his hungry kisses, allowing the warm flood of excitement access to her heart.

A smile curved her lightly glossed lips. She opened her eyes, softened now with a dusty blue glow, and glanced into the mirror. She put her palm flat on the glass, expecting to feel the heat of his image there. Of course, the glass was cold.

Again she wondered if she could keep at least a part of her emotions unfettered in this relationship. And again, deliberately, she directed her thoughts toward the day ahead to keep from having to answer her own questions. She would never make it to the office at this rate.

She shook her head in an effort to dispel the distracted mood and reached for a tiny bottle of fragrance. Today was not the time for introspection; there were too many other things to concentrate on. She wouldn't be able to avoid thinking about her own feelings forever. But later, when the minister's visit was over, when she wasn't so rushed...

Bree was never more thankful for Louise than when the woman had to be out for a day or two. A young red-haired man was sitting at Louise's desk when she entered. The telephone was caught between his chin and his shoulder. He put a hand over the mouthpiece and whispered the name of a client. She nodded and went through to her office, listening to his practiced voice tell the person smoothly that she had just come in. If the client didn't mind holding, she would be right with him. Her messages were on her desk, and the coffee was made. She took a moment to pour herself a cup.

The brief encounter had assured her that the temporary help was able and efficient, and she breathed a sigh of relief. She also had Louise to thank for that. If she'd called she would have accepted what they sent her; Louise always questioned the agency carefully to make sure the substitute was, among other things, versed in the ways of computers and of the particular software they used, knew how to answer a telephone properly and was capable of brewing a cup of coffee without making an issue of it. She always asked for a graduate of Katie Gibbs.

Thank goodness for Katie Gibbs, thought Bree. Katherine Gibbs Secretarial School was one of Boston's most underrated resources. Generations of secretaries had been trained there and had gone on to positions of importance in Fortune 500 companies. But often, while they waited for placement, they would register with a temporary help agency.

As soon as she hung up he joined her to introduce himself as Charles Combs. Charles looked as if he were about half her age. In fact, he was twenty.

Together they went through her messages. She cautioned him about others that might be forthcoming. "Did Louise explain that I am involved with Minister Saber's visit?"

"Yes, ma'am," he answered, making her feel as if she were his mother. "She said she knew you would be out of the office most of the day, so she will stay by the phone in case I have any questions. I have a copy of your schedule and a list of numbers where you might be reached."

"Good. Just remember that anything related to the visit has priority. Minister Saber has a TV interview at eight, then I have a meeting at nine with his aide to discuss the last-minute details of tonight's dinner, which is being hosted by the minister. I'll be at the Ritz-Carlton for at least an hour.

From there the party will be on the Freedom Trail, but I'll call in periodically.''

When she was satisfied that he understood, she gathered up her briefcase and purse and left the office. Dismissing the half-formed idea of taking her car, she headed instead for the nearby subway station. She took the Green Line, which went through the heart of downtown Boston, to Arlington Street, where the elegant old hotel was located.

After the interview Bree left Saber in his suite to talk business with the mayor. Saber's aide, Mr. Frizia, who she had noticed at once was really more than an aide, waited for her in a room off the lobby that had been set aside for their use.

Bree was uncomfortable around this man for some reason. Though Saber clearly relied on him, he seemed to be nervous, always hovering in the shadows of the party, as though he would escape if he could. And she had yet to see a smile on his face. They greeted each other politely and were joined almost immediately by the floral designer who was to decorate for the dinner and soon after by the hotel's chef.

Along with its exquisite silks, embroidered damasks and unsurpassed golden caviar, Karastonia was celebrated for a particular variety of flower, called the *Path to Heaven*, which it exported all over the world. Saber had brought an extravagant supply of them with him on his plane.

What tulips were to the Netherlands, the Path to Heaven was to the small country on the Mediterranean. Hearty and stylized, the blossom was similar to a Bird of Paradise except that its colors ranged from azure to indigo, with touches of ivory at the throat instead of the vivid orange tongue that was characteristic of the Pacific island flower. The floral designer was delighted with his commission. The blossoms were seldom used in such profusion because of their cost.

After receiving his badge for security clearance, the florist left them, going off to inspect the room where dinner would be served.

The caviar, which Saber had also brought with him, and certain other delicacies typical of Karastonia would be supplemented by specialties from the hotel's master chef for tonight's dinner. When everything had been settled he, too, left.

Bree and Frizia remained behind to work on the seating charts, using tiny magnetized name cards on a large board.

Saber had indicated that he preferred several round tables to a long head table. The only problem was that circles had limited seating; the largest of the tables, where the minister would sit, would accommodate twelve comfortably. But the remaining tables were only suitable for ten. The original sixty guests had grown to eighty, which meant adding two tables or crowding the ones they had to a point that was unacceptable.

Bree moved the cards around for a minute until she was satisfied. Then she leaned back, examining her work with a critical eye. "I suggest we seat the mayor and his wife, the governor and his wife, Senator and Mrs. Black, Senator and Mrs. Robertson, Representative James and her husband and Mrs. Karman from your consulate at the minister's table."

The aide nodded somberly. They had been working for only a few minutes when a black-clad arm reached between them to rearrange some of the cards. Bree looked up, surprised, and the aide stumbled to his feet.

"Excellency!" the man cried, bowing deeply.

When she started to rise, Saber placed one hand on her shoulder and the other on the man's, firmly directing them back down into the chairs. "No, no, old friend. I did not mean to interrupt." His smile was for both of them, but it was to the man that he spoke. "You must get over this disconcerting habit of bowing every time I see you."

"Old habits die hard, Excellency."

"But if we are to become a democracy we must learn to treat each other as equals. This time next year I shall be begging you for your vote. Doesn't that sound good, my friend?"

Bree wondered if Saber saw the cloud that passed over the man's brow. "Certainly, Excellency."

Saber sighed and returned his attention to the board in front of them. He moved a few more cards, one of which had Bree's name on it. "Let's separate some of the dignitaries. Being politicians, I'm sure they will understand if I ask for them to act as host at some of the other tables," he said smoothly. "There. I prefer a beautiful woman at my side tonight. And you, my friend, also?" He shifted the consul to another spot, next to Frizia's place.

The man blushed. Bree bit back a smile, revising her opinion. She remembered meeting the lovely woman last night. She was a divorcée.

She noticed that he had placed Ryan at his table, on her other side. "Protocol will be outraged," she warned.

The aide looked worried; Saber laughed. "Good," he said. "I enjoy outraging Protocol. My secretary has the name cards and will see to their placement." He glanced at the exquisitely thin watch on his wrist and rubbed his hands together in anticipation. "Are we ready?" he asked, smiling.

Bree checked the time. "Yes, sir. The limousines should be waiting outside."

"Then come along." His long, impatient strides took him to the door.

Bree stopped in the lobby to speak to the concierge, asking him to lock the door of the room where they had been working and not to allow anyone to disturb the board until Saber's secretary arrived. He assured her he would take care of it. She hurried after the minister.

In the first limousine behind the lead car, Saber rode with one of his aides and the mayor and his wife. A security officer rode in front with the chauffeur. Bree was in the second car with the consul, Mrs. Karman, three men from Saber's party—she wasn't sure of their function—and two more security officers. She held her breath as the limousines skirted the corner of Boston Common, praying that there would be no disturbance to mar this day.

Sure enough, there were the protesters. She presumed they were the same people Saber had discussed with Ryan last night, the ones who had picketed the hotel the day before. But the group seemed disciplined, not rowdy, as they marched with their hand-lettered placards—she couldn't read what they said—in an elongated circle. Uniformed police, some on horseback, were very much in evidence.

Nothing in the orderly demonstration indicated a possibility of violence. Intensity, yes. They were mostly young—students, she imagined. Seeing them, she wondered at Ryan's concern about this well-behaved group. They couldn't possibly be a threat. She sat back, relieved.

Even the mayor was quickly impressed by Saber's knowledgeable comments and enthusiasm as the entourage progressed from one point to the next along the Freedom Trail. They examined the archives at the new State House—as opposed to the Old State House—paid homage both to the Park Street Church, where the first antislavery address was delivered, and to the final resting place of John Hancock, Samuel Adams and Paul Revere next door to the church at the Granary Burying Ground.

Saber was thoughtful and sober during lunch; and later, after they had resumed the tour, he gazed sadly at the ring of cobblestones marking the site of the Boston Massacre. There the death of nine patriots had aggravated events that had led to the explosion of the Revolution.

Ryan showed up unexpectedly during the stop at the Old Corner Book Store, where such great literary figures as Longfellow, Emerson and Hawthorne used to meet and chat. He gave Bree a wave and a smile but, motioning for Sam Dalton to join them, he headed for Saber.

Bree watched as the three men talked for a few minutes. They were all about the same height, all well-groomed, all handsome as sin, but her eyes were drawn only to Ryan's thoughtful face. His navy-blue suit jacket was held open by his hands, which were planted at his waist. The stance displayed a broad expanse of white shirt bisected by a striped tie of rust and blue.

Finally Saber nodded earnestly and shook hands with Ryan. He seemed to be pleased about something.

On the way back to the entrance Ryan detoured to where Bree was standing beside one of the small-paned bay windows. "Hi," he said softly when he reached her side. "How's it going?" He touched her sleeve briefly, as though there had to be some physical contact, then let his hand drop.

Do you know how much I want you to kiss me? "It's going very well." She gripped the edges of her scarf to keep from touching him and smiled up into his eyes. "I'll have to admit, even traveling from place to place in a limousine, the trail is still impressive."

He looked blank for a second; his eyes were riveted on her mouth, and clearly his mind was focused there, too. "That's quite a concession," he said. Then he added in an undertone, "Do you know what I'm thinking?"

"Yes, I think I do," she whispered, listening to the inappropriately seductive tone in her voice with a kind of horror. This was neither the time nor the place for such games. She gripped the ends of the scarf tighter, putting creases in the silk that would never come out. "How's it going with you?" she forced herself to ask lightly.

Leisurely he raised his eyes to meet her gaze and gave her a rueful grin. He thrust one hand into the pocket of his slacks and raked the other through his hair. "Sorry," he said, and she didn't have to ask what the apology was for. "The leaders of the protest group have accepted Saber's offer for a meeting," he explained.

Bree frowned. "When? Where?" She knew how crowded the schedule was; she'd drawn it up.

"Tomorrow morning seems to be the only possible time. He was to meet at ten with the importer over on Newbury Street, but the man was agreeable to a change. Now the group's leaders will come to the hotel at ten tomorrow and Saber will make a last stop at the importer's place on the way to the airport Sunday morning."

"Do you need copies of the new schedule to distribute?"

"I don't think it's necessary, Bree. The meeting with the importer was a private one, anyway, so the press won't need to know. Newbury Street will still be checked out early Saturday morning and we'll leave a man on duty there until Saber leaves Sunday."

There was a general movement toward the door. "I've got to go, honey. See you at dinner." He touched her again, lightly; it was barely a graze against her sleeve, but she felt it.

"Bye." Her gaze followed him out. She wasn't aware of anyone beside her until Mrs. Quinlan spoke.

"He's such a fine man, isn't he?" she said. "It's a pity we can't keep him."

Bree felt a knot tighten in her midsection at the reintroduction of the troubling topic. She wondered why she hadn't mentioned Mrs. Quinlan's comments to Ryan.

"Washington is already looking at him very closely. The mayor just hopes an offer won't come for a couple of years." She sighed. "Ryan O'Hara is destined for great things, but I don't suppose I have to tell you that, do I?"

Bree wondered at the evenness in her voice when she spoke. "No, it doesn't surprise me. I've always admired Ryan."

"Well," Mrs. Quinlan went on in a confidential tone, "there were two other men besides Ryan who were under consideration for the job of commissioner. You know the mayor likes to promote from within. But he felt that neither of them was *quite* ready. The city might as well get the benefit of Ryan O'Hara for as long as possible." She waved at her husband. "Yes, dear. I'm coming."

A few hours later, Bree unobtrusively slid one foot from her shoe and flexed her toes. How she would love a long hot bath to soak the weariness from her body. She knew she wouldn't have that luxury, though. She would have to pick up her car at the office and rush home to change for dinner at the Ritz-Carlton. She'd be lucky to have time for a quick shower.

On the hillside overlooking Charlestown, Saber and Mayor Quinlan stood apart from the group, talking and gesturing as they replayed the Battle of Bunker Hill. The security detail, which had been fairly inconspicuous until then, became visibly nervous at their charges displaying themselves so clearly in the open. They didn't bother to hide their relief when the men were safely back in the limousines, headed for the last stop.

The site of the Boston Tea Party wasn't officially a part of the Freedom Trail, but Bree had included a stop there at

Saber's request. Feet apart and arms crossed, he stood on the deck of the replica of the brig *Beaver* and watched with amusement as modern-day Bostonians, disguised as protesting colonists disguised as Indians, hurled fake chests of tea into Boston Harbor. He seemed to be thoroughly enjoying himself.

The party broke up at dockside. Before the limousines left to return the minister and his entourage to the hotel, he made it a point to single Bree out for a private word. "It was a meaningful day for me, Mrs. Fleming," he said. "I thank you for it."

"I'm very glad you enjoyed the tour, sir."

Everyone, even Mrs. Quinlan and clearly the members of the security detail, was glad that the day was over. Tomorrow's tour of Harvard would be much easier to patrol.

Bree berated herself for not having brought her clothes into town as she'd threatened to do. She'd barely gotten into her favorite red silk dress when Ryan stopped in front of her house, blowing his horn. She didn't question his presence; she just grabbed her jewelry and purse, raced down the stairs and out the door. "I didn't remember that you were to pick me up," she said as she swept her skirts into the car. Then she turned to face him and froze in her seat.

Ryan O'Hara in jeans or a softball uniform was sexy, in a suit was handsome, but Ryan O'Hara in dinner clothes was spectacular. He smiled and leaned across the seat to cover her parted lips with a warm, hungry kiss. "God, I wanted to do that all day. In the bookstore, I—"

She smiled against his lips. "Yes, I did, too."

His hot gaze barely flickered over the rest of her before returning to her mouth.

"You look—" Her words were smothered by another kiss.

Finally, reluctantly, he drew back. Smiling, he ran his tongue over his lips to get a last taste of her. "Toothpaste never tasted so good." He put the car into gear.

"Wait," said Bree. "I'm not zipped all the way. Would you?" She turned in the seat, presenting him with her back.

Ryan growled softly. "This is cruel and unusual punishment, lady." He zipped her, fastened the tiny hook and left another kiss at her nape. "Fasten your seat belt."

The press was out in full force at the entrance to the hotel. Ryan scanned the crowd, satisfied to see that the security detail was in place.

"I feel like I'm at the Academy Awards," muttered Bree out of the side of her mouth. "Is that one of the network reporters?"

Ryan's gaze followed her slight nod. "Probably. One of my men saw a mention of Saber on one of the national news programs."

She heard him even through the din surrounding them. "We expected it," she reminded. One flash caught her directly in the eyes, blinding her for a moment.

In response to her gasp, Ryan covered the hand on his arm with his warm grasp and leaned down protectively. "Are you okay, honey?"

"Commissioner, look this way, please," said a voice from beyond the silver streaks across her vision.

"I'm fine."

"Damn," breathed Ryan under his breath when they entered the comparative quiet of the lobby. "Will you look at that?"

Bree looked. He was referring to a copy of the evening paper on the concierge's desk. Plastered over the top half of the front page was a picture of Saber and the mayor at the Bunker Hill Monument. The picture was grainy, as though taken through a long lens. The darkroom must have worked quickly to get this in tonight's edition.

"If a photographer could get that shot, so could an assassin. Where the hell were the security detail?"

Bree felt his anger in the tension of the arm she held. She recalled the moment, and the nervousness of the men guarding Saber, vividly. "They were trying to get them to move."

But Ryan's anger wouldn't be appeased. "That's no excuse. I want to see Dalton. You go on inside, Bree."

Saber greeted the guests alone at the door to the candlelit dining room. He was a charming host. "Mrs. Fleming." As Bree reached him, she noticed he couldn't control an involuntary glance over her shoulder. She wasn't offended. "I can't believe your escort would forsake such a beautiful woman. Where is the commissioner, Mrs. Fleming?" he asked smoothly. It was no casual question; he really wanted to know.

She hesitated, unwilling to mention Ryan's anger at the sight of the newspaper picture. If Ryan wanted the minister to know he was incensed, *he* could tell him. "The commissioner had to attend to something, Mr. Minister," she explained. "He'll be right in."

Saber nodded, satisfied, and turned to greet the senior senator from Massachusetts.

Bree moved forward into the room and caught her breath. She had often been to meetings here, had dined here on other occasions, but she had never recognized the potential for intimacy achieved this evening by the use of smaller tables, subdued lighting and exquisite flowers.

The floral designer had done a magnificent job. Arrangements using the Path to Heaven were centered on each of the eight tables. Their amazing beauty was reflected in wide circular mirrors placed beneath their cut-crystal containers, and the colors of the blossoms were also reflected in the indigo-and-ivory napery. Gold-edged china, shimmering crystal and heavy flatware enhanced the perfection of the tables. And the colors might have been used in decorating the room itself. The carpet was a rich indigo and the walls were papered in an elegant design of ivory and gold.

Conversation around the dinner table was surprisingly relaxed for such a notable group. Saber had a remarkable ability to put people at their ease. And those who might have a tendency to take their own importance too seriously were ashamed to do so in the presence of this very down-to-earth man. But Bree noticed that, though Ryan had subdued his anger, remnants lingered in his tense manner.

He consumed the rare caviar as though it were peanut butter, ignored the wines that accompanied dinner, both white and red. He did sip the champagne that was served with dessert.

At one point Saber apologized to Bree and spoke quietly across her to Ryan. "Do you mind staying after the others have left?"

Ryan agreed, as though he had a viable option. The picture and the accompanying story had both infuriated and frustrated him. The paper questioned everything from the murder investigation to the handling of security for the minister's visit. It seems they weren't permitted as much access as they would have liked to have.

Was Saber going to add his voice to the criticism of the Boston police department? Well, this might have developed into a politically related crime, but he wasn't ready to call in the FBI yet.

He felt Bree's hand close over his where it rested on his thigh and turned to look at her. Her mouth curved in a small smile of understanding.

Suddenly he relaxed. Turning his hand, he squeezed her fingers in gratitude. She understood him so well.

Too damned well.

Without any warning, Ryan began to feel stirrings of disquiet. The progression of this relationship was to be decided on his terms, wasn't it?

Bree was getting too close. He didn't like, couldn't accept, depending on her for comfort and understanding.

He couldn't trust her again.

Chapter 10

Pandal was staying at a chain motel across the river in Cambridge. He didn't rent a car, and no cabbie can identify him from the picture you gave us. The flight attendant remembers him. She says he told her no one was meeting him, and she saw him later at the baggage carousel. Alone. So we're assuming he took the Blue Line into town from the airport. He would have had to switch trains, pick up a different one to Cambridge. That would take some time. But not as much as it apparently did, unless he got lost on the way."

"He knew the Boston 'T' very well," inserted Bree. "He seemed fascinated with the efficiency of the system and the people he saw on the trains. He rode a number of times while he was here. We even—oh, never mind, it isn't relevant." She broke off, suddenly and painfully remembering Pandal's eager interest the day they had taken the Green Line to a student beer hall near Boston College for lunch. And the horribly mutilated body in the Charles.

Saber leaned forward in his chair to cover the hand resting on her knee briefly with his. "He obviously had a friend in Boston," he said kindly. "I'm very grateful."

Ryan watched the exchange without expression, dismayed at the intensity of his disapproval. He wasn't jealous. Hell, he *liked* Saber. But he didn't want the man's hand anywhere near Bree's knee.

In the formal ambience of the dining room downstairs, she had looked exceptionally beautiful. Here, in the more relenting atmosphere of the hotel suite, she looked sexy and warm. He couldn't describe why—he and Saber had doffed their jackets and loosened their collars, but she hadn't taken off a thing. Her lids, with their heavy shield of lashes, did droop slightly with weariness; her posture was more relaxed, her lips, bare of defining color, seemed softer. Maybe those subtle differences were enough to alter her whole demeanor.

He refocused on the matter at hand. "So he didn't get lost," he went on. "But he didn't check into the motel until four hours after his plane landed. He had only a small flight bag with him."

Saber returned to his previous position, elbows on the chair arms, hands linked lightly across his stomach, and frowned thoughtfully. "He would have had more luggage than that, surely."

"Three cases, none of them small," Bree furnished in a soft, amused voice. "He was loaded down with souvenirs to take back home."

"Have you remembered anything else? Anything at all?" Ryan asked her.

"Not really. I remember how nice he was, how excited about the trip." She glanced at Saber. "He missed his wife, Saber." She still didn't feel quite comfortable using the familiar form of address, but Saber had insisted. "He kept saying how much she would have enjoyed the trip."

A smile of deep sadness reached Saber's eyes. "She would have. We both tried to convince her of that. Unfortunately she felt it was not a good time to leave her children."

The short comment said it all, thought Bree. A woman who put her family above herself would be devastated without her husband. Her own mother was such a woman. But Frances had learned to draw on strengths she hadn't known she had. Bree prayed that the unknown woman in Karastonia would find those strengths.

She wondered if she would have found such capacity within herself if she hadn't been a coward twelve years ago? With the advent of maturity she would like to think so, but it was something she would never know.

Unbidden, her gaze traveled to Ryan to find that he was watching her as though he had followed her thoughts. Deliberately she lifted her chin, faced him fully, a bold sureness in her eyes.

Saber cleared his throat, recalling them both to their surroundings. He grinned when both pairs of eyes whipped to him. "'The first sigh of love is the last of wisdom,'" he quoted. "Go home and go to bed." He covered his mouth with his hand.

Stunned, Bree schooled her features not to reveal her turbulent thoughts. Had she fallen in love with Ryan again? Or had she never stopped loving him?

"...or whatever," Saber went on. "I presume there isn't anything more we can do tonight that your police department hasn't already done."

"No," Ryan answered, grateful for the simple reply. Saber's words, coupled with his own earlier disquiet, had sent a thousand-volt shock through him. It took a superhuman effort to maintain his calm. "We got hold of the credit card company to find out where he'd been staying in California. We've contacted the hotels out there for copies of his bills, to check any phone calls he might have made through the switchboards. Of course, he may have used a pay phone. If so, it would lead to nothing."

"I keep coming back to why."

Ryan had finally worked through that one. "That was the question that had me stumped, too. But I think the answer is clear. If, as you say, you trusted him implicitly." He waited for Saber's firm nod. "Then he'd learned something that led him to believe you were in danger. I suspect it was something he discovered right before he left Boston, otherwise he wouldn't have left. Maybe something he didn't recognize as suspicious until he had time to mull it over. He decided to come back here, to ask some questions. His curiosity scared someone."

"We're interviewing the motel staff here, trying to find who saw him last. Maybe he met the killer at the hotel. Maybe someone saw them together." He spread his hands. "I know it sounds like a lot of maybes, but with nothing more to go on—" He shrugged. "It's frustrating as hell."

Saber thought for a minute, then nodded. "It makes sense. We both have enemies in our country, of course. Any change of government provides a great opportunity for the wrong kind of people to try to take over. And Pandal seemed more sensitive to such a danger than most." His voice dropped an octave. His pain was obvious to both his listeners, but his shoulders were straight, his eyes unwavering. "I even accused him once of seeing a fascist under every rock. I blame myself. If I had been more open-minded, he might have called to talk this over with me first."

To break through the tension produced by so grave an admission, Bree spoke comfortingly—she hoped. "From your description and from what I knew of him, Pandal was a loyal friend. He wouldn't want to accuse anyone until he had something more than speculation.''

"Yes, well—" Saber hesitated for a moment then smiled his thanks and stood. Despite the familiarity that had developed between the three of them, it was an imperial dismissal. She smiled to herself, wondering if he was aware of the remnants of royal prerogative that still lurked in his democratic soul.

Bree had remembered to turn on the radio alarm, and when the soft strains of Mozart filled the room she returned slowly to consciousness. Content to lie there for a minute, savoring the warmth, relishing the sensation without identifying it, she was only half-aware of movement next to her.

Ryan. Suddenly her eyes opened wide, not because his presence was a surprise but because she was surprised he was there at all after Saber had opened his big mouth last night. Ryan. She loved him still—again, it didn't matter. Before her mind had completely accepted that he was really there, he was turning her from her spoon position to face him.

He looked rugged with a night's growth of beard, his hair tousled, his eyes dark with purpose and desire. She realized that he didn't share the sleepy look she was sure she wore. "How long have you been awake?" she asked huskily.

He scraped the dark cloud of hair away from her face. "Just for a few minutes," he answered. His unsmiling gaze wandered over her sleep-swollen features, lingering on each one.

Self-conscious, she tried to turn away from the thorough study. She knew what she looked like first thing in the morning, slit eyed and disheveled. She was no longer a dewy-eyed twenty-two-year-old. "Don't," she whispered against the skin of his neck. "I look awful."

"You didn't mind yesterday."

"Yesterday I didn't have time to mind."

Ryan smiled at her uncertainty, touched his lips to her brow and brought her close. "You're much more beautiful than you were twelve years ago."

She muttered something that sounded like "bosh" and he grinned and tightened his arms. He'd stared at the ceiling for a long time last night after she had slept, trying to make sense of his emotions. Though Saber had misunderstood, it was obvious that his words had left an imprint on them both. Their lovemaking had contained a suggestion of desperation that left Ryan feeling unsettled. He hadn't come up with a reason. What the hell, he thought. They had this. For a while. Until things got too deep.

Ryan's sigh against her temple was an echo of Bree's. Here, for a brief moment before the hectic day began, was a small island of quiet. But even as her thoughts took shape, her dismay crept in.

Saber's observations last night had left her with a savage kind of melancholy. She had seen Ryan's response to the older man's words. And she felt things drawing to an end between them before they'd really begun.

His lovemaking was wonderful, tender and exciting. He couldn't make love to her like that if there weren't feelings there. But one day soon he would recognize that her response to him was not desire but love.

He had made it clear that any deeper emotions on his part were impossible.

She wasn't even sure she wanted it changed, she told herself. Her love for him was going to complicate her life immensely.

Recognizing her last thought for the lie it was, she hid her face in the secure curve between his neck and his jaw, feeling the abrasive beard at her temple, against her cheek, inhaling the last faint traces of his shaving lotion, the pure male smell of him. "We have to get up," she murmured.

"I know. I just want to hold you like this for a minute more." There was something, a trace of surprise, in his voice....

She was surprised herself that she was satisfied to be held. Desire had whipped them both wildly during the night. She wasn't even sure what time they had finally drifted off to sleep. But this morning the feelings were different. She was comfortable with his strong arms wrapped around her. She smiled against his skin. Comfort wasn't a feeling she often experienced in the presence of this dynamic man.

He felt her smile; his arms tightened imperceptibly. "What are you thinking?"

"That I'd like to stay here this way for hours and doze. Sunday morning, when Saber is safely on that plane, I'm going to come back here and sleep for days."

She felt the laughter through his body before she heard it. "If we stayed like this you wouldn't doze for long." He paused. "I have to be downtown in a couple of hours," he added.

She yawned, a huge, skin-stretching yawn that he watched in amusement, and angled her head back to look up at him. Her smile was bright and wide. She was determined he wouldn't know she was breaking up inside. "So we have time for breakfast or sex. Which will it be?"

Ryan's eyes narrowed at the smile and the blunt question. It was so unlike her that he shook his head. "Which would you prefer?" he asked, as formally as though he were asking her preference for a meal.

The sound of her soft laughter was warm and sexy. He felt the decision being taken from him as his arousal grew. Lord, how many times had they made love last night? He couldn't believe there was anything left in him, but obviously there was.

She felt it, too, and her laughter turned playful. "Like you, I would prefer sex. But I think my body might protest the lack of food today."

He tamped down his desire—mentally, at least—and his doubts, for the time being. The sharing of quiet, gentle humor in the early morning was a unique feeling, something he'd never experienced with any other woman, and very pleasant.

Had she and what's-his-name enjoyed these kinds of tender moments? Had they lain like this, exchanging early-morning secrets? The image his mind came up with was enough to hurt and to quell his desire suddenly and completely. He released her, threw off the covers and sat up on the side of the bed. Damn. How had he let himself get so deeply involved with this woman again? A fool would have more sense.

"Ryan?" Her voice held a trace of vulnerability, and he realized how abrupt his movement had been.

He glanced over his shoulder to see her holding the sheet to her breast; the question in her eyes wrenched at his heart. He reached across the bed to touch the downy softness of her cheek. Forcing a heartiness he didn't feel, he smiled and said, "I'll cook breakfast if you'll let me shower first."

Bree relaxed, but not completely. There had been something in his posture for a minute as he'd sat, broad shoulders slumped, staring at the floor. Still, she met his smile. "That's the best offer I've had all morning," she said lightly.

She was putting the last touches on her makeup when the smell of bacon reached her nostrils. She clasped her watch on her wrist and subdued gold hoops at her ears and stood back to survey the effect. The rich tangerine color of her suit warmed her skin, and the high-necked Victorian-style blouse was flattering. She felt and looked both feminine and capable, and today she needed to be both.

She hurried down the stairs, stopping at the front door to collect the newspaper. "Have I dawdled long enough to get out of helping with the cooking?" she asked as she entered the kitchen. The table was set with her mats and her plates, but it was as though he were the host. How odd, she thought. "I see you've raided my roses." Three deep, velvety crimson buds from her Mr. Lincoln bush had been arranged in a jelly glass. Their scent mingled with the smell of bacon and fresh coffee.

"You can butter the toast while I scramble the eggs." Ryan turned from forking bacon onto a folded paper towel. He paused at the sight of her, so crisp and refreshed, her eyes shining, her makeup like no makeup at all, her hair perfectly arranged at her nape, a newspaper tucked under her arm. In the professional dress she wasn't the young girl, wasn't the Bree he'd known and loved when she'd been at the threshold of womanhood. The one who'd been his Bree. This was another, a mature Bree who'd had a big chunk of life that didn't include him.

"You get to do the dishes," he said, wishing he hadn't sounded so harsh.

She made a face. "Thanks a lot. Boy, are you a grouch this morning."

"I feel grungy when I look at you," he complained goodnaturedly in an effort to throw off the feeling of being haunted by her dead husband.

"You're fine," Bree answered inadequately. He wore the same clothes he'd worn last night, and his hair was still wet from the shower. He hadn't shaved, but he smelled like her lilac soap. The sleeves of his white dress shirt had been rolled back over his muscular forearms; the onyx studs were open halfway down his chest, revealing the soft, curling hair there. He looked totally masculine and very sexy.

She crossed to the toaster, but the picture of him in her mind's eye was more than sufficient to keep her heart tripping in double time. She buttered toast and poured coffee. He scooped the light, fluffy eggs onto a waiting platter and arranged the bacon around the edges. They moved separately but in tandem, and both finished their tasks at the same time.

Bree sat, shaking out her napkin. She offered him part of the paper. The hated picture wasn't on the front page, thank goodness.

He declined. "I'll see it at the office."

"This looks wonderful," she said, at ease with the domestic scene, the incomparable scent of bacon and coffee, the quiet rustle of the morning paper. She wondered if she could live with being a policeman's wife. And then had to clutch her fork tightly to keep from dropping it. Impatient with herself, she let the paper drop. Where on earth had that thought come from?

She answered her own question: because despite all the barriers, marriage was a logical progression after admitting love.

She should have known herself better. Marriage had been rejected by them both very vehemently as a possibility. She herself had felt relieved when he'd made it clear from the beginning that he didn't want permanency. She should have known she would fall in love with him and would want to be his wife.

What would he say if he knew where her thoughts were leading this morning? She almost laughed aloud at the thought. He wouldn't like it worth a damn. Or maybe he would. Maybe he was just waiting to pay her back for the heartache he'd suffered twelve years ago.

She forced the fork to her mouth. No, she thought as she chewed the bite of egg. She refused to believe that of him. He couldn't make such tender love to her if his motive was revenge. She allowed her gaze to stray to him. He was eating heartily—no hesitation there. She dropped her eyes and stirred her coffee, sipped it, then broke off a corner of toast and got butter on her finger. She licked it off, glanced up idly. And froze.

His gaze was riveted on her mouth. Quickly she withdrew her tongue and closed her lips.

Ryan cleared his throat. He had been watching the emotions flit across her face and wondered if her feelings were in as much turmoil as his. One thing was for sure. They were going to have to rethink this situation.

He dropped his napkin on the table and stood. "I'd better get going. I've got to change clothes," he explained unnecessarily. "See you at ten." He wanted to kiss her goodbye, not a passionate kiss but an affectionate one, the kind of kiss a husband would give his wife before he went off to work.

The realization scared him to death. He grabbed his tuxedo jacket and left through the kitchen door.

Bree sat where she was for a long time, not moving at all except to breathe, except for the breaking up of her heart within her breast. "See you at ten." Was that all he had to say? Not even a "Thanks for the sex, babe." What had happened to the kissing and the touching and all those other things he'd regretted they hadn't had time for yesterday? Maybe he had acknowledged some of the things she was beginning to see, that it was going to be almost impossible to continue this relationship.

Finally, through the disorder in her mind, she heard the front doorbell. Her head whipped around. He'd come back. He hadn't left her without a word, a kiss, anything. She rushed into the hall, her high heels tapping on the hard-wood floor, and swung open the door, a smile of anticipation on her lips.

"Morning, Mrs. Fleming. I'm collecting for the paper," said Johnny Duggan.

She dug through her purse and came up with the right change. When she closed the door behind the child she looked longingly at the stairs. If she could go up them, into her bedroom, climb in and pull the covers over her head, she might, she just might, survive this day.

Bree drove across the Summer Street Bridge, her emotions still astir. She made the right turns, parked her car in her appointed place and couldn't remember driving there. Determinedly she shook off the worried feelings that were so distracting. She had to get through this day; she had to function efficiently. And she couldn't do that if she allowed emotion to govern her actions. She would think about this when the minister's visit was over.

"Louise!" Bree practically fell on the older woman with relief. Charles was nice, but Louise was her rock. "At least one thing is going right today."

Louise looked at her employer curiously. "Mrs. Quinlan called. The minister has agreed to another press conference immediately after this morning's meeting with the protesters, and he'd like you to be there."

Bree rolled her eyes toward the ceiling as though searching for deliverance. "Okay."

Ryan parked his car in the space labeled with his name and got out. His long legs took the steps two at a time, and he pushed open the door to the building with the flat of his hand. But just inside the door he stopped and turned back.

A young boy, probably no older than eight or nine, stood outside in the parking lot, uncertainty in every line of his thin body. His sandy hair had been slicked back with a comb. His clothes were neat but obviously cheap. He didn't know what to do with his hands, first jamming them into the pockets of his jeans, then taking them out and crossing his arms over his scrawny chest.

Eyes narrowed, a smile tilting his mustache, Ryan sought an explanation for the sense of familiarity he was feeling. He retraced his steps. "Can I help you, son?" he said, hunkering down beside the boy.

The boy seemed to brace himself. "No, sir. I'm just waiting for the auction," he said, assuming an amazing dignity for one so small.

The police auction was a twice-yearly event at which the department sold recovered but unclaimed goods. He remembered seeing a memo last week. VCRs, TVs, jewelry, all kinds of goods were up for grabs, sometimes at bargain prices. This explained the familiarity he'd felt when he saw the boy. "And you're shopping for a bicycle," he said gently.

The child's gray eyes widened in astonishment. "How did you know?" he breathed.

Ryan tried to look wise. "Well," he said. "I am a detective."

The arms came down now to his sides in a stiff parody of military attention. "Yessir."

Ryan gave way to the grin that had been playing around his mouth. "But I'm not that good. Fact is, my first bicycle came from a police auction." He slid a sideways glance at the child. "Man, was I scared that day."

The idea that this large man had ever been afraid of anything was obviously reason for skepticism. "I'll never forget it," Ryan went on. "I only had a little money and I was afraid I wouldn't get that bike. But worse than that, I was even afraid to come into the building. I guess I thought they would arrest me if I looked at them crooked."

"Did you get the bike?" asked the boy.

Ryan hesitated. He looked at the boy, who could have been his own, the coloring was so similar, and swallowed around the lump that suddenly clogged his throat. Thoughts of Bree, thoughts of a family, wanting thoughts, needing thoughts, flooded him. Could he risk falling in love with her again?

"Yes, I did," he lied. In fact, the five dollars that he had saved from running errands in the neighborhood hadn't been nearly enough. "It was a red one."

The boy nodded seriously. "That's the color I want. I hope twenty dollars is enough. Do you think they'll have any red ones today?"

"There's always a red bike," said Ryan positively. "Come on in with me and I'll show you where to wait."

Fifteen minutes later, on the way to his office, Ryan surprised a uniformed officer who was lounging against the coffee machine. When he saw Ryan, the man came to attention. "Good morning, commissioner."

"Good morning." Ryan glanced at the identification badge clipped to the man's shirt. "Sergeant, there is a youngster downstairs waiting for the auction to start. Eight or nine years old, jeans, sneakers, a gray Celtics T-shirt. He wants to buy a red bike. See that he gets it."

"Yes, sir."

"At his price. I'll make up the difference between his twenty dollars and what the highest bicycle brings. But he isn't to know. He's to bid on it. Do you understand?"

"Yes, *sir.*"

You would have made a good father, said a voice from somewhere within Ryan as he settled behind his desk.

He remembered another conversation with himself on this very subject. He had satisfied himself then that a family was not high on his list of priorities.

It isn't too late. Saber saw it; why won't you admit you still love her?

He ignored the voice and picked up the telephone. "Get me Austin Maxwell, please."

Bree stood at the door at the back of the room and listened with great relief to Saber's strong voice. He seemed to have regained control of the crowd. Where was his press secretary? This meeting should never have been handled in this way. She had thought from what Saber had said that he would meet with only the leaders of the group; instead, the whole mob had been admitted.

At a comfortable distance she had been very liberal in her conception of the protesters' right to voice their opinions, but this was a totally different group from yesterday. She would have sworn to it. Where those had been young, these were mature men; where those had been disciplined and neat in appearance, these were unkempt and strung out.

They had marched in carrying the appropriate banners—More Jobs in Karastonia, Fight Inflation, Housing for the Poor. Today she was beginning to realize the banners didn't mean a thing.

Up close, these people frightened her. They physically jostled anyone who got in their way. They were protesting for the sake of protesting—or for the sake of stirring up trouble. And they were getting plenty of media coverage. Reporters and photographers lined the wall. Some, with still cameras, tried to get the perfect angle. Minicams labeled with the logos of local television stations panned the room. She wondered who had informed the press of this meeting.

Ryan had said the protesters were dangerous. Seeing them in action, she had to agree. She also fully understood Ryan's anger at the picture in the paper last night and his concern for Saber's safety.

Even with security solid and overt, the situation was volatile and dangerous. More than once the meeting had threatened to deteriorate into a shouting match.

Without her being aware of his presence, Ryan came up behind her. "What the hell are you doing here?" he demanded, taking her shoulders to move her firmly out of his way. He had come on the double when he'd been informed of the situation.

Now he moved forward, intent on breaking this up before it got any worse.

Bree stopped him with a hand on his arm. "Listen," she said.

Saber had moved the crowd to quiet, if not submission. His strong voice rang out. "This new democracy can only work if all its citizens take part in governing. You will have your chance to really make your protests work where it counts—next year, at the ballot box. Thank you." He left the podium, a scowl like a cloud on his handsome face.

"Come on." Ryan took her arm and steered her toward the door where Saber had disappeared.

"Would someone mind telling me what happened here?" he asked when they reached the group of men surrounding the minister. "I was under the impression that you were to meet with the leaders of the group, not let in the whole mob."

Saber turned to give him a cynical smile. "My press secretary responded to a challenge—on my behalf," he said mildly.

"I hope he'll know better next time," answered Ryan in an equally mild tone.

"Was he the one who called the press?" asked Bree.

"He says he didn't," Saber said, but he looked thoughtful.

Chapter 11

Minister Saber," Ryan said as he entered the suite with Bree.

Saber was standing with his back to the room, looking out the window, either across to the Public Gardens or to the street below. The formal mode of address brought his gaze immediately back over his shoulder to Ryan. Bree shot him a questioning glance, as well.

"Yes, commissioner?" Saber responded.

The opulent suite, where he had felt perfectly comfortable last night, cloyed at Ryan for some reason today, perhaps because it was crowded with talking, gesticulating people. The rowdy group downstairs had been dispersed, but the more civilized group up here had not been so easy to get rid of. The minister's aides and other members of the official party milled around. Ryan had the impression they were rather aimlessly trying to look busy so they wouldn't be banished. Curiosity, he supposed, or was it something more sinister? Was someone in this room waiting, watching, not out of interest but driven by a nefarious purpose? His trained eye cataloged them even as he spoke again. "We have a promising lead in the murder case."

Ryan's statement was delivered in a quiet undertone, but as though he had dropped a bomb in their midst, the room suddenly became as silent as a tomb.

"I should like to hear about it," said Saber into the stillness. His accent was slightly more pronounced.

Ryan lifted a brow of inquiry.

Saber answered the unspoken question. "Yes, in front of all these people. They have my welfare at heart." His expression was uncommunicative, and there was no trace of sarcasm in his voice, but Ryan could feel the emotion in the air between them.

"I was called in this morning to meet with a confidential informant who had done some vague boasting on the street. We've been trying to find the man for a week. This morning we came down hard on him."

At Saber's raised brow, Ryan smiled. He held up a placating hand. "Please don't misunderstand. No rubber hoses, just intensive questioning. He was able to give us a description of a young man he saw running away from the river the night of the murder. We have a hold-for-questioning order out on him."

"Do you have a name to go with this description?"

"No. But the description is pretty specific. Black hair, brown eyes, just under six feet—"

From somewhere in the room there came a muted sound of scorn. Bree wasn't surprised. That description could have fit half the people in this room, and the group surrounding the minister had been making unsubtle comments about the efficiency of the Boston police ever since the meeting with the protesters.

Ryan ignored the derision and went on, "The man is young—early twenties, possibly late teens—and walks with a limp, stiffly, as though the right leg might be a prosthesis."

The gasp was not muted at all. It came from the consul, Mrs. Karman, who had sat at their table during dinner last night. Saber turned slowly to fix the woman with a stare. "Your brother?"

She regained her composure quickly. "Excellency, I couldn't say. I haven't seen him since I arrived."

Ryan knew! Not even a flicker of surprise crossed those steel-gray eyes.

"Would you mind answering a few questions, perhaps look at some pictures, Mrs. Karman?" he asked carefully. "I realize that you don't have to cooperate with us; you hold diplomatic immunity. But any information you have could possibly be very helpful."

Bree felt his frustration, sympathized with it. A lead, any lead in this case, would have been a premium. She and probably the rest of the people in the room expected to hear Mrs. Karman refuse, but instead the woman looked at Ryan, then at Saber. Then she nodded.

Bree let out a breath she didn't know she'd been holding.

"Thank you very much, Mrs. Karman. We appreciate your cooperation. I will try to make the ordeal as brief as possible."

As soon as Ryan had left with the consul, Saber turned to Bree. His expression was unreadable, but there was a wry quirk in his voice. "I understand we are to have lunch at the New England Aquarium. The sharks await. Shall we go?"

Curiosity plagued Bree throughout the afternoon. It took an effort to keep her mind on her duties. She had heard nothing from Ryan, and Mrs. Karman had not returned.

When she went home to change for the evening she called his parents' home. She let it ring and ring, but there was no answer. She tried again just before leaving to meet Saber's group for the dinner at Elmwood. Still there was no answer. For a moment she was puzzled; then she remembered that Ryan's mother and father had gone to California. She hung up and left the house.

Outside she met Gig. He was either going out or coming in from one of his jaunts. She looked closer; he was a little ragged around the edges. "There's food on the back porch," she told him. "You'd better keep your strength up."

Elmwood was the perfect spot for this last dinner, thought Bree later as she mounted the two steps, thoughtfully illuminated by a lantern post, that led from the front walk to the threshold. The trim, from the window casings to the widow's walk, was a clean white, in soft contrast to the pale yellow walls. Older than the country itself, the gracious old home had once quartered Benedict Arnold, and its Federalist flavor gave a viewer the sense that it had been here forever.

A number of Cambridge notables were already present when the minister's party arrived. Bree met the president and his wife, accepted a glass of sherry from a white-gloved butler and looked around with interest at the paintings and polished floors, at the exquisite antiques, which glowed with the patina of age and loving care.

She was familiar with the house but had never been inside. When the calls had begun to come in from the mayor's cronies requesting a meeting with the minister, she'd suggested to Mrs. Quinlan that she drop out of this last dinner to make room for someone else.

Mrs. Quinlan would not hear of it. "My dear, next to an available man, a beautiful woman is the most important element in a successful dinner party."

Now Bree was glad she'd been overruled. Not only was this an opportunity to see the house, but the mix of people that Mrs. Quinlan had come up would be more than entertaining. The six-foot-eight-inch former ambassador to India was the only person present who could come close to the height of the Celtics star who stood beside him. Two men, one a Nobel laureate and the other the author of a series of detective novels featuring a popular and surprisingly sensitive hero, waited together to be introduced to Saber.

The dress was informal, almost casual, compared to the regalia of last night. She'd always heard that in Cambridge what you had to say for yourself was more important than what you chose to wear while saying it. Most of the men wore suits; a few, sport coats. The women had opted for simple dresses or skirts and blouses that bore the unmistakable stamp of Peck and Peck. Bree was dressed in a tailored ecru silk blouse, and her skirt was a nubby blend of silk and linen in natural colors. Her only jewelry was the modest string of pearls Dirk had given her when they'd been married.

"For a lady who doesn't drink, you seem to be imbibing a lot lately," a voice teased from behind her.

Bree whirled, feeling her face flush with unmistakable pleasure. Her heart accelerated to the now-familiar cadence that announced his nearness. "Ryan! I wondered where you were." She touched his lapel lightly, briefly, but necessarily. "Did you have any luck?" she asked.

"Nothing. Mrs. Karman was cooperative, but we've been unable to locate the kid," he murmured. "I have to report to Saber, and I don't have anything to tell him. This is the most frustrating case I've ever been involved in," he added, his tone evidence of his bafflement. "It's like chasing a shadow."

His hand at her elbow was warm and so welcome. His thumb stroked carefully, if absently, over the bone there. But his mind was only half engaged. She read the disappointment in his eyes, in his body language, in the deepening grooves that framed his mouth. She moved closer until her arm was pressed between their bodies and looked up at him. "You've done all you can," she said, her clichéd words a lame attempt at encouragement, which he acknowledged with a smile.

"Thanks, but no brass ring," he said, drawling the words in his exaggerated Texas twang.

The weariness in his expression was like a pain in her own heart. She tried again. "Ryan, Saber has been here three days. With the exception of the meeting with the protesters this morning, there has been nothing to upset the harmony of the visit, certainly no danger of physical harm to him. Everything has gone exceptionally well."

"Too damn well," said Ryan. "It isn't over yet." He heaved a tired sigh. "I might as well get this over with. Then I have to get back to headquarters. I'll be there most of the night."

"Headquarters?" she said, and could have bitten her tongue for the distress she heard in her own voice. If they were to continue this relationship, she would have to be content to leave him free and accept his job as a part of his life. With his authority, Ryan no longer had to be on the front lines of police work, but he would be.

To her relief, Ryan didn't seem to take offense. In fact, he looked down at her, his eyes filled with a sincere and unmistakable desire for her to understand what he was about to say. "I have to go, honey," he said softly. "I'd rather be with you; you know that, don't you?"

She didn't hesitate. "Yes, I know that," she answered.

He caught his breath. His smile was no more than a flash of white teeth under a quirk of the mustache, but when it reached his gray eyes their color turned to hot smoke. "Maybe there's hope for us yet," he said quietly and very seriously.

"I think so," Bree agreed, unsure how she got the words past her numb lips. Lord, she was being brave. Her heart had bolted within her chest, and now it sent the blood splashing through her veins like a raging river. She hoped his words sounded like what they meant. Or meant what they sounded like.

He seemed disinclined to leave her. "I'll miss you tonight. Maybe we'll take a picnic and drive out to the Cape tomorrow after Saber leaves."

Suddenly Briana Regan Fleming reached deep inside herself and found that the strengths she had longed for were there. Slowly she drew her arm free, smiling gently to remove any idea he might have that freeing herself was what she wanted. "Go on, Ryan. I do understand. Finish up what you have to do. We can talk later. A picnic sounds like fun."

The hot, smoky gaze blazed with fire and promise. "God, I love you, Briana," he said simply and huskily.

Bree stood as though turned to stone for a full minute.

They were inches apart, shoulders almost touching, heads turned, eyes locked. She was shaking like a Vermont aspen inside, but she was determined that none of the inner turmoil his words had evoked would be visible on her face.

Finally she took a large sip of sherry, felt its potency release the words that were stuck in her throat. She faced him fully, turning her back on the room, and planted one fist on her hip. "Well, this is a *hell* of a time to tell me that, Ryan O'Hara," she muttered. "Right here in the middle of sixty of the most proper Bostonians."

Ryan searched her face for a minute. He wasn't sure himself where the statement had come from. He certainly hadn't meant to tell her in the middle of a party. Maybe his subconscious had decided he'd waited long enough. At last he spied the tiny depression at the corner of her mouth. He laughed under his breath and bent to give her a kiss good-bye. "Yeah, it is, isn't it? See you."

"See you," she echoed, looking up at him with her heart in her eyes.

He finally dragged himself free of the soft blue gaze that spoke volumes to him and went to find Saber.

The luggage had been sent ahead to the airport. Saber was saying a personal goodbye to the staff of the hotel. Bree waited by the open door of the limousine, her arms crossed casually, her lips curved in a small smile. Her expression, she knew, announced to everyone within sight of it that she was in love. She could not have hidden the emotion.

Looking worried and impatient, Ryan paced back and forth along the sidewalk in front of the hotel, his long strides eating up the distance. He pivoted to retrace his steps as he had done dozens of times in the last few minutes. If the sidewalk hadn't been concrete he would have quickly worn a path there.

She glanced at the sky, hoping the weather would hold. Gray clouds had begun to gather at dawn, but there had been no rain so far. Soon Saber would climb aboard the plane that would take him to Philadelphia. The mayor and Mrs. Quinlan had said goodbye last night at Elmwood, leaving her and Ryan to see the minister off.

Soon they would have time for each other.

Ryan halted in his tracks as the glass doors of the hotel opened. Saber and his aide exited. Since this was a private visit, they would go alone and meet the rest of the party at the airport.

"Let's go," Saber said tersely as he climbed into the car.

Ryan held the door while Bree joined the two men in the back. The security men took the jump seats, and he climbed into the front seat beside the driver.

The few blocks to the importer's place of business were traveled quickly and silently. Bree watched the parade of shoppers along the section of Newbury Street devoted to unique shops and sidewalk cafés. Even with the threat of rain, Newbury Street was thick with people, young and old, sauntering along the narrow boulevard or lounging at tables. The black limousine drew more than one glance as they moved on toward the less commercial end of the street.

When they arrived at their destination they stepped from the car between two black-and-whites parked at the curb. Bree wondered about the necessity of such visible protection. This was the first time, with the exception of a traffic escort during the travel along the Freedom Trail, that a police car had been in evidence.

Karastonia Imports sold wholesale to distributors and retail outlets, so the building was devoted mostly to warehouse space, but she was delighted to see that the owner had maintained the charming old building, which was so typical of the businesses in the area. Like many others it was tall and narrow, four stories, Victorian in style, the entrance five steps up from street level. In a floor-to-ceiling bay beside the entrance was a window display of the food and textile products imported by the company, a long swatch of scarlet silk as the focal point.

Bree hung back as a round little man flung open the door and spread his arms, welcoming Saber expansively from the landing. "Your Excellency. You do my humble place of business a great honor. I can not tell you how much I appreciate—''

Saber looked up. "Yes, yes, Plato. You are kind to invite me," he said quickly.

"Plato?" murmured Ryan to Bree, placing his palm flat against her spine in a possessive, protective gesture. The worried expression on his face eased slightly as he smiled down at her.

Saber had heard. He spoke in a barely audible voice. "I wonder, too, but that's what he calls himself. He's married to my late wife's sister."

Ryan wrenched his gaze away from Bree's. "Saber, you have ears like a bat."

The minister met his grin. "You're both invited to come inside. You'll enjoy this."

"I think I'll pass," said Ryan, seeing Sam Dalton approaching.

"Bree?"

"Yes, I'd like to."

"Come along, then," said Saber.

Bree glanced over her shoulder as they moved away. Ryan had been joined by Sam Dalton. The worried expression was back. She followed Saber, his aide and the security men up the steps.

Ryan was listening to what Dalton had to say, but his gaze remained on Bree. The blue dress shifted interestingly over her hips, around her knees, as she climbed the steps behind the men. He'd give a hundred bucks right now to see her in jeans with her hair loose and curling, her smile relaxed.

It won't be long, he reminded himself. They'd stop to change clothes, pick up lobster rolls at one of the small places near the beach. They'd lie in the sun all afternoon, soaking its healing warmth into their bones, and they'd talk. He cocked his head to glance at the threatening sky. Well, if it rained they would find somewhere else to go. A place where they could be alone.

They would talk openly and freely. About the past, about their feelings. They would set it all out in front of them. And then they would decide if they had a future. He knew beyond doubting that the love was there for both of them. Though she hadn't said the words, the love shone from her sapphire eyes, along with confidence and maturity. Things would be different this time. Love alone hadn't been enough twelve years ago, when certain other vital elements had been missing. This time they would make sure everything was there.

He hadn't meant to spring it on her like that last night. He'd gotten carried away, and that wasn't something he often did.

He grinned, remembering her reaction. God, she'd been magnificent. How many other women would turn on you, cursing and smiling at the same time, when you told them you loved them?

"...O'Hara?"

He realized that Sam Dalton was speaking to him and that he'd missed it. "Yeah? What did you say?"

Sam cupped his hand around his lighter and inhaled on a cigarette. Lifting his head, he thumbed the lighter closed and repeated, "I said I'm glad this baby-sitting job is over. Aren't you?"

Ryan gave a noncommittal shrug. But he would be glad, very glad. This whole visit had been a nightmare of waiting, watching, afraid something would happen, feeling helpless to stop it. He'd told Bree it was like chasing a shadow, but a more apt description would be a specter, a phantom of evil just out of reach, that eluded your efforts like a handful of fog.

The case was close to breaking; he could feel it. When they found the boy they would have some answers. They'd all been grateful for his sister's cooperation yesterday. Austin had treated the woman with kid gloves, thank God. They certainly didn't need a diplomatic incident.

She had been concerned about the boy. He was a serious type, a straight-A student, but he'd been disturbed over something for weeks and he wouldn't tell her what. He was a good boy, she'd told them. He'd heard that before. But, oddly, he'd believed her. Especially when she'd given them the names of all his friends in this country that she could remember. She hadn't held back.

"It isn't over yet," he said.

"Well, almost," said Sam. "We've done everything to keep him safe, but—I don't know—I'm still jittery."

"Yeah. Me, too. The man you left on duty had no problems here last night?"

"Not a one. It was as quiet as church on Monday." He ground the cigarette into the sidewalk beneath his heel and turned in response to a hail from a uniformed policeman standing beside a black-and-white. The officer held up the mike. "For you, commissioner. Says to hurry."

Both men were galvanized into action. Ryan reached the police car first. He thumbed the button that would send his voice to headquarters. "This is O'Hara. What have you got?"

From the speaker inside the car came Maxwell's voice, loud enough for every one of the men to hear. "Ryan, Austin." His friend didn't waste words. "We got the boy. He's implicated the importer."

Ryan's eyes shot up to the innocuous building, a horrible feeling of dread coursing through him. A dozen men snapped to attention.

"I'd get them out of there if it was me."

The advice was unnecessary, and Ryan didn't bother to answer. He was already moving as he thrust the mike at the cop. "Get them out. Now," he ordered harshly.

No one questioned him, but he was halfway up the steps before anyone moved.

Bree followed the men into the dimly lighted building. To their left as they entered was a stairwell with steps going in both directions. She presumed there was a basement below, and there were noises of activity from above. To their right was a large room dominated by an imposing desk; glass-fronted cabinets held sample books, empty jars and pots of what she took to be the sizes available for caviar, fabric swatches. Several comfortable chairs were grouped around a large coffee-height table piled high with colorful brochures.

"Please feel free to look around, Excellency. The warehouse is in the basement. This is our showroom, but most of our work goes on upstairs. We now employ a dozen seamstresses to sew the beautiful fabrics from our country," the importer explained expansively with a wide, toothy smile. The smile faded and his eyes narrowed when he saw Bree at the rear of the party. But he recovered immediately and resumed his chatter.

The security men roamed about the area in search of whatever such men look for.

"Would you like to see the upstairs?" asked their host. "I know my employees would be most honored by a word from you."

"Of course," said Saber.

Saber had one foot on the stairs when a tiny, wizened old woman appeared from below, walking carefully because of the huge brass tray in her hands. It held a large coffeepot, white china mugs, a bowl of sugar and a half pint of cream in a waxed cardboard container. The thing must have weighed twenty pounds, judged Bree.

"Nina, what are you doing? I told you we would have coffee after the tour," said the importer, frowning at the interruption. Or was he? He made a great show of taking the tray from her hands and introducing her.

Saber acknowledged the introduction kindly.

"I thought the men outside might like coffee," said the woman to her employer. She seemed extremely nervous. Now that her hands had nothing to do, she twisted them together in front of her white apron, raised one to her grizzled hair, touched her thin upper lip.

Bree supposed the woman's agitation was natural, but she frowned absently, tucking her hands into the pockets of her blue linen skirt. Why did she have the feeling that this whole show was choreographed a little bit too carefully?

The importer beamed. "That was thoughtful of you, Nina, but this tray is much too heavy for you to carry." He lifted his shoulders in a what-can-I-do gesture and smiled his toothy smile at Saber. "Please go right on up, Excellency. I will be with you in a moment."

Saber nodded and started to climb the stairs. His aide followed, then the security agent, then Bree. The other agent remained below at the foot of the stairway.

When they reached the second floor Saber glanced around, but it seemed to be deserted except for some storage. Without a pause he continued upward, leading the small party toward the sound of voices and the steady hum of sewing machines.

They were halfway up the next flight when Bree had a thought. Sewing on Sunday? Her foot paused on the next step, her hand stilled on the smooth, worn banister. Surely the ladies were entitled to a day off. Even if the employees were anxious to meet the Karastonian foreign minister, they could have done so. Maybe the importer wanted to provide a demonstration. Still, it didn't *feel* right.

"Saber…" Suddenly she heard a sound from below their feet, like a quick, loud smack, followed by a strange rumbling that seemed to shake the whole building. Before she could turn around to see what had happened, a powerful force hit her in the back, knocking her down. Her foot slipped off the tread of one step, and her cheek hit the nosing of another. Sprawled as she was, she clawed for purchase to keep from falling back down into the unknown catastrophe below. Plaster fell, its dust obscuring her vision. Her hand encountered something—she didn't know what—and she hung on.

For a moment everything was quiet, and then the clamor began—voices shouted from below and cried out in confusion from above. She swiveled her head to look back over her shoulder. Oh, God. Smoke was being sucked through the stairwell, which acted like a chimney, to mingle with the plaster dust.

Through the haze she could see tongues of flame already licking at the first flight of stairs. There was no way anyone could get through that. They were trapped above the fire. This was the nightmare of all downtown Boston residents. These old buildings went up like tinder. She couldn't seem to tear her eyes from the scene. And the thought that rose to the forefront of her mind was, thank God Ryan is outside.

A hand grabbed her wrist, pried her fingers loose from whatever she'd been holding and hauled her to her feet. "Come on," said a voice. The aide, Frizia. She had been gripping his ankle.

The mixture of dust and smoke obscured her vision as she raised her eyes, but she could see that Saber was also on his feet. The agent wasn't. She immediately scrambled up the stairs that separated them to kneel beside the man. She felt for a pulse and found it; it was fast but strong.

"Is he all right?" asked Saber, coming down on one knee beside her.

"His pulse seems strong." She combed back a strand of hair that had become dislodged from her chignon. "I don't know, Saber."

"We've got to get him out of here!"

"We aren't leaving that way," said Frizia with a jerk of his head toward the floors below. "We'll have to go up," he decided.

Saber and his aide moved the man up the remaining stairs and over to the corner opposite the landing. A huddled group of women, twelve or so, watched in fright. One or two were crying softly.

Bree went to them. "Don't cry," she told them in a tone that sounded more confident than she felt. "The fire department will be here soon and they'll get us out. Until then we must remain calm." All the platitudes she had learned in first aid class came back to her. To her surprise, they were effective.

While she had been talking to the women, Saber and Frizia had conferred. Now they approached. "Whoever planted this knew what he was doing. The windows are sealed. We have to get up to the roof," said the aide, indicating a permanent ladder attached to the back wall of the building. A small trapdoor was set into the ceiling overhead.

"It's padlocked," said Bree, her heart plummeting to her toes. Were they trapped here?

"Don't worry about that," Frizia growled.

Saber wiped his face, smearing the grime there. "The access to the fire escape is blocked. There are no partitioning walls in this damned place. If we break open any windows we'll have a draft straight up the stairwell to feed the fire. It's the only way out,'' he agreed.

"The door will do the same. We'll have to hurry and close it again." Bree took a moment to look around. Already the front of the building and one side were in flames. "The sprinklers—" She looked up at the shiny steel fixtures that were a requirement in buildings of this age.

"Don't work," said Saber. "Obviously." He attempted a smile. "We need a sling of some sort to get this man out."

Bree looked around. "That's no problem." They were in the sewing room. Colorful silks spilled off every surface. She picked up a piece of fabric and a pair of scissors. One of the women saw what she was doing and came over to help. "Is there an alley in the back?" she asked as they worked, slashing and knotting the fine silk, which would have the strength of iron if it didn't burn.

"A narrow one," the woman answered.

"I hope it's wide enough for a fire truck," said Bree grimly, not holding out much hope. The space between the buildings was often infinitesimal.

In only minutes they had a makeshift sling. Saber and Frizia lifted the man while Bree and the woman fitted it under his armpits and between his legs. She tightened the loop that would keep the sling secure when they lifted him.

The heat from the blaze on the front wall was becoming uncomfortably hot; soon it would be unbearable. "Let's get going," Saber said, herding the group of women toward the ladder. "Hurry!" When they reached its foot he turned to them, rather like a father—or a coach, thought Bree.

"You will have to climb the ladder as quickly as possible and move out of the way for the next person. Do you understand?"

They nodded raggedly.

Frizia had climbed to the top of the ladder. He waited for Saber's signal. Then, reaching inside his coat to a holster at the back of his waist, he drew his gun and shot off the padlock. The sound of the gun reverberating in the room startled Bree, who was still crouched over the still form of the agent. For a heart-stopping moment she was afraid the door was not going to give, but the man put his back into it and it flew open. He quickly descended the ladder.

They sent up the older women first, hurrying, encouraging and occasionally pushing without a thought of modesty. The room grew hotter and thicker with the smoke being pulled up from below. Bree's eyes stung.

Saber indicated that Bree should go next. She hesitated, and before she knew what was happening he and Frizia had her feet on the rungs. A firm hand on her bottom pushed. She scrambled out of the way, breathing huge gulps of the fresh air. Had she really wished for the rain to hold off? Now she said silent prayers for a deluge.

Saber followed and turned immediately to reach for the sling. With Frizia pushing from below, Bree added her muscle to help haul up the deadweight of the agent. He was not a small man, but finally they had him through the opening. Frizia was right behind him. He slammed the trapdoor shut.

Bree started to smile. But then her gaze followed the others'. Diagonally across the roof, the flames had eaten away one corner of the building completely. As the horrified group watched, the fire sent out sinister fingers, groping across the roof toward them.

Ryan had stepped back to let the wizened old lady pass. A dozen men were waiting for the importer as he followed her out, bearing a tray. "What—?" said the man as Ryan pushed past him and took the steps two at a time. The force of the blast almost knocked him down, but he held fast to the railing and pulled himself to the landing.

He slammed into the door with his shoulder and heard a cry of fear and pain. The agent who had been standing at the bottom of the stairs reeled toward him, his clothes aflame, his face scorched black. He fell at Ryan's feet.

For a split second Ryan looked helplessly at the devastation behind the man—Bree and Saber were somewhere behind that curtain of flame and smoke, and he had to get them out. He whipped off his own jacket and smothered the agent's burning clothes. Gently he took his elbow and tried to help him to his feet. The man didn't seem to have the strength. Ryan kept his voice calm but firm. "I'm going to get you out of here, son. Can you stand up?"

Sam Dalton was there suddenly with a uniformed patrolman. Between them they got the man outside. The agent couldn't possibly see, but he turned his head to Ryan. "Upstairs," he whispered through lips already beginning to swell.

Someone was screaming into a mike to get the fire trucks over here and the ambulances.

But Ryan looked at the flames already licking at the facade above the entrance to the building and knew he couldn't wait. He forced his mind to dominate his fear, to work with its deliberate speed and ability. Cool under fire, that was his reputation, and now he prayed to God to help him think that way, to keep all his emotional feelings at bay.

He strode to the building that abutted on the importer's on the right. People were streaming out the door. He caught a man by the elbow. "Who owns this building?" he barked over the din of shouting.

"I do."

"Can I get to the roof?"

"Sure," said the man. "There's a deck up there. At the top of the stairs."

Sam was issuing orders before Ryan could ask. Men appeared with ropes, block and tackle, safety harness. "I need a ladder," Ryan shouted back at them as he disappeared into the building.

He came out onto the roof in time to see Bree and Saber pulling up what looked like a body from a trapdoor in the roof. At the sight of them, whole and healthy, he closed his eyes for a second.

Then Sam was coming up the steps behind him, bearing the front end of a miserable excuse for a ladder.

"It's sturdier than it looks," said Sam, reading his mind. And it was long enough; that was what mattered.

He and Sam positioned it across the span, and Ryan took the first step toward the other side.

Chapter 12

Ryan, get this stubborn woman out of here. She won't listen to me," Saber shouted.

Ryan's first inclination was to do just that. But then he was caught by Bree's gaze, brave and determined, and by the angle of her stubborn chin. He looked at her for a long moment, a moment they couldn't afford to waste. If they were to make it together this time she'd have to give him her confidence, her trust and belief in the importance of what he was doing. And with her continuing sense of responsibility toward Saber, didn't he owe her the same confidence?

He made the decision without further contemplation. The fire was roaring around them. It had eaten away the section of the roof diagonally opposite, and the tar and gravel beneath his feet was sticky and hot. The rest of it wouldn't last long.

"Sorry, Saber. Protocol, you know. You're next."

Saber was furious, but he didn't waste time arguing further.

The space between the two buildings was less than ten feet, but it might as well have been a mile. They had devised a ladder bridge between the adjacent buildings, but they were afraid to test its strength by moving more than one person at a time across. A safety harness helped protect against a thirty-foot fall, but it was still a risky maneuver.

The unconscious security agent had been the most difficult to transfer, but they had finally gotten the man to safety. He was already on the way to the hospital. The women had been next, and now only the four of them remained.

As soon as the last of the women had shuffled across the ladder, Saber stepped on it.

On the opposite roof Sam Dalton protested, holding up a hand to halt his progress, indicating the safety harness. But Saber was having none of that. He walked across the shaky ladder with the style and grace of a cat, never looking down.

Bree and Ryan watched with Frizia, their hearts in their throats. When Saber was across, he turned to wave. Everyone breathed again.

Ryan grinned across the intervening space. "A damned fool thing to do. Okay, let's go." He caught the harness as it was tossed to him and slipped it over Bree's head. She had watched this maneuver twelve times, but he still talked to her as he helped her up onto the parapet. "Take it slow and easy, honey. One step at a time. Here, give me your shoes. I'll toss them over and they'll be there waiting for you."

"O'Hara," she interrupted dryly, and he met her eyes. She stood above him, one hand on his shoulder for balance as she removed her pumps and handed them to him. "I'll be all right. You just get yourself across in a hurry." Without waiting for a reply, she stepped onto the side rails of the ladder and took hold of the rope, inching forward with a shuffling movement.

He grinned. His woman was one gutsy lady, he decided. Though the harness would prevent a bad fall, he still watched with his heart in his throat as she maneuvered the narrow rails.

The wind was a surprise to Bree. Whirling up between the buildings, it brought with it dust and grit. She narrowed her eyes against its sting and moved forward steadily. Hands waited to grip her elbows and divest her of the harness. She whirled to meet Ryan's eyes across the gap.

Frizia, too, declined the harness. He was ready to move as soon as Bree stepped off the ladder.

Bree put a fist in front of her mouth. Ryan smiled at her, holding her gaze, sending his love across the distance. *I won't lose you by dying, my love. Not now when we've waited so long.* Her fist relaxed, the hand dropped to her side and she smiled back. Hurry, she mouthed.

Frizia was half the distance across when Ryan felt the building under him shudder violently, the roof shaking like Jell-O under his feet. He stepped up onto the parapet and slid out of his shoes. As he tossed them across, the support beneath him began to sway.

Bree felt the vibrations, as well, through her feet, through her heart—she wasn't sure. Ryan didn't wait for the harness. He was on the ladder immediately after the agent's last step.

"Damned fool thing to do," she muttered. The ladder was so rickety. Then she saw the tower of flame spurt toward the sky behind him and realized why. She bit back a scream. The bricks of the parapet holding the other end of the ladder began to crumble.

Everything from that moment seemed to happen in slow motion. Bree watched in horror as the ladder lurched, sank a foot, its support disintegrating before her eyes. Ryan paused for a split second to regain his balance. Now he was heading uphill. He took another step, and another.

Bree stood at the edge of the roof, bit through her lip, praying silently as she watched the man she loved more than life make his unsteady way toward her. She willed him on. Eight feet, seven, six.

And then the wall gave way. The ladder dropped toward the street below in a slow end-over-end tumble, and she closed her eyes and screamed his name, and screamed, and screamed.

Saber was holding her in a binding embrace as though he feared she might jump into the inferno after Ryan. "No, no, Bree. He dived for the wall. God knows how he made it, but he did. He's all right. Look."

She opened her eyes. Two men were hauling Ryan up. Up from the chimney of flame that was a backdrop behind him—up, it seemed, from the very depths of hell—up and away from the verge, onto the safety of the roof.

When he looked for and found her in Saber's arms, his strong white teeth split the grime that blackened his face. She tore free from Saber and flew into his arms. He crushed her to him; his mouth covered hers for one white-hot moment before the others were upon them, laughing with relief, pounding each other's backs.

"We made it!" shouted Saber, enclosing them both in a bear hug.

Bree found herself laughing, too, in relief, in thanksgiving, and with a tinge of hysteria that she had under control but, try as she might, she couldn't completely quell. But it was all right, because she heard the same note in several other voices.

Ryan kept her under his arm, his hand gripping her shoulder, as they made their way down the steps. She was grateful for his support. Her knees didn't seem to want to lock the way they should have done as she walked.

The press was waiting behind a police line at the entrance to the building. At the sight of Saber they broke through. Microphones were thrust into their faces, questions were screamed above the pandemonium of sirens and strident voices. They were jostled none too gently.

Sam Dalton forced his way through the crowd. "We have ambulances waiting," he shouted.

"No ambulance," said Saber.

Ryan agreed. A first aid kit was all they needed, and he knew the limo was equipped with one. He held out his arm to form an aisle so that they could reach the car, stopping only once for a word with Austin Maxwell, who had arrived on the scene to take the importer into custody. "Meet us there," Bree heard him say.

Just before they climbed inside, Bree turned to the protesting reporters. "Ladies and gentlemen, please. I'm sure the minister will have a statement for you later at the hotel. Give him a little while to catch his breath."

Ryan's expression was grim on the short ride back to the hotel. His hand gripped Bree's on the seat between them. Saber sat on the other side of her, his features equally harsh, his head against the plush upholstery. A few minutes ago, they were elated but now they were empty. The adrenaline had done its job, but with its ebb they felt drained of energy, drained of fear, drained of talk.

The elegant suite had been cleaned and was open for them as though they had always planned to return. The three collapsed on the sofas with no thought at all for the effect of their filthy clothes on the delicate fabric. Frizia joined them and, for the first time since Bree had known him, forgot his place. He collapsed on a side chair.

The reason for the man's sour, restrictive demeanor had become apparent to her when he'd pulled his gun to shoot off the padlock. He was no more an aide than she was; he was a bodyguard.

Slowly power returned to Ryan's limbs. He rotated his head and looked down to find he was still holding Bree's hand. Or she was holding his hand. Their fingers were laced so tightly their knuckles were white. He lifted them and kissed her fingers. "If you'll let me go I'll get you a brandy."

"I don't drink," she answered automatically. The mechanical phrase broke the tension in the room.

Saber laughed. "I'll get the brandy." He filled three snifters, handed one to Frizia and one to Ryan and raised the other to his own lips.

Before Ryan could drink, Bree stretched out a hand for the snifter. "Maybe this once," she said. "We do have something to celebrate."

"We certainly do." Grinning, he handed her the snifter and went to get himself another.

The brandy stirred the blood that seemed to have been frozen in her veins. She savored the taste of the potent liquid and its effect. "There's a lot to be said for fine brandy. Now can anyone tell me what happened?"

Sprawled back on the opposite sofa, Saber made a fist and pounded his knee. "One of your men burned, another with a concussion. What did happen, Ryan?"

Suddenly serious again, Ryan stood staring into his glass for a minute before he answered. "I don't know all of it. Maxwell will be here shortly to fill us in." As if on cue, the bell rang. He went to the door to let in his chief of homicide detectives.

Maxwell entered and settled in a chair. In response to Ryan's question he explained, "First, Mrs. Karman's brother is in the clear. He has been able to help us a lot. Actually, the plans were pretty simplistic. The importer wanted to kill you during your visit to the United States—they love to hate us, you know. You would have added value as a martyr to their cause. Their plans were to stir up trouble both here and at home. As much and for as long as possible, in hopes that when the New Year arrives and the king steps down there will be disorder and chaos instead of a disciplined change of government."

"Anarchy," said Saber angrily.

"At the very least," agreed Maxwell. "The boy didn't like the feeling he had about the planned protests and about some of the people who were taking part. He felt the cry for more jobs was a legitimate one. I understand unemployment has been a problem in your country."

Saber nodded. "Lack of job training."

"But that wasn't an excuse for the rumblings he was hearing. He became suspicious and began to nose around. The night of the murder, he followed the importer to the river to meet Pandal. He was a witness to the murder. He was scared and he ran. I can't blame him too much. He's just a kid, an alien in this country. He thought if he came forward he would be suspected. Finally he couldn't take being on the run anymore. He contacted his sister last night, and they both came to headquarters this morning. As soon as I heard his story I got on the horn and warned Ryan."

Swirling the liquid in his glass, Ryan spoke. "If that warning had come half an hour earlier—" He shook his head as if to clear his memory of the ordeal they had endured. "Sam Dalton says the bomb wasn't in the building yesterday, and I believe him. We aren't sure how it was brought in, but we have a pretty good idea the old woman who prepared the coffee was involved. We didn't strip-search everyone who entered this morning.

"We aren't sure how deeply this thing goes, Saber. But we'll find out. I guarantee you that." Ryan's tone had taken on a hard edge. "We'll find out to a man how many people are involved and who they are."

Listening, Bree knew that he would do what he vowed, down to the last perpetrator. She looked at Saber.

"I have no doubts that you will, my friend. Thank you," he said. He turned to Frizia. "Has anyone notified the rest of our party at the airport?"

The man looked aghast. "Excellency! I forgot!"

Saber waved away his apologies. "Understandable. But you'd better call them now."

"Shall I tell them to return to the hotel, Excellency?"

Bree sent mental commiseration winging south to her unknown counterpart in Philadelphia.

Ryan set the brandy glass on the table in front of him. He let his hands dangle loosely between his knees. "Saber, we can still get you to the plane with a reasonable chance of keeping to your schedule."

In an instant Saber was on his feet. "Then let's go. If the damned fools think they can scare me off, they'll have to think again."

The doorbell rang. The sunlight wasn't streaming in through the windows this time. Ryan had left her at her car a scant half hour before.

Bree had rushed home to shower and wash the lingering smell of smoke out of her hair. Now she wiped damp palms on the seat of her jeans and opened the door.

Ryan stood with one arm on the doorjamb at shoulder level. He wore faded jeans and a formfitting white polo shirt. His hair was damp from his shower. "Can we walk?" he said quietly.

She looked beyond him to the sky, which was still threatening rain. "Sure," she said.

They walked for hours, tracing the paths of their childhood. They passed the church and the school and the movie theater. They paused at the playground to swing and wandered through the deserted park.

And they talked, not of the things lovers talk of but about their families, their friends, their memories. When the rain began, the drops were gentle upon their faces. They stuck out their tongues to catch them, laughing together. Finally they talked about his job and his ex-fiancée, and her late husband. They weren't easy subjects for them to discuss, but love eased the way.

Ryan turned at last to Bree. "Let's go home," he said.

Through a curtain of joyous tears she saw his expression. No trace of hardness or bitterness marred the love there. "Yes," she said softly. A slow smile touched her lips. "Yes, my darling, let's go home."

The click of the dead bolt lock was loud in the silence of her house. They faced each other. Ryan tucked a wet strand of hair behind her ear. His fingers slid to her nape and he angled his head, bent toward her.

She swayed toward him, her face tilted up, lips parted in anticipation, eyes shining.

Their mouths touched.

The doorbell rang again.

"Briana?" called a voice through the door. "It's your mother."

"Mother?" said Bree, opening the door.

"Good afternoon, Briana, Ryan," said Frances, sailing past them without waiting for an invitation.

Ryan watched in amusement. He was going to stay out of this.

"I can see that you're . . . busy, so I won't keep you but a minute. Ryan, your car was here all night for two nights this week." She held up a hand when Bree opened her mouth to say something. "Let me finish. I know it is none of my business. I know you're a grown woman. I know that I've encouraged the two of you to . . . be together."

Bree watched her mother, hoping that her expression was noncommittal. She wasn't about to apologize or explain.

"I also know all about the so-called 'new morality'—we used to refer to it as sin."

"Mother." There was a warning in Bree's voice now that was unmistakable. She prayed Frances would heed it, because she didn't want an argument, not now, not here.

"But we were wrong to call it that," Frances went on in a rush. "A relationship between two people is nobody's business but their own. I have but one bit of advice to offer. Don't get pregnant." She reached over to kiss her daughter on the cheek. "Have a nice day, dear. Bye, Ryan." She left.

But before she could get down the steps, Ryan had gone after her. He took her by the arm, leading her firmly back into the house. "We're getting married," he announced flatly when he'd closed the door again and brought Bree close under his arm.

"That's the smart thing to do," Frances agreed.

"There are a few ground rules we intend to lay down, and we might as well get those out of the way right now. No dropping in unannounced. I don't want my mother-in-law catching me with my pants down. If Bree and I decide to have children we'll let you know, but we don't want any hints about grandchildren. Do you understand?"

Until now Bree had avoided looking at her mother, sure that she would see triumph in the faded blue eyes. But the emotion there went much deeper.

Frances folded her hands together in front of her breast. Her eyes glistened with unshed tears. For once she seemed to be deprived of speech. She nodded her agreement vigorously, shaking one tear loose. It trickled down the side of her nose.

Ryan smiled tenderly and caught the moisture with his finger. Then he circled Frances's shoulders, bringing her close until she was part of their embrace.

*   *   *   *   *

Silhouette Special Edition

THE O'HURLEYS! CHANTEL'S STORY

from
Nora Roberts

Skin Deep

Available September 1988

The third in an exciting new series about the lives and
loves of triplet sisters—

In May's *The Last Honest Woman* (SE #451), Abby
finally met a man she could trust . . . then tried to
deceive him to protect her sons.

In July's *Dance to the Piper* (SE #463), it took some
very fancy footwork to get reserved recording mogul
Reed Valentine dancing to effervescent Maddy's
tune. . . .

In *Skin Deep* (SE #475), find out what kind of heat it
takes to melt the glamorous Chantel's icy heart.
Available in September.

THE O'HURLEYS!

**Join the excitement of
Silhouette Special Editions.**

SET SAIL FOR THE SOUTH SEAS
with
BESTSELLING AUTHOR
EMILIE RICHARDS

This month Silhouette Intimate Moments begins a very special miniseries by a very special author. *Tales of the Pacific*, by Emilie Richards, will take you to Hawaii, New Zealand and Australia and introduce you to a group of men and women you will never forget.

In Book One, FROM GLOWING EMBERS, share laughter and tears with Julianna Mason and Gray Sheridan as they overcome the pain of the past and rekindle the love that had brought them together in marriage ten years ago and now, amidst the destructive force of a tropical storm, drives them once more into an embrace without end.

FROM GLOWING EMBERS (Intimate Moments #249) is available now. And in coming months look for the rest of the series: SMOKESCREEN (November 1988), RAINBOW FIRE (February 1989) and OUT OF THE ASHES (May 1989). They're all coming your way—only in Silhouette Intimate Moments.

IM249-R

ATTRACTIVE, SPACE SAVING BOOK RACK

Display your most prized novels on this handsome and sturdy book rack. The hand-rubbed walnut finish will blend into your library decor with quiet elegance, providing a practical organizer for your favorite hard-or soft-covered books.

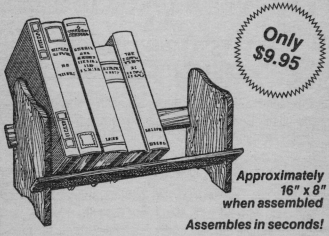

Only $9.95

Approximately 16" x 8" when assembled

Assembles in seconds!

To order, rush your name, address and zip code, along with a check or money order for $10.70* ($9.95 plus 75¢ postage and handling) payable to *Silhouette Books.*

Silhouette Books
Book Rack Offer
901 Fuhrmann Blvd.
P.O. Box 1396
Buffalo, NY 14269-1396

Offer not available in Canada.

BKR-2A

*New York and Iowa residents add appropriate sales tax.

COMING NEXT MONTH

#253 THAT MALCOLM GIRL—Parris Afton Bonds

Rob Malcolm had been a rancher all her life, and her only dream was to have her own spread someday. Then Hollywood—and Jed Pulaski—came to Mescalero, and she fell in love with a man as different from her as night from day. Only time would tell if these two opposites could merge forever in the glory of the dawn.

#254 A SHIVER OF RAIN—Kay Bartlett

FBI Agent Luke Warren burst into Rachel's quiet life, insisting that her former husband had been a thief. Worse still, the sexy man planned to stick around until the stolen money was recovered. Soon Rachel found herself the target of the real thieves and of Luke's latest campaign—to win her heart.

#255 STAIRWAY TO THE MOON—Anna James

Ella Butler, widow of a famous rock star, was sick of publicity, and then she met Nick Manning, a prominent diplomat. His career placed him in the limelight, and she was certain they could never have a future together. But Nick would do anything to keep her—even climb a stairway to the moon.

#256 CHAIN LIGHTNING—Elizabeth Lowell

Mandy Blythe didn't want to be anywhere near the Great Barrier Reef. She didn't like the water, diving made her nervous—and she certainly didn't trust Damon Sutter. He was a womanizer, and the last man she could ever fall for. But the tropics were a different world—and paradise was only a heartbeat away.

AVAILABLE THIS MONTH:

#249 FROM GLOWING EMBERS
Emilie Richards

#250 THE SILVER SWAN
Andrea Parnell

#251 SUSPICIOUS MINDS
Paula Detmer Riggs

#252 BETTER THAN EVER
Marion Smith Collins